The de Lacy Inheritance

The de Lacy Inheritance

ELIZABETH ASHWORTH

Myrmidon Books Ltd
Rotterdam House
116 Quayside
Newcastle upon Tyne
NE1 3DY

www.myrmidonbooks.com

Published by Myrmidon 2010

A catalogue record for this book
is available from the British Library.

ISBN 978-1-905802-36-4

Typeset in Sabon by Ellipsis Books Limited, Glasgow

Printed in the UK by CPI Cox & Wyman, Reading RG1 8EX

1 3 5 7 9 10 8 6 4 2

For Ben

Chapter One

Kneeling on the stony ground, his head bowed in prayer and his hands clasped before him Richard FitzEustace tried with all his will not to release a finger to scratch at the persistent itch beside his nose. It was as if the very devil were tormenting him, even as he knelt outside the chapel and listened to Father William reading the Mass of Separation.

"I forbid you to ever enter a church, a monastery, a fair, a mill, a market or an assembly of people."

How can I live without ever entering a church, thought Richard as his fevered mind translated the Latin words into Norman French. *How can I pray to God for forgiveness and for a cure if I am to be denied entry to His house?*

"I forbid you to leave your house unless dressed in your recognisable garb and also shod. I forbid you to wash your hands or to launder anything or to drink at any stream or fountain, unless using your own barrel or dipper. I forbid you to touch anything you buy or barter for, until it becomes your own."

Dear God, prayed Richard silently as his left hand strayed to the side of his face and scratched at the ulcerated skin, give me strength to face this tribulation. *Forgive me my sins and restore me to Thy grace and to my health.*

"I forbid you to enter any tavern; and if you wish for wine, whether you buy it or it is given to you, have it funnelled into your keg."

I will live simply and will not ask for wine – only for a spring of clear water where I may pray each day and wash away my sins, if it be Thy will.

"I forbid you to share your house with any woman but your wife."

I will never touch a woman again, I pledge, if only You will forgive me my sins and cleanse me of this unwhole-some disease. She tempted me, Lord. Like the snake tempted the woman, Eve, in the Garden and brought about the downfall of Adam, she has brought me to the devil.

"I command you, if accosted by anyone while travel-ling on a road, to set yourself down-wind of them before you answer. I forbid you to enter any narrow passage, lest a passer-by bump into you. I forbid you, wherever you go, to touch the rim or the rope of a well without donning your gloves. I forbid you to touch any child or give them anything. I forbid you to drink or eat from any vessel but your own."

Richard clasped his hands before him once more and though he kept his eyes tightly closed he could still see the redness around the knuckles and feel the incessant itching that plagued him day and night. Itching that tormented him until he wept along with the sores on his body.

The priest touched his shoulder and he was grateful. How long was it since anyone had dared to touch him, even through his clothing? Had she been the last person, he wondered, unable now to erase the image of her dark skinned body from his memory. She had tempted him and he had been weak. Now his punishment was visited upon him. But surely, he thought, God's mercy was great towards those who had fought alongside King Richard in the Holy War. Surely he could be cured, by the grace of God, through prayer and washing and fasting and repentance. After all hadn't the Lord Jesus touched the leper and declared him clean? Through prayer, it was possible for him too.

"Will you say goodbye to your family?" asked the priest gently. Richard opened his eyes and looked up at the anxious faces of the women who waited near the chapel door. His mother looked aged, he thought, since the day he had kissed her farewell as he went off to the Crusade. She was weighed down by the burden the Lord had asked her to carry, grieving for his father and anxious too for his brother Roger, who had also left for the Holy Land, leaving his pregnant wife, Maud, in her care. Beside her stood his elder sister Helen, married to Dutton, his father's steward, and his younger sister Johanna. They had all hoped to be kept safe under his patronage, but his return with this plague meant he was unable to stay to care for them, let alone take them in his arms and give them comfort.

His grandmother, widowed and deprived of her eldest son and now one if not two of her grandsons, stood resolute. She was in charge of this family now and, as his fingers touched the pouch at his waist containing the letter she had given him the previous night, he vowed that he would accomplish the task she had set for him.

Richard rose slowly, his knees sore and his legs stiff

from the prolonged prayers. He hung the wooden bowl and clapper from the thick belt that held the coarse woollen habit to his itching body, then raised the dark hood to conceal his face before pulling the gloves over his reddened, flaking hands. Slowly he approached his family, keeping a distance from them.

"I will pray for you day and night," said his mother, "and although the priest and laws decree that you should be as dead to me now, I have had my fill of death and I pray that one son at least will be restored to me."

"Pray hard and fast, mother," he said. "And I will remember you also in my beseeching, both day and night. I pray that one day my brother will return to hold you close and gladden your heart. Hold fast meanwhile to Helen and Johanna – and to your faith."

She thrust a leather purse at him, which jingled with the sound of coinage. She was unafraid of touching him but Helen took the bag and tossed it to the ground near his feet, restraining their mother from running forward and taking him in her arms.

With tears stinging his swollen eyes Richard turned away from the women. The sight of his mother clinging to her daughter like a feeble invalid hurt him more than anything else he had endured since his return. But he knew that he must leave them and that a prolonged farewell would only make it harder. Adjusting the hood so that no portion of his face was visible, he bowed his head as the priest crumbled earth at his feet and gave him his blessings.

Then he set out – not to the leper house of St Giles as he had promised his mother – but northwards, to cross the river into the newly named county of Lancashire. His destination, skirting the huge marshlands of Martin Mere to the west, was the township of Cliderhou where he would seek out his grandmother's cousin, Robert de Lacy.

The mud squelched beneath the unaccustomed shoes that were already rubbing a new sore on the back of his left heel as Richard headed north. He shivered in the chill wind of the ensuing autumn as he walked. In Palestine the sun had been so fierce overhead that, sweltering in his chainmail harness, he had longed for the cold westerly winds of his homeland. But now he longed for the warmth and shelter of his family house – a house denied to him – as he trudged down towards the river crossing.

Richard had resolved not to look back, but the drifting smell of a distant fire caught his nostrils and he turned for one last look at Halton Castle. Near the chapel a plume of smoke rose, and he wondered for a moment what Father William was burning, until he realised that it was all of his own clothes and possessions being consumed by the cleansing flames so that the affliction could not be passed on. On the path that led from the chapel to the main keep his younger sister was helping their grandmother home. Even in the distance he could see that she was leaning heavily on Johanna with every step, and he realised that she was no longer young. He wondered what would happen to them all with no man to protect them.

Beyond the village he saw a string of ponies, laden with salt in panniers, coming down the road behind him. They would catch up with him in a little while, he thought – meantime he had to go on. The journey would take several days and he had no idea how he would eat and where he would sleep along the way. He could only put his trust in God.

It seemed only moments later that Richard heard the steady beat of hooves as the ponies came up behind him.

"Get out of my way! You filthy wretch!" Richard stopped and turned to see who was the recipient of the drover's wrath. "You! Get off the road!" The drover, whom Richard vaguely recognised, waved a stick in his direction. "Get back! Keep away!"

One of the ponies passing him on the narrow track trod on his foot as it went by, adding to the pain and misery already caused by the chafing of his shoe. Richard sank down in pain onto the damp grass bank and watched as the swishing tail of the last pony diminished into the distance and the drover turned to shake the stick at him once more.

"Unpalatable cur," he muttered as he watched them go. "I remember the time, not that long past, when you would have scraped and bowed in my presence. You mangy upstart!" he called after him. But his voice was lost to the beat of the hooves and the jangling of the bells on the reins as the snorting ponies trotted on towards the ford with their precious loads. And as he watched them go Richard recalled something that the woman had said when he was telling her of his home.

"England is a rich county. You have plenty water; plenty salt."

Soon he could smell the salt on the air as he approached the tidal waters of the Mersey with some trepidation. It wasn't the first time he had crossed here and on horseback the ford across the river held no fears, but so many had drowned attempting the perilous crossing on foot that his father had employed a ferryman who, for a few coins, would row travellers across to the far side. But Richard knew that the man would refuse to take a leper like himself. His only way ahead was to wade across to the other bank.

As he approached he saw that the tide was already rising. Glancing up at the sky he also noted that it would be growing dark soon which would add to the danger, but he was determined to cross that night rather than wait for the next morning's low water. He found it hard to keep a foothold on the stones that littered the steep down-hill track and wished that he had had the foresight to bring a knife so that he could have cut himself a staff to support his descent. He glanced around for a loose branch that might serve that purpose, but the trees were thinning as he neared the river and he continued to slip gracelessly as he went down.

The sun was already low on the horizon when he reached the water but, not wanting to wait, Richard sat on a smooth rock and gently eased off the shoes that chafed his feet. As he stepped in, the shocking cold of the water made him gasp and faint clouds of blood swirled and were dispersed by the tidal pull that dragged at his aching legs. The saltwater stung at his wounds and the pebbles struck sharply at the soles of his already painful feet, but as he held up his long cloak around his thighs and waded further into the Mersey, the cold began to numb his feet and legs and provide some relief. He waded into the deepest part of the channel as the sun sank into the sea, creating a swirl of orange and yellow low in the sky. He couldn't help but pause and stare at God's wondrous creation until the sucking of the tide almost tipped him off balance and he staggered a little as he faced the far bank, the image of the sinking sun now flashing a black spot in the middle of his vision. Hitching the rough cloth of the leper's garb even higher he tried to feel a smooth path beneath his feet and raised his prayers to ask that he should not fail in his mission so soon by drowning.

Beyond the river Lancashire appeared as a vast forest and it was almost dark when he stumbled out of the cold river, panting and relieved. The strength of the water had been frightening and he was exhausted.

He left off his shoes and climbed up far enough to avoid the incoming morning tide. Then, having checked that his grandmother's letter had stayed dry inside its pouch, he settled down under the shelter of some bushes to try to sleep until dawn.

At first Richard welcomed the discomfort of hunger as a trial that would test his endurance and make him stronger. The sensation was not new to him. He had been hungry before, and he knew that once the obsession with bodily needs faded his enhanced mental perceptions would bring him closer to God. After all, hadn't the Lord Jesus fasted in the desert for forty days and forty nights? And God had not abandoned him but, on the contrary, had spoken and clarified what his destiny was to be. Christ had been tempted too, remembered Richard as he walked on. God had tempted him to turn the rocks into bread and assuage his hunger. But he had resisted. He had been strong. *Unlike me*, thought Richard. *I was weak and I strayed from the ways of the Lord – and this is my punishment.*

He bent to pick up a rock that was round and flat, like bread, but he knew that even if it was in his power to turn it into food he would resist. To give in to temptation once more would surely condemn him to the flames of everlasting Hell – a far worse fate than that of a rumbling stomach. He threw the stone forcefully into the nearby undergrowth, disturbing a bird which flew with an alarm cry into the clear blue of the afternoon sky.

As night fell once more he found a relatively dry place in the undergrowth, not far from the road, and gathered some grass in an attempt to soften the ground a little. He wasn't afraid of discomfort though – he had learnt the art of living simply as he'd journeyed with other knights across the unforgiving terrain of the Holy Land. He knelt and made his prayers before quenching his thirst at the nearby stream, remembering to use his dipper so as not to infect the water from the oozing sores around his mouth. As he settled to sleep, with the thick hood of his cloak making an ample pillow, he reflected that he felt the presence of God very close to him. It was as if the Lord walked hand in hand with him, supporting and strengthening him along his way and leading him to the salvation that He promised all those who turned to Him and truly repented.

Richard remembered that when he had arrived in Palestine he had expected to feel closer to God, but often God was lost to him there – amidst the fighting and blood-spill of war. Nor had God seemed that near as he had travelled through France – the land of his ancestors. But here, curled under this English hawthorn, where the thrushes and blackbirds had feasted on the rosy berries, he felt God's presence nearby, comforting and strengthening him.

A bright crescent moon rose slowly into view as he lay and studied the sky that hid Heaven. It reminded him that the Infidel was still undefeated, and he pulled himself once more to his knees to pray for the soul of his dear departed father, who had died at Tyre the previous year, and for the safety of his brother, Roger, still fighting on Crusade.

He woke early with the sunrise, and having washed, prayed and drunk – in that order – he set off again on the interminable journey north. Although the hunger was good for his soul it wasn't so kind to his body and his legs felt almost too heavy to lift as he plodded on. Every incline seemed to be a mountain, and he knew that before long he would have to find something to eat.

There were a few brambles growing near the roadside but nothing of any substance and, as the track and his heightened sense of aroma, led him towards a small settlement he resolved that he must go in and try to buy some bread rather than skirting around it.

The attitude of the drover had hurt him more than he was willing to admit. As the son of a Norman landowner he was used to the locals treating him with respect – at least to his face. But his was a face that was now to be kept hidden. He was nobody, and therefore could not command, nor deserve, respect from anyone. It was a harsh lesson and one with which he was struggling.

Perhaps it is for my pride that I am being punished, he said to himself as he watched one foot after the other step the road in front of him. *For is not pride also one of the seven deadly sins?*

Richard approached the settlement with some unease. Smoke was rising from the fires and its smell mingled with the familiar aroma of baking bread. He felt the saliva rising in his mouth and he took the gloves from where he had tucked them inside his belt and pulled them on.

He untied the wooden clapper that he must use to warn of his approach and pulled the hood further forward to hide his spoiled face – the face which his mother had caressed when he was a child, the face she had told him would break hearts, the face he had allowed Leila to kiss on those summer nights in his tent in Palestine.

"You are so pale," she had said. "Even in the sun you do not turn brown – just red, then your skin flakes away. I shall kiss it better." And she had kissed him, trailing her long, dark hair over his cheeks, his neck, his naked chest until he could resist her no longer and had clasped her close as she laughed and kissed him even more.

A dog barked a warning of his approach, interrupting Richard's thoughts and making him angry for allowing such memories to surface and torment him. It was bad enough when the Devil used his dreams to plague him with the temptations of the flesh, but to let such feelings take over his mind during the daylight hours was proof indeed of his weakness. He shook the clapper hard to warn the villagers of his approach and as a punishment to himself. It would be only what he deserved if they sent the dogs to chase him away hungry, he thought.

A woman appeared in the doorway of the bakehouse from where the smell of the baking bread emanated. He stopped some distance from her.

"May I buy some bread?" he called in English. "I have

money and my hands are covered. I will not approach you, but if you can put some bread on the stone there I will leave the coins for you."

"You put the money down first, then back off," she replied. Richard proceeded towards the flat-topped stone that the woman had indicated some distance from the building. His gloved fingers fumbled with the coins and, unsure how much to pay, he placed down a silver penny and then stepped away.

The woman, who had watched him with the corner of her apron held across her nose and mouth, glanced around furtively to ensure she wasn't overlooked and then hurried to the stone where she scooped up the coin and dropped it into her purse.

"Wait there," she said.

She returned to the bakehouse and, despite the obvious heat, closed the door firmly behind her. His legs trembling with weariness and emotion Richard sank to the ground to wait, fearing that she would simply take his money and not return. A dog sniffed around him and he was too afraid to kick out at it or throw a stone. A few other villagers watched from a distance, muttering amongst themselves and casting looks of contempt in his direction. He wondered how long he could prevail under their undisguised disgust before he was forced to stand and leave.

He was just contemplating what he should do when the door opened in a cloud of vapour and the woman, sweat running from beneath the cap tied around her hair, emerged with a large loaf of steaming bread held in a cloth.

"Stay back!" she warned, as he struggled to his feet.

He waited, still, until she had placed the dark rye loaf on the stone and run back to the door where she watched through an open crack. She reminded him of his mother trying to tame the robins in the courtyard garden of the castle with her crumbs. He walked slowly so as not to alarm anyone and took the bread. He broke off a chunk and pushed it, hot, into his mouth, although it was not usual to eat bread the same day that it was baked.

"Thank you!" he called when the overwhelming hunger pangs had somewhat abated. "God bless you for your kindness to me. I will remember you in my prayers." Then he turned from the edge of the village to walk around the periphery of the houses and continue northward, lowering his hood once he was out of sight of the village and wrapping the rest of the bread in the cloth to eat later.

Next morning Richard woke early. The rooks in the nearby trees were already awake and arguing with their neighbours as he rolled stiffly onto his back and shielded his sore and sticky eyes from the brightness. It would be another fine day, he thought, once the sun had burnt off the early mist.

He prayed first and then hobbled down to the stream and dipped his cup into the water to fill it. It was cold and fresh, relieving his mouth from the sticky coating of its sleeping hours. He drank again and fumbled for the remains of the bread. It had been rather squashed in his sleep, but at least his lying on it had kept the mice and insects from nibbling a share and as he bit into it and chewed he praised God for the kindness of the woman.

Leaving behind the lowland marshes of the Martin Mere, the ground now rose as Richard headed northeasterly towards moorland and the township of Bolton le Moors. As the packhorse route rose and the treeline was left behind, the chilly and damp westerly wind easily found its way through the coarse weave of the leper's cloak and Richard held the dark cloth tightly to him as he walked onwards, watching as the church of St Peter came slowly nearer. He felt drawn to the stones that housed the place of prayer and wished that he could go in to try to make his peace with God within a holy place, but he knew that he dared not and he would have to trust that God could hear the prayers he offered as he glanced in at the altar through the squint.

Dropping down later on the far side of the hill, he was sheltered a little from the prevailing wind and paused to pick berries from the wayside, although the sharp pangs of hunger had faded to a dull ache of familiarity and the desire to find something to eat was not so sharp now. Instead, his mind was focussed on his journey's end. He felt an urgency to reach Cliderhou soon.

The route led ever higher over the moorland and, as he paused to catch his breath, Richard gazed at the land that rolled away on either side of him. The mournful baaing of the sheep, the lambs now as full grown as their mothers but still following them hoping for a taste of the ewe's milk, and the last calls of the curlews before they flew down to the coast for the wintertime were the only sounds – apart from the howling of the wind that he hoped was not the distant cry of wolves. How different it was from the lowland plains of his home.

As he descended, following a river valley towards the woodland that flourished at a lower level, he surmised that by the afternoon he could reach the outskirts of

Blackburn – the town after which this hundred was named and where he would find the church of St Mary.

The land here was flatter, and as he walked the track was flanked on either side by beech woods; the fluttering golden leaves cascaded down from the tall trees and some caught at the cloth of his cloak. He stopped to brush one from his shoulder, pausing to scratch at a persistent itch on his lower leg that drew blood as he clawed at it. Shaking his head at his own lack of self control he pressed on towards the town which he could see in the distance. It was the only major settlement for miles around, most of the countryside he had passed consisting only of remote farmsteads with shepherds and other abandoned or burned out villages, fallen victim to either raids by the Scots or his own people, the Normans, who had fought here. For what, he wasn't sure. There seemed to be nothing but sheep, hundreds if not thousands of sheep for every human being, but then the sheep didn't run and hide when they saw a black hooded figure, a spectre of the living dead, coming in their direction.

As he approached the town he could hear the shouts and merriment of a market day. Just beyond the church the local Saxon farmers were gathered around the sheep pens as they traded the lambs that had been born in the spring. Below the church, by the side of the road, was an inn where people were drinking the local ale and a sheep was roasting on a spit. The smell of the meat drew Richard nearer, the juices of his ravenous hunger competing with the dripping, sizzling juices of the mutton.

"What do you want? Get away from here, leper!" someone called as he approached.

"I need food. I will not touch anything. See, I am gloved and covered," he replied, holding out his shrouded hands to reassure the people.

"Get away!" called another man, picking up a stone from the ground and throwing it in his direction.

"Yes," said another. "He sounds like he's a Norman anyway, so serves him right."

"Yes, we don't want you filthy Normans bringing your diseases here. Go away!"

Another stone hit the ground near him followed by more as the crowd copied the example of the first farmer in their effort to repel him. Richard, his mouth now dry with fear, backed away as one well aimed stone glanced off his shoulder causing him to stagger, lose his balance and fall. The roars of laughter rang in his ears as he tripped over his long cloak in an effort to regain his feet and get away from the malicious crowd. There was at least one blessing, he thought, as he hurried away past them: at least they were too afraid to touch him and it was that alone, he surmised, that saved him from a severe beating at their hands. As he felt at the purse of coins hanging from the belt of his tunic he was relieved that he hadn't pulled it out in their sight; for if the peasants had seen the amount of money he carried they may have even risked the plague to rob him.

Unharmed except for his bruised shoulder – and he had suffered far worse from the Turks – but hungry and weary he continued along the road towards Wallei where he hoped that the villagers would treat him more kindly.

He had around ten miles to travel and as he wished to arrive before nightfall Richard lengthened his stride as he walked on. The countryside was greener here, more fertile and much of the land had been ploughed and cultivated to bake bread and provide feed for the sheep that were now being herded and brought down from the high hills for the winter.

Ahead of him he could see a hill that rose, he thought, near to his final destination. He kept his eyes fixed on it, willing it to become nearer with every step, but as the light faded it seemed to remain as elusive as ever.

Lost in reverie and prayer it was some moments before he heard the sound of hoofbeats approaching. He turned, blinkered by his hood, and saw a hunting party coming up behind him.

The man who led the way wore a cloak of wolf skin and a matching hat. His horse was not a large destrier of the type that could carry an armed knight but a smaller well bred courser. He studied the animal in the twilight, thinking for a moment that he would very much like to own and ride such a mount on a hunting expedition.

The rider reined up as he passed him and spoke. "Where are you headed, friend, at this late hour?"

"I'm hoping to reach Wallei before the darkness falls completely. Is it far ahead?" asked Richard.

"Not far. It's where we're headed," replied the man. "I take it you were struck down with this affliction whilst doing the Lord's work?"

"Yes, I was fighting the Holy War, but..." Richard hesitated; this wasn't the time or place to reveal his story to a stranger.

"I am Robert," said the man.

"Robert de Lacy?" asked Richard, surprised that he should have found his grandmother's cousin so quickly on his quest. The man above him shook his head.

"No. I am Robert de Wallei, the Dean," he explained. "You look tired and hungry," he went on, "follow us home and I will find you a meal and somewhere to sleep for a night or two. Though I take it that your final destination is the Holy Well?"

"Yes, yes, indeed," replied Richard after a moment's hesitation. He hoped that God would forgive him for telling less than the whole truth, but he knew nothing of this Holy Well and though he wished fervently to know its location he felt disinclined to tell this man too much. Although he was obviously well placed, there was something about his gaze, despite his generosity, that Richard found unsettling.

The Dean rode off ahead and Richard followed, quickly overtaken by the other hunters on horseback, including a well dressed young lad of around fifteen or sixteen who he thought might be the Dean's son.

The huntsman slapped his whip against his leather boot and called the excited hounds to heel. The fresh doe's carcass dripped blood from a single precise sword wound where the huntsman had killed it after the chase, and the dogs knew that although the Dean and his household would eat venison that night the entrails would be their supper. And, limping in their wake, Richard hoped that they would save some for him.

He followed the hunting party as they rode down towards the river and over the wooden bridge. Nearby he saw the squat stone church in the fading light and, just beyond it a manor house surrounded by wooden outbuildings and stables, all contained within a stone wall.

As he approached the gateway to the manor he hesitated. He doubted that he would be invited inside the house, but the Dean's promise of food and shelter had seemed genuine and he was too hungry and tired to wonder if the man had any ulterior motive or was just performing his Godly duty by ministering to the sick.

Whilst leaning heavily against the wall and wondering what to do next he saw the young lad who had ridden with the hunting party coming towards him. He had taken off his hat and Richard could see that he was fair skinned with a tinge of red in his thick wavy hair, but his eyes were dark brown rather than the penetrating blue of his father's and they held a warmth that the Dean's did not. His smile was hospitable as he approached.

"I am Geoffrey, the Dean's son," he introduced himself. "Come this way and I will find a dry place for you to sleep in the stables."

Thankfully, Richard limped after him, past the barely disguised glances from the grooms who were busy unsaddling and brushing mud from the horses. The boy led him to a space where the dogs were being given fresh water and straw bedding by the young apprentices.

"Bring some clean straw over here," the boy called to one of the children who cared for the dogs. He was an English boy of around nine or ten years old and he regarded Richard's sore encrusted face with curiosity as he pushed the bedding into sacks to form a mattress. "Bring him some ale too," Geoffrey said, and Richard noticed that the instructions were given in a kindly voice and he touched the boy's arm in a gesture of thanks as he spoke.

"I have my own cup," said Richard when the boy returned with a jug. "Pour it into here," he said, noticing that his hand shook with fatigue as he held it out. The boy filled it to the brim and Richard drank thirstily as his hosts watched and then held out the cup for more.

"Have you come far?" asked the Dean's son.

"I have been travelling for several days," said Richard, reluctant to reveal too much. He had a feeling that the Dean may have sent his son to discover what he could about their visitor, perhaps thinking that he would speak more candidly to the boy. "I've been sleeping in the open, but the nights are becoming colder and I am very grateful for some shelter tonight."

"And have you far to go?"

"Not far I hope." Richard hesitated and then decided to take the chance. "The Holy Well your father mentioned. Is it far?"

"No, only a few miles farther on at Cliderhou," he replied.

"And have people been cured there?"

"So I have heard," replied Geoffrey, "although I have never seen the proof."

"But you have faith?"

"Yes. I have faith," said the boy, with an emphasis which made Richard wonder who didn't. "I will send you some food," he went on after a moment's silence.

"God bless you," said Richard. "You are a generous young man."

As he rested and waited he watched the dogs and saw

that, like the horses, they were fine animals that belonged to an obviously wealthy man. They were a mixed pack he noted, the bloodhounds with their long ears to sniff out the scent of the kill and the swift, lithe greyhounds that could chase a stag or boar until it was exhausted enough for the huntsman to move in for the kill.

A little later, as Richard was dozing on the pallet listening to the chewing of the hounds and the clatter of dishes, one of the apprentices came with a plate of steaming venison and fresh white bread, which Richard transferred to his own platter to eat. The food filled his stomach with a warmth that gradually spread through his tired body and afterwards he fell into a sleep disturbed only by the snoring and whimpering of the dogs and words muttered in the sleep of the boys who looked after them.

He dreamt of a Holy Well, filled not with water but sweet white wine from French vineyards that could cure any ills, but towards morning the straw bed seemed to intensify the itching of his skin and he woke at dawn to find blood on his hand where he had been scratching at his leg in his sleep.

Close by, the church bell was ringing for Matins and, sad that he could not walk to the church to attend the Mass, Richard rose to his knees and recited the prayers alone. He watched and waited as the boys fed and watered the dogs and let them outside. Then the same young lad of the previous night brought him a simple breakfast of bread and ale.

Afterwards, coming blinking out into the morning sun, rubbing at his sticky eyes Richard almost walked into the Dean.

"Forgive me!" he said, jumping back swiftly. "I am afraid that sometimes I forget my affliction and the responsibilities that it brings."

"Rest easy, my son," said the Dean. "Come, walk with me to the riverbank and tell me a little about yourself. You said you have been fighting the Holy War?"

"Yes, I am recently returned from Palestine," said Richard.

"How does it go?"

"Slowly," he told the Dean, "though I was there to see the city of Acre surrendered to the king." But as he described the events to the Dean and the sun rose higher above the trees, its warmth just about penetrating his dark cloak, he saw, in his mind's eye, not the river sparkling in the English sun, nor the Crusaders falling to their knees on the hot sand to give thanks, but Leila, framed against the entrance to his tent. "Afterwards I was sent home," he said. "The king did not want me spreading this affliction amongst the men." Richard almost went on to tell the Dean more about himself. The man was a skilled listener who didn't ask too many questions but nodded encouragingly as he walked closely by Richard's side, encouraging an intimacy that had been sparse in his life of late.

"With prayer and fortitude you will find salvation," said the Dean after a moment's awkward silence. "I sense that something troubles you, my son, and I am willing to hear your confession when you are ready to make it."

Richard looked up to meet the Dean's shrewd and appraising eyes. Could this man see through his outer clothing and tormented skin into the inner reaches of his soul, he wondered.

The Dean smiled. "When you are ready," he repeated. "Now tell me that you will rest here for a few days to gather your strength before you continue your journey. You look exhausted."

"I am anxious to reach my destination," Richard told him.

"Ah yes...

"The Holy Well," he blurted out into the ensuing silence and then regretted the words, but this man was so easy to confide in; too easy; maybe dangerous, he wasn't sure. "I don't think I am far from it?"

"Not far at all," agreed the Dean, briskly. "In fact I will ask my son Geoffrey to guide you to it. Tomorrow if you wish?"

"Yes, thank you," replied Richard, surprised at the Dean's sudden change of tone. It was as if he had suddenly realised that Richard couldn't or wouldn't tell him more, not now anyway.

"Then that is settled," said the Dean with a smile. "Can you find your way back? I have business at the church."

"Of course," said Richard, and with a brief nod the Dean strode off away from the river and Richard turned to sit on the fallen branch of a tree and watch the swirling pools as the water ran over rocks hidden beneath the surface, wondering why he had the impression that the Dean knew exactly who he was and why he had come.

Chapter Two

Johanna watched as the dark hooded figure paused to look back. Even at this distance and concealed by the leper's hood she would have recognised her eldest brother easily. She would have waved him a last farewell except for her grandmother, who was leaning heavily on her arm with her crooked fingers pressing into her wrist. Albreda sighed and shifted her weight slightly as they paused outside the wooden steps that led up to the main doorway of the castle keep.

"Will he fare well?" asked Johanna as her grandmother turned awkwardly and followed her gaze towards the north.

"I hope so," she said.

"What is it like at the leper house?"

"Where?" asked her grandmother, seeming distracted as they watched the solitary figure disappear behind the trees.

"The leper house," she repeated, hoping that her grandmother was not becoming aged of mind. She needed her help more than ever as she knew that her mother planned to arrange a marriage for her now that Richard was gone. "What is it like there?"

"You stay away from that place," warned her grandmother turning to look her fiercely in the eye. "I do not want to lose another grandchild to disease."

"I have no intent to go there," she replied. "I was only curious."

"Come," said her grandmother, digging her fingers into her arm and leaning so heavily that Johanna stumbled and almost fell herself. "Stand up straight and help me up the steps."

A chill met them as they stepped into the sunless interior where a smoky fire was being coaxed into life by a servant in the centre of the great hall, but her exhausted grandmother insisted on being helped up the steps to her own private chamber.

The heavy door creaked open as Johanna pushed hard with her free hand before half lifting her grandmother over the threshold and helping her to sit on the leather strung bed topped with a thick feather mattress. Her grandmother's fingers were swollen and bent and she could barely grasp anything with them, so Johanna unfastened the clasp of the heavy woollen cloak which she had taken to wearing summer and winter as she grumbled about the constant cold and the pain in her swollen joints. She hung it up on a wooden peg and turned back to help Albreda unfasten the ankle straps of her shoes and ease them from her deformed and slightly smelly feet so that she could rest a while on her bed.

As she studied her grandmother's hands and feet with a fascinated distaste, Johanna hoped that she would never grow old.

"Why does someone have to be declared dead if they

have leprosy?" she asked as she deposited the shoes in a far corner of the room and pushed lovage leaves inside them to freshen them. Then she made a great show of plumping up the pillow that was stuffed with dried meadow flowers to dispel the stink.

"It is not your place to question the word of God," Albreda told her.

"But Jesus touched the leper and healed him so why cannot Richard be healed?"

"Perhaps he will if he has enough faith."

"But he still could not come home, could he?" she asked.

Her grandmother shook her head. "You ask far too many questions, Johanna, and I am far too tired to answer them. Let me rest now. Go and comfort your mother. She needs you more than I do this day."

Reluctantly Johanna left the chamber, closing the door gently behind her. Her grandmother's eyes were closed and she thought, but could not be sure, that she was already sleeping. The air was fresher at the bottom of the stone cut steps that led up to her mother's solar and she knew that it would be fragrant there but she lingered, putting off the visit.

Her mother was always weeping. It had begun when Johanna's father had gone on Crusade and worsened when Richard had followed him. And now that her father was dead, Roger also gone to fight and Richard come home a leper, her mother was inconsolable. She sat dolefully in her solar all day with Maud, and her sister-in-law was no different. The whole castle was filled with their sobbing and awash with their tears. Sometimes Johanna wished that she had been born a boy, then she too could have taken the cross and gone on Crusade rather than having to listen to their lamentations. Of course she was saddened, as was her grandmother, but they did not make a great show of it.

As she stood brooding and staring out of the narrow window she wondered how far Richard had travelled and whether he had reached the leper house. She had a vision of him being confined in a long low room filled with the gradually decomposing bodies of the living dead. A cold shiver ran through her and she made another silent prayer for his wellbeing. Out of all her family Richard was the one to whom she felt the closest, the one to whom she had always gone when she was perplexed and needed someone to listen and advise. She missed her father too. He had been kind and used to spoil her, taking her on his lap, hugging her and giving her presents and sweetmeats; though he had never seemed much interested in talking to her, preferring to drink wine and discuss politics with his sons around the charcoal brazier in the great hall until late at night after the women and children had retired to the bedchamber.

Her other brother, Roger, she did not miss. He had been the youngest until she was born and he was jealous of her and bullied her: not so obviously that her parents would notice, but in cruel and subtle ways. Despite her prayers Johanna still could not forgive him for the time when she was five years old and he had stolen into the bedchamber where she slept and taken the soft brown blanket that she kept folded there and burned it. When she had discovered the remains in the hearth he had scoffed at her tears and told her not to behave as a child and that it was only a piece of cloth. At that moment she had felt, not for the first time in her life, a rising anger that had made her try to snatch up his sword from the top of the coffer where he had been polishing it. Her intention had been to ram it through his guts but he had laughed at her feeble attempts to lift the heavy sword in her two small hands and, still laughing, had picked it up single-handedly and gone outside to practise his fighting skills – a boy then on the threshold of manhood with a streak of cruelty that became more apparent by the day. Johanna had spat after him in frustration and vowed that she would never forgive him; and she never had.

Her mother had always turned a blind eye to such taunting, but Richard, if he was around had always taken her side, once punching Roger squarely on the nose for pulling her hair and refusing to let her go despite her screams of protest. Roger had run to their mother with blood dripping from his chin but she had refused to believe that Richard could have done such a thing and had maintained, to Roger's fury, that it must have been an accident. Then she had turned on Johanna and berated her for teasing her brothers and making them angry. Johanna had felt like spitting then as well, although she knew her mother would slap her if she did, so she just swallowed down the bile of her anger and frustration and vowed that one day she would be revenged on her mother too.

Then, when the news had come of her father's death and her mother roamed about the castle weeping and speaking to no one, Johanna wondered if the sick feeling she felt in her stomach was guilt. She had prayed for years that something bad would happen to her mother, but she had never intended to harm her father. How could God let such things happen, she had asked Richard, but he had just shaken his head and told her to pray.

She too had wept when Richard went to Palestine; not openly as her mother had but quietly, in the privacy of her bed where nobody could see or hear her, which was how weeping should be done. Grief, she believed, was a private matter, not for public exhibition.

Now, as she approached her mother's solar, the crying assaulted her ears. She knocked, but receiving no reply apart from the noise she turned the handle and went in. Neither her mother nor Maud seemed to notice her as they clung together, sniffing and wiping their faces on the corners of the cloaks that they were both still wearing.

She stood and watched them dispassionately for a moment until her mother looked up and saw her. With a wave of her hand she dismissed her and Johanna, having fulfilled her grandmother's command, backed eagerly out of the doorway and returned down the stairs to the hall and out through the courtyard to stare at the vacant spot where she had last seen her brother. Without Richard to speak up for her and protect her she was suddenly afraid for what her future would hold. Already she had heard whispers about betrothals and suitable matches and the thought of a husband and the half discovered truths about what marriage entailed terrified her.

It was in fact only a few days later that her fears were realised. She was lurking in the bedchamber keeping out of her mother's way when she heard the sound of horses approaching the castle, and when she drew back the shutter at an outer window she saw a procession of strangers making its way across the inner courtyard.

Minutes later there was a confusion of excited voices outside as the horses snorted and a knight with his squire and men-at-arms rubbed their hands and stamped their feet in the cold mist after what looked like a long ride.

Then she heard her mother's voice and saw her curtsey to the man in the dark green cloak and fur hat, smiling at him with her most charming manner and ushering him inside.

She watched as the visitors stepped from her view up the steps and into the hall and the horses were led away to the stables. She turned as Megan, one of the servant girls, came hurrying in with a basin of hot water and cloths.

"Mistress, your mother says you must wash and put on your best blue tunic and come down straightway," she told her.

"And why do you think that is, Megan?" she asked, leaning against the cold stone of the wall and watching as the other girl dashed about, shaking the gown from the clothes coffer and laying it out across the bed.

"There are important visitors for you to greet," said Megan.

"Who are they?"

"I do not know, Mistress."

"No, neither do I, but I suspect I know why they are here."

Johanna sighed as she watched Megan scurrying around the chamber finding shoes to match the dress. Now that Richard had been disinherited and Roger's whereabouts were unknown, she might be the heiress to her grandmother's lands and such an incentive was sure to bring a stream of potential husbands sniffing around her like the hounds when the bitches were in heat.

Slowly, Johanna dipped and squeezed the wash cloth in the tepid water several times, allowing the drops of scented water to run over her forearms and drip from her elbows onto the floor. She washed her face and ears and the back of her neck then under her arms before allowing Megan to lift the blue undergown over her head and lace it tightly around her slim waist. Then the girl helped her on with the loose surcoat of a paler blue which was shorter and allowed the darker material to show at the hem and the wrists. She sat on the small wooden stool beside her bed and brushed her long dark hair before allowing Megan to braid it over one shoulder and pin it with a silver tippet.

"There," said Megan at last, stepping back. "You are ready."

"Like a lamb to the slaughter," remarked Johanna as she left Megan to tidy the chamber and made her way down the stone steps to the hall in the new leather shoes which squeaked at every step.

Seated in a chair before the fire with a jug of wine and a platter of meat, cheese, fruit and bread was a stranger, dressed in a fine woollen tunic of dark red that not only clashed with the green cloak he had thrown aside but also with his thinning gingery hair and sparse beard. Her mother, hovering nearby, motioned her to come forward and greet the man.

Johanna approached and was repulsed by the sight of a huge wart with two hairs springing from it on the man's cheek. She made a quick bob of greeting and stood with her arms folded protectively across her chest as her mother spoke.

"This is my daughter, Johanna. Johanna, this is William FitzNigel."

The man appraised Johanna from head to toe and back again with his watery blue eyes as if he were eyeing up horseflesh on market day. She stood, uncomfortable and resentful under his gaze. Her stomach rumbled and she was more interested in her own dinner than making polite conversation with this gruesome suitor.

"So, how old are you, Johanna?" he asked.

"Fourteen."

"A good age," he replied with a nod towards her mother. "And what do you like to do? Do you like to sew?"

"Yes, I like to sew," she replied as if she were answering a catechism where the answers were set and there was no choice but to give the required responses. In reality she despised sewing and liked nothing better than to ride her chestnut mare as fast as she could urge the animal to go, bareheaded, with the wind tugging her hair from its roots. She liked to visit the horses in the stables and help to groom them; she liked to sit with the stable boys and pages cleaning the harnesses, playing with the dogs and feeding the hawks. She wanted her own bird to train, but her mother forbade it, saying that it was dangerous to ride out alone to hunt and insisting that she spent her afternoons confined in the stuffy solar with her and Maud making endless tapestries to decorate the walls that depicted the battles she would have preferred to be fighting.

"Stand up straight with your hands by your sides," ordered her mother.

"Good," said the man, his roving eyes taking in her body and her breasts as she shifted uncomfortably under his gaze and fiddled with the ties of the belt around her gown. "Good," he repeated to her mother and raised a cup of wine to his lips as if a deal had been struck.

"Go now," said her mother, waving her away again as if she were a child and not party to an adult conversation.

Johanna turned and stomped down to the kitchen where she helped herself to a chunk of the fresh bread that was cooling on the table and a piece of cheese.

"You look nice today," said Eleanor, the cook. Johanna merely snorted and went to sit near the fire where she watched the boy turning meat on the spit for their dinner and stared into the flames as she ate, wondering how she could avoid her fate.

Later, her mother sent Megan to fetch her and Johanna trailed up the steps to her mother's solar, already knowing what she was to be told.

"I shan't marry him!" she announced before her mother had a chance to say a word. "And you cannot force me!"

Turning from her desk, her mother irritably threw down the quill with which she had been writing.

"You are an ungrateful and difficult child!" she told her. "Your father yearned for another daughter, yet how disappointed he would have been with you now. Here am I, left alone without the protection of either husband, father or son and all I have from you is petulance and ill temper! William FitzNigel is a good man who is prepared to take you and care for you, though little does he know what a wildcat he is taking to his house. I advise you to accept him and be grateful."

"I shan't marry him!" repeated Johanna, before running from the solar, hesitating only to slam her mother's door behind her as hard as she could, making the sound reverberate all around the walls of the castle, shaking it to its rocky foundations.

She ran down to her grandmother's chamber where she burst in without knocking and flung herself at her grandmother's feet, biting back the tears that made her throat ache with their pressure.

"Don't make me marry him. He is a disgusting old man," she pleaded. She buried her face in her grandmother's lap and felt her gnarled hand softly stroking her hair where the braid was already unravelling.

"He seems a good man."

"But I do not love him."

"We cannot always marry for love, but often love comes with time," soothed her grandmother.

"I will marry for love or not at all," vowed Johanna.

"It may not be that simple."

"If Richard was here he would not make me marry him," said Johanna.

"That's probably true," agreed her grandmother, still stroking her head. "But Richard is not here and you are your mother's responsibility now."

But why did it have to be so, thought Johanna, her face still pressed against her grandmother's dark gown. Richard had always protected her against their mother and brother. Their mother would do anything he asked and Johanna knew that if he asked their mother not to marry her off to this man then she would listen. In fact Richard was the only person she would listen to. And he wasn't really dead. He was only a few miles away. She could easily ride to the leper house and find him and ask him to send a message to their mother. It would only take half a day. She could go now.

Johanna jumped up from her grandmother's embrace.

"I must go," she said shortly and ran back to the bedchamber where she peeled off the close fitting surcoat and tugged from beneath her mattress the boys' clothes she had begged from Will in the stables, which she liked to wear to ride astride her horse. She laced the braies around her waist and struggled into the knee length tunic before pulling the woollen stockings onto her slim legs. Over the top she dressed in her own boots and cloak. She tucked her hair inside a net and pulled up her hood before creeping down the stairs, leather riding gloves in hand, and running across to the stables where Etoile snickered a greeting when she saw her.

She rubbed a hand over the mare's velvety muzzle and kissed the white star between her eyes. "Come quietly," she cautioned the horse as she saddled her and led her out into the yard before mounting and trotting out past the gatehouse where the guard was absent, having been tasked to carry tables and chairs into the great hall for the coming feast. She glanced back apprehensively before urging Etoile forward to a gallop, but everyone was so busy preparing a feast to announce her betrothal to William FitzNigel that none saw her leave.

The mare's thick mane bounced against her muscular

neck as Johanna leant forward and enjoyed the rhythm of the horse's sleek body beneath her. The leper house at Spital Boughton was to the south, outside Chester, and as Johanna turned Etoile onto the road and gave the mare her head it suddenly occurred to her that when she last saw Richard he had been heading north. As she rode, lulled by the rhythm of the mare's beating hooves, she dismissed the thought from her mind. Maybe Richard had taken a more circuitous route to St Giles to avoid being seen by anyone who knew him. After all, where else would he have gone?

As Johanna approached Morgan's Mount she saw the prior come out to greet her. She pulled hard on Etoile's reins circling the excited horse around as she brought her to a halt. The mare flung back her head, almost giving Johanna a bloody nose as she pranced and chewed at the bit. But despite the noise of the horse Johanna still heard the prior's gasp of surprise and disapproval as she turned to face him and he saw that she was a girl.

"This is a leper hospital. I beseech you not to come closer," he called.

"I am seeking my brother, Richard FitzEustace," she told him. "Please tell him that his sister Johanna is here and must speak with him."

"Richard FitzEustace is not here, Mistress. What makes you seek him here?"

"Well this is the leper house."

The prior nodded. "Yes, indeed, and I was told that your brother had returned from the Holy Land with this cursed affliction, but he has not come here. Yet..." the prior hesitated, "you believed that he had?"

"Well, yes," said Johanna, searching her mind for an explanation. If Richard was not at the leper house then where was he, she wondered. Surely some harm could not have befallen him on his journey here.

"Do not be alarmed," said the prior, responding to her worried looks. "I am sure there is some explanation. When he arrives I will give him your message. In the meantime I suggest you return home where you will be safe."

Johanna watched as he retreated inside and shut the door firmly behind him. She sat on her horse and stared at the closed door and the building for some time wondering what to do next.

Having made her decision to resist the arranged marriage she was determined not to return meekly home to be awarded to the ugliest man her mother could find without a word of protest. She soothed Etoile by stroking her neck and murmuring into the mare's flickering ears. She would not return home, she decided. If Richard could not be found then she would ride north and seek out her grandmother's cousin in Lancashire and ask him for protection instead.

So she urged Etoile back towards Halton where she skirted the castle and the surrounding village by taking a lesser used track through the woodlands until she eventually reached the ford where she could cross the river.

The sinking sun towards the west warned her that there was not much daylight left as, hungry and tired, she loosened the reins and allowed Etoile to pick her own way down the slippery and stony track that approached the crossing. As the path evened out Johanna gazed across the estuary and saw that the tide was high. Although she had never crossed here before she had sometimes ridden this far to watch the merchants and travellers come and go, and she knew that she was obliged to wait until low tide before she could attempt to reach the other side.

On the riverbank she slid down from the horse's back and with the reins in her hand led Etoile down to the edge of the water. The ferryman came out from his hut when he heard their approach.

"You cannot cross yet, Mistress. The water is too high."

"How long will it be before the tide goes out?" she asked.

"A couple of hours or so at least," he replied, studying her with interest, "and by then the dark will be drawing in. Do I know you, Mistress?" he asked.

"I doubt it. I am not from these parts," she told him.

"Have you come far then?"

"Yes, a long way – and I have a long way to go which is why I am anxious to cross soon," she replied, irritated by his questions.

"And you are alone? You have no maid or servant with you?"

"Do I look like someone who would have a servant?" she demanded.

"No," he agreed, "but you speak like someone who would have a servant and your horse is not an animal that a peasant might ride." Johanna felt her face blush and she raised her hand to disguise the colour rising to her cheeks.

"It's none of your business," she responded, angry with herself that her manner of speech might have given her away. At least the man had not accused her of thievery.

Johanna turned her back and walked upstream a little way where she loosened Etoile's girth and allowed her to graze. Then she sat down on the damp grass and willed the river water to retreat so that she could cross safely into Lancashire.

She had often heard her grandmother speak of her cousin Robert who owned much land and castles in the north, including one at a place called Cliderhou. On winter nights she would sit by the fire just before bedtime and tell the children about their family: about Ilbert de Lacy who had come from Normandy with the Conqueror; about Henry, Walter and her own grandmother after whom she was named. Her cousin, the second Robert de Lacy who had lived at Cliderhou, was the son of Henry de Lacy. There was some scandal she recalled concerning the eldest son, Ilbert, and she could not remember what her grandmother had told her about Walter, if anything. What she did know was that Robert de Lacy and his wife had no children and that her grandmother hoped to inherit the de Lacy estates to add to her own. As heiress to her grandmother's fortune it was no wonder she was seen as such a valuable catch by a procession of greedy old men, thought Johanna. But if she could persuade cousin Robert that he must ensure his lands passed to a worthy successor she might be able to make him her protector in this matter – at least that was her plan.

Johanna jumped as a twig cracked behind her and she leapt up and around to find herself face to face with Dutton, her father's steward and husband to her sister Helen.

"What do you want?" she demanded reaching for Etoile's reins.

"I have come to take you home," he said briefly.

As they rode in under the portcullis at the gatehouse Johanna saw her mother standing at the bottom of the steps to the hall with a cloak clasped tightly around herself against the cold. The gathering gloom of the evening was nothing compared to the dark anger on her face.

Dutton threw Etoile's reins to a stable boy and Johanna had no choice but to slip from the saddle and watch as the mare was led away.

"Thank you, Dutton," said her mother tersely. "I am glad you found her before darkness fell."

"She was waiting to cross the river as the ferryman said," he replied before giving a swift nod and withdrawing himself to avoid the gathering storm.

"Get inside!" her mother muttered, reaching out to slap Johanna as she passed and, although Johanna saw the slap coming and ducked, her mother's hand still connected with a resounding smack.

She ran up the steps and into the great hall, pulling off her cloak as she went to reveal the boys' clothes beneath.

"What in the name of heaven are you wearing and where have you been?" screamed her mother.

"I went to the leper house to find Richard," said Johanna, and then she paused as she stared her mother straight in the eye. "And he was not there!"

The bold statement that she had been rehearsing in her head during the uncomfortable ride back from the river was delivered with an assurance that would not have shamed one the finest minstrels, and it had the desired effect. For a moment her mother could only open and close her mouth like a fish pulled from the river in a net and Johanna made the most of the advantage by striding off to the bedchamber without another word.

Once in her own curtained alcove she flung herself onto the bed and, with the bolster over her head, she wept long tears of anger and frustration until her sobs became barely controlled and she sat up and wiped her face miserably on the covers. She was cold and she was hungry and she knew that her mother would set the servants to watch her like hawks circling prey. She wondered if she dared creep down to the kitchen to look for something to eat, but decided that she preferred to be hungry rather than risk having to listen to more of her mother's chiding.

As she lay on her back and watched the clouds reveal and obscure by turns a small crescent moon outside the partly shuttered window, she suddenly wondered what had happened to William FitzNigel. He must have ridden away when she could not be found, she decided, as there was no sign of him or his retainers and there was a strange silence all around the castle as if both the inhabitants and the buildings were holding their breath in anticipation of the almighty row that was to come. Johanna imagined his foxy face, contorted with disappointment as he realised that his prospective bride had escaped. It made her smile despite her abject misery, though it was the thought of how angry it must have made her mother that gave her the most pleasure.

Johanna's mother had, as she knew she would, set Megan to watch her every move. From the moment she brought her water to wash in the morning until after she had helped her to bed at night Johanna was made to feel as if she was a prisoner. Yet the worst thing was that she was forbidden to go to the stables to even see Etoile, let alone take her out for a ride, and she was subjected to the torture of sewing with her mother and Maud every afternoon. The two women would talk amiably between themselves but exclude her from the conversation as if she were a deaf mute. One consolation was that the darkness came soon on the winter afternoons, and long before the Vespers bell was rung at sunset the women could no longer see the colours of their threads and the tapestries were put away until the next day. The other consolation was that Johanna would sometimes sit with her grandmother, whose failing sight meant that she no longer plied her needles but would often talk about her childhood in Yorkshire, her marriage to Johanna's grandfather Richard FitzEustace and her journey to Halton. She liked to listen as her grandmother told tales about her father John and what he had been like when he was a boy: how he used to ride and hunt with her uncles Robert and Roger and how her grandmother had sat and sewed with her aunt Mary. It made her feel that she belonged and she hoped that one day she would be able to pass on these stories to children of her own – children who were fathered by a man she could love and respect.

No more suitors came during the winter when the snowfalls piled up against the stone walls of the castle and balanced precariously along the branches of the bare trees until a weakly sun or some passing crow out foraging for food shook it loose and made it cascade sparkling to the ground.

Johanna often wondered where Richard was and how

he was surviving the relentless cold. She thought of him wasting away at St Giles, but no word had come and no one spoke of him. Her mother merely tightened her lips and blinked back the ever present tears if Johanna so much as hinted that she might say his name and her grandmother deftly changed the subject whenever she tried to ask about him.

Christmas came and went with little cause for celebration, yet the days showed no sign of lengthening and the darkness appeared more intense as Johanna awoke each morning and shivered at the narrow window as she looked out on the castle bailey below.

It was from here, one afternoon after it had become too dark to sew but when she was reluctant to join the others by the fire in the hall, that she saw the messenger, wrapped in furs against the cold, come trotting up on a damp, grey palfrey that blended almost perfectly with the white winter world. Praying that he might bring word of Richard at last, she ran to pull open the door of the bedchamber, letting it bang back against the wall and leaving it shuddering on its hinges as she ran down the stairs.

She was surprised to see that the messenger had been brought inside and was dripping a spreading puddle in front of the fire whilst her mother and Maud pored over a damp parchment in the half light of the flickering candles.

They glanced up as she came down, lingering on the edge of the tableau, and returned to their urgent whispering. Hearing the mention of her own name Johanna became even more convinced that the message was rightfully intended for her and she stepped forward to snatch it from Maud's hand.

"Let me look!" she demanded, seeking the well known signature and seal of her brother that would reassure her that he was well. But a cold greater than the one outside clenched its menace around her guts as she recognised the hand not of Richard, but of her other brother, Roger. "How can this be?" she asked as the words jumbled and danced before her eyes making them impossible to decipher. "What does it say?" she asked, thrusting the parchment back into Maud's trembling hand.

"I am summoned to Nottingham," she replied in a tremulous voice. "My husband has returned and he has sent for me to join him."

Maud sank onto the bench before the fire. Her face was white in the light cast from the flames and Johanna suddenly realised that she was very afraid of Roger, and probably with good reason judging by her own past experience.

"You cannot go until the weather improves," said her mother, tearfully. Johanna knew that it was because she could not bear the thought of being parted from Maud. "I cannot think what Roger means to send for you in such foul weather. I shall write to tell him and say that you will come with the thaw." Then she turned to Johanna. "And I shall also ask him to consider taking you, my lady, for your constant distemper is too much for me to bear alone."

Johanna looked from the two mournful women to the messenger who was still dripping on their hearth and felt an icy cloud of despair settle around her shoulders.

She was dismayed at the idea of being sent to Nottingham to dwell in the household of her accursed brother Roger but, short of running away again as soon as the snows began to melt, she was at a loss to know how to prevent it.

Chapter Three

Richard had expected Geoffrey to ride ahead of him to show him the way to the Holy Well but the boy arrived on foot at the entrance to the stables and asked politely if Richard was ready to go.

"I will walk with you. It is not far," he said.

Richard gathered his few possessions from the floor, including a stick he had found on the river bank that was about the right length and thickness to help him walk, and thanked the kennel boys who had brought him food and ale before pulling the cloak and hood around himself.

"Lead the way and I will follow," he told Geoffrey.

"I am not afraid to walk with you," replied the boy, fiercely.

"You are a good and kind young man," Richard told him, warming to the independent spirit of his young companion, "but I would not wish people to see you walking with a leper in case they should choose to shun you as well."

"They would not dare!" replied Geoffrey with the innocence of youth and Richard smiled a rare smile that pulled on the dry sores at the corners of his mouth and hurt his cracked lips.

"Walk ahead," insisted Richard surprised at how stiff his body felt after a day of inactivity, "and I will follow in your steps."

They set out north with the low sun behind them and the boy preceded him reluctantly along the well worn track leading around the side of a hill that reminded Richard of a hunting dog or a wildcat crouched to pounce on its prey.

"What is the name of the hill?" called Richard.

"We call it Penhull Hill," replied Geoffrey over his shoulder without slackening his pace. "The peasants say it is haunted by spirits."

"I can almost believe that," said Richard as he gazed up to where the early morning mist still shrouded the summit.

"They won't go up there after dark, not even for lambing. They say they can hear the spirits howling, though I think it is wolves myself."

"That's probably as good a reason as any to avoid it unless you have a horse that's fleet of foot and a fine pack of hounds like your father's."

"That's true," laughed Geoffrey. "But you will find that the peasants are full of superstition around here. They come to church and make a show of following our Christian beliefs, but they are pagan at heart."

"But they do as they are told?"

"When it suits them – and when we are watching – but there's not many I would trust," said Geoffrey.

"But you are English too," said Richard.

"My mother is English; my father half French," he replied. "He is related to the Lady Isabel, the wife of

Robert de Lacy who has the castle there you can see on the hill."

Richard stood a few feet behind Geoffrey as he stopped to point out the stone keep rising above the village. "So that is Cliderhou?" he said.

"Yes. The Holy Well of St Mary is there, just below the castle hill. I will show you."

As they approached Richard could see that the castle was built on an outcrop of limestone that rose like one of the sores on his body from the flat plains all around. He could understand why the site had been chosen as it gave an ample view of the far countryside and any invader would be unable to approach it from any angle without being seen whilst still miles away.

The limestone knoll fell steeply away below the keep but nearby, where the hill was more gentle, there were several stone and wooden buildings nestling within the confines of the castle walls and a gatehouse was set at the base of the hill, above the village. On a smaller knoll outside the castle walls stood a stone built church and around this was a motley collection of whitewashed dwellings with thatched roofs.

As they passed the gatehouse Geoffrey turned and said: "This is where Robert de Lacy lives. The well is at the bottom of the hill," he explained, before leading Richard down past the church to the village.

As they approached a small stone pit Richard stopped and pushed back his hood slightly as he tried to discern from which of the huts the bad smell was coming. But the unpleasant odour of bad eggs grew stronger as they approached the well.

He watched as Geoffrey bent to gather water into a bucket on a frayed rope, then moved forward with his cup in his gloved hands to allow the boy to pour some into his own vessel.

"There is sulphur in the water," he explained as Richard recoiled from the stench of it.

"Is it drinkable?" he asked, studying the liquid that looked clear enough but smelt repulsive. "Surely water that stinks so bad must be filled with evil?"

"The locals say that it is the smell that makes the cure; that the bad smell chases the devils from the body," he replied.

Richard slowly raised his cup to his dry, chapped lips and tasted it. The taste of it in his mouth was abhorrent but he swallowed it down quickly like a medicine. Geoffrey laughed.

"You are braver than most pilgrims," he said. "They are usually content to just wash in it."

Slowly Richard pulled the irritating leather gloves from his sore, chapped hands and poured the remainder of the icy cold water over each one in turn, watching as the warmth of his hands turned the moisture to a fine vapour that momentarily mixed with his breath before dispersing on the wintry air.

He looked up to see Geoffrey staring at his reddened hands. "Do they hurt?" asked the boy.

"They itch – like the devil!" confided Richard. "But I will wash in this water every day and, by God's grace and with prayer and repentance, I will be granted a cure."

The boy nodded as he watched Richard gently pat dry his hands on his inner tunic and ease them back into the gloves. "You will need more than a cup to draw water to wash," he said. "I will bring you a bucket, and you will also need somewhere to shelter."

Richard suddenly realised that the boy was talking good, practical sense. He had been so keen to find Cliderhou and make contact with Robert de Lacy that he had given little thought to what else he would do and where he would stay once he had arrived.

"Where is the nearest leper house?" he asked. Geoffrey shook his head.

"There's none nearby," he said. "But I do know a place where you can stay. I sometimes played there when I was a child whilst I waited for my father to talk with Sir Robert. Shall I show you?"

Richard nodded at the eager boy and fell into step behind him as they skirted the houses, where eyes peeped out like the stars appearing in the evening sky as they passed by; and a whispering like the wind through the moorland grass tracked their progress to the north of the castle walls where the escarpment met the flat pasture, tilled into long strips, barren now where the autumn crops had been gathered in. Looking up Richard could see that there were several hollows in the rock face that might accord him some protection, but Geoffrey passed them by until he reached a place, half hidden behind some shrubs, where he turned, panting slightly, and called, "This is it."

The boy stood back as Richard bent and looked into the low entrance of the cave. It did not look promising and Richard would probably have dismissed it immediately if his young guide had not been standing a few feet from him with a smile that stretched the whole width of his fresh face.

"Well?" demanded Geoffrey, pushing his wind whipped hair back from his dancing eyes. "What do you think?"

"It is dark," remarked Richard doubtfully as he bent double to peer in. "Do you think it is used by wolves?" He heard Geoffrey laugh out loud behind him as he edged a little nearer.

"Go in. Go in," urged the boy. "I used to play in there for hours. It is huge when you get inside."

Richard crouched down though still managed to graze his cheek as the hood of his cloak snagged on a rock and pulled him to one side as he ventured further. Once inside, he sensed rather than saw that the roof was high enough for him to stand and once his watery eyes had cleared a little and adjusted to the darkness he could vaguely see that the chamber was not only large, but well protected both from the weather and from prying eyes.

"What do you think?" called Geoffrey from outside. And for the second time that morning Richard found himself giving an unthinking and painful smile.

"It will do very well," he called back, stretching out his arms above and beyond him to judge the dimensions of his cell. "It will do very well."

He ducked back outside to where even the weak winterish sunlight stung at his eyes. He wiped them on his sleeve and pulled up the hood again as his sight cleared and he saw Geoffrey staring at his ravaged face.

"You will need some bedding and some rugs," said the boy, "and a brazier to make a fire for light and warmth and to cook on – and some pots to cook and a bucket for your washing water. I will bring them to you."

"Geoffrey!" Richard held up a hand to silence the boy. "You have done enough for me already. I do not want to burden you."

"Since when has helping a fellow human being been a burden?" asked the boy quietly. "It will please me to help you."

Richard stepped forward to touch the boy on the shoulder, then remembered his affliction and allowed his hand to fall away. Yet he noticed that Geoffrey had not flinched and would have allowed the touch.

"God bless you," he whispered, wondering how the Dean had produced such a brave and honourable son. "I am in your debt – and one day, if I am able, I will see that your kindness to me is repaid tenfold."

Having listened to the quick footfalls of the boy fade down the slope, Richard fell to his knees on the hard stone floor and gave thanks to God for sending him such a help-meet. He recalled the words of Jesus himself, who told his disciples not to worry about what they should eat or drink or clothe themselves in but that, if they would only trust in God, then their every need would be supplied.

"I have put my trust in you, O Lord," he prayed out loud, "and, by Your grace, You have led me to this place and given me the friendship of this boy. Now give me the strength to complete my mission and, if it be Your will, accept my penitence and grant me a cure by the water of the Holy Well."

Later that day, as good as his word, Geoffrey returned with a large bucket and a couple of woollen rugs.

"I took them from the stables," he confessed as, bent double, he peered into the cave, his hair falling around his face. "I hope they do not smell too much of horse but I doubt they will be missed. I will bring the other things when I can. And here..." He handed Richard a roughly wrapped cloth with a loaf of bread and some scraps of meat. "I stole these from the kitchen."

"Thou shalt not steal!" Richard reprimanded the boy, who grinned and then stood upright so that Richard could only see his brown leather boots that were caked with mud.

"I will come again," he called, "but my father has noticed that I have neglected my duties today. He suspects that I am enamoured of a girl and has lectured me on the sins of the flesh."

With that, the boots moved swiftly away and Richard was left alone, clutching his supper, to meditate on the consequences of such sins.

He slept badly, with every stone and crack of the floor piercing his body and the coldness of the stone seeming to creep into the marrow of his bones. He itched and raged and shivered in turn until, as the first hint of sunrise broached the edges of the hill and the first bell of the day rang across the valley, he pulled himself to his knees to pray. Then before breaking his fast he took the bucket and, wearing only the cloak and gloves, he stumbled down the steep side of the rocky cliffs to the Holy Well.

The village was still slumbering. One or two of the huts showed meagre puffs of smoke above their roofs as the covered fires were coaxed back to life and a mangy mongrel raised its head and gave a half-hearted attempt at a bark as Richard passed by. In the half light, Richard used his staff to break the thin layer of ice that coated the well water. As the winter drew on he would need to find a stronger one.

He lowered the well bucket and pulled it up full, averting his face from the stink as he poured it into the bucket Geoffrey had brought him. Then, glancing around to ensure he was not observed, he quickly pulled off his gloves and shoes and unfastened the cloak, throwing it aside before quickly raising the bucket to tip the foul, icy water over his head. He gasped as the water drenched his body, the shock making him empty his bladder, mixing warm liquid with the cold that ran down his legs. Then, steaming and shivering in the morning air, ashamed and humiliated, he wrapped the rough cloak over his wet skin, raised up the hood over his dripping hair, donned his shoes and cursed the gloves that stuck to his wet hands as he tried to pull them on. He was aware now of being watched from the huts some distance away and he quickly drew some more water to carry back to his cell, retrieved his staff and made his way back past the villagers to the cave.

At the nearest hut a woman pulled back an inquisitive child from the doorway as he passed. A breeze tugged back his hood a little and he met the woman's eyes.

"The well beyond has sweeter water," she said in English, indicating the other side of the village.

"But not the healing power," replied Richard. "But God bless you. Go in peace."

"Go in peace," replied the woman as he passed and she crossed herself in defence.

He returned up the steep slope, sliding on the icy mud

and spilling much of the water before he reached the cave where he prayed again and ate some stale bread. The warmth he had felt after the effort of the climb soon evaporated and even though he dressed himself in all his clothes he still found that he could not prevent the shivering. He longed for a fire to warm himself and light the dank walls, for thick furs and leather boots and soft linen underclothes to soothe his fevered skin, wine to drink and hot venison stew to warm his stomach. How much he had had in the past without ever appreciating it, he thought, and now the Lord was wreaking His punishment.

Some time later as he mused on his own shortcomings he was disturbed by a noise outside. He thought it was Geoffrey, but was surprised to see a pair of plain leather shoes, wrapped over thick woollen hose and the uneven hem of a coarse brown skirt. A hand pushed a package towards him and then was gone. By the time he had crawled into the open the woman was almost at the bottom of the hill. She glanced up quickly as he stood at the entrance to his cave looking down on her and, without any acknowledgment, she turned and ran to the village. Richard bent and retrieved the package. It was a freshly baked loaf of bread and some dripping. He fell to his knees and praised the Lord for the kindnesses shown to him by these northern people.

Having eaten, his thoughts turned to his grandmother and the letter she had given him. She had come to him the night before his Separation as he had slept in the cellar on a straw stuffed pallet to protect his family from his disease.

The gentle knocking had not awakened him, as sleep

had proved elusive in that long night that was to be his
last as a member of the FiztEustace family. At first he
thought it was a rat; then his grandmother's voice clearly
called his name.

"Grandmama?" he whispered, pulling up the old blanket
around him.

"Richard. Open the door. I need to speak with you."

"Speak from there, Grandmama. I have no wish to pass
on this contagion to you," he replied, partly fearful that
it was an apparition from the devil who had come to
haunt him.

"Open the door," she commanded in the voice from his
childhood that he could not disobey and Richard had got
up from the bed and removed the plank of wood he had
used to wedge the door shut against he knew not what evil.

Dressed in a gown beneath her customary thick brown
cloak, his grandmother had entered the room like a spectre
and closed the door behind her. Breathing heavily she had
pressed a letter into his hand.

"There is something you must do," she had said. "You
must take this letter to my cousin, Robert de Lacy, at
Cliderhou Castle in the new county of Lancashire. He is
an old man with no heirs and many lands. They are lands
that are rightfully mine and my family's. You must give
him this so that he knows I am still alive and you must
ensure that he writes a will that names me as his heir, or
I am afraid that the wealth may be lost to us forever. I
have heard that there is an Englishman who plots to take
the land as his own."

"I have heard you speak of this cousin," said Richard.

"Then promise me that you will not go to the leper

house of St Giles, but will go north with this message instead. Your grandfather, father and brother are all lost to me, and now you as well, my sweet Richard..." He drew back as she reached out to cup his face in her outstretched hands.

"Do not touch me, Grandmama," he pleaded. "I could not bear it if you caught this plague."

"I am an old woman," she sighed, "and soon my place will be with the Lord. But you must do this for your mother and your sisters. I will not have them robbed of their inheritance. Promise me you will do it. And promise me that it will be a secret between you and me alone. If your mother hears of it she will beg you to stay close at hand where she knows you are safe."

Richard stared at the letter in his hand, turning it over and over in a shaft of moonlight. He looked up and met his grandmother's pleading eyes.

"Do this for your family," she said. "Even though tomorrow the priest will declare you dead to us, it will never be so. You will always be a FitzEustace."

He longed to take his grandmother in his arms and feel and smell the body that had nurtured him since childhood, rocking him on her lap, telling him the old stories, soothing his fevers of both mind and body and finally watching him ride off to the Crusade with a proud tear in her eye only to have him creep back diseased and unclean. Richard restrained himself and pulled the blanket tightly round his itching, irritated body.

"Of course I will go," he said simply. He would have entered hell itself if he had thought it would give her peace of mind.

Now, he reached through the slit in the side of his cloak and opened the leather pouch to take out the letter, a little crumpled now and damp in one place, and resolved that his task must be completed with no more hesitation.

With cloak and gloves concealing him he took the staff and stumbled once more down the slope and walked up the path to the gatehouse, unsure of his welcome. A guard stepped forward as he approached and called out in accented English: "Get away from here, you cur!"

"I have a message for Robert de Lacy," he replied and the guard hesitated a little at his reply in French.

"Who are you?" he asked.

"I cannot reveal myself to you. But I have an important letter for Sir Robert. I must speak with him."

"He isn't here," replied the guard. "He is at Pontefract and we don't expect him soon."

Richard hesitated. He wasn't sure if this was the truth or if he was being dismissed with an excuse. As he looked up at the castle any occupants were well hidden from his gaze, but it was obvious that he was not to be granted an audience with Sir Robert that day and all he could do was wait and watch until an opportunity presented itself.

Frustrated, he turned and walked slowly back to his cave, the sore on his left heel making every step an agonising one. Yet, he had known, he told himself, that this task was never going to be as easy as his grandmother had surmised. All he could do now was watch and wait.

As the weather turned Richard woke each morning to find a fresh topping of snow, like the flour on a loaf, dusting the summit of Penhull Hill. He still went down to the Holy Well at first light each morning to wash. The villagers continued to watch from the secrecy of their huts and the woman brought him their offerings each day.

As he had promised, Geoffrey had returned with a brazier and helped Richard gather wood to store in the cave. In the firelight they were both amazed by how large the cavern was, though when Geoffrey found a fissure at the back of the cave that appeared to lead deeper into the hill and wanted to explore it, it took Richard all his will power not to physically pull the boy away and in the end it was only a reminder that his father would be wondering which girl he was with today that made him give his shame-faced grin and agree to go home.

When Geoffrey had gone, Richard lit one of the precious beeswax candles that he had brought and carefully fixed it into the horn lantern. Then he went back to examine the opening for himself. It was about wide enough for a man to squeeze through and in the faint light he could see that the passage extended up a gentle slope and out of sight around a corner. Although it looked natural, as he held the lantern to the rock face Richard could see places where the stone appeared to have been marked by chisels where it had been widened. Slipping out of the cloak, he squeezed through the gap and followed the passage to its first turn. Holding the lantern higher he could see that it led on, the floor rising to meet a lowering roof so that a man would have to crouch to negotiate it. Although he noticed that the floor was dry, it was still probable that the passage, as well as the chamber of the cave, had originally been made by water seeping through the porous rocks. Intrigued, he went on, his thighs aching as he walked, bent like an old man, until the passage turned and opened into a larger inner cave. Here he saw the steps that were definitely man made and raised his lantern to light them to the top where he saw the heavy wooden door. Richard crept up the steps and first put his ear to the wood. There was only silence. He pressed an eye to the keyhole but could see only blackness beyond. Then, with a pounding heart he raised the handle and turned it. A latch raised easily with a loud click that reverberated all around the cave and Richard waited, trembling, for hoards of guards to come running from the other side and haul him off to the gallows. But the echoes faded away and Richard chanced a push at the door, though, as he suspected, it was barred and locked on the far side and did not move at all. An escape route from the castle, guessed Richard. There was a similar one at Halton which came out near the river. And he could not help a half smile as he pictured the faces of the occupants if they ever had to choose between facing attackers at the top of the castle or traversing the cave of a leper below.

Chapter Four

With the melting of the last snowfall from the summit of the hill the peasants came out of their huts to plant their oats and beans and barley in the ploughed fields and Richard emerged with long hair and beard from his cell.

All through the freezing weather he had descended each day at dawn to break the ice on the well water and wash his body. After a few nasty slips he had ceased trying to negotiate the slippery track back to the cave with a slopping bucket of icy, stinking water, but had once again stripped naked at first light to wash at the side of the well.

The villagers had taken to surreptitiously watching him with a mixture of awe and admiration as he had shivered in the soft light of the morning and they had continued to leave food for him, either at the entrance to his cave or by the well, although none would speak to him or look him in the eye, but would rush into their huts and cross themselves repeatedly if they saw him approaching.

As the days became longer Richard rose each morning when the church bell rang for Matins to wash and pray, until one morning in early April he felt the warmth of the sun on his back as the sulphurous water dried and he paused for a moment to enjoy the hint of a summer to come before re-clothing himself. As he lifted and shook his linen braies, another gift from Geoffrey to help keep out the cold, he caught sight of his own flesh, something he always tried to avoid. But now he paused, garment in hand, and examined himself anew. The skin across his abdomen had grown white but smooth under a scattering of dark hairs and when he looked at his legs and arms he could see that the redness had subdued and there were expanses of smooth skin between the scaled and itchy sores that had covered him before.

"Praise to the Lord!" he called at the top of his voice, lifting his arms to the sunrise and throwing back his head until he could feel his hair between his shoulder blades. "And thanks to God for the miracle!" With this he fell naked to his knees amongst the stones and mud, buried his face in his hands and wept tears of joy that his faith had not been found wanting and that God had granted him a cure. "For this I am Yours!" he cried. "I dedicate my life to You in thanks for the compassion and forgiveness you have shown me. Alleluia! I am Yours!"

As he turned triumphantly to face the morning sun he was aware of a frisson of whispered voices and excited movement from the villagers as they spied on him. Smiling for the first time in months, and without pain, he quickly dressed and drank from his cup before vowing to return to his cell to spend the rest of the day in prayers of thanks for his forgiveness and deliverance.

As he gathered his staff and bucket he saw the woman from the village, whom he had come to recognise, approach him slowly with the familiar bundle of bread and dripping. He waited as she crept closer, like a wary but inquisitive animal, ready to run at any movement. A crowd of villagers huddled together to watch, one elderly woman holding back a small girl who was keen to follow her mother. He stood, still, and watched the woman come towards him. Her eyes remained downcast as she came gradually nearer and nearer until she was within a few feet of him. Here she stopped and looked up. Her blue eyes met his and she crossed herself as she held out the food with her trembling hand.

"For the Holy Hermit," she whispered.

Richard stepped forward and took the bread from her.

"God bless you. Go in peace," he said, in English, as he had on the first occasion that they met.

"Go in peace," she repeated, before scuttling back to her family, who smiled and hugged her and patted her about the head and shoulders for her bravery. Richard smiled back at them and made the sign of a blessing on them before walking back to his cave with a feeling growing inside him that he took some time to identify as happiness.

He ducked down under the overhanging rock and waited a few moments for his eyes to accustom themselves to the gloom after the intensifying brightness of the spring morning outside. As his rudimentary cell revealed itself in the colourless half-light he located the high shelf where he stored his food out of reach of vermin and carefully placed the bundle up there. He would eat when the sun went down. Meanwhile he would pray and fast to the glory of God.

Beside the rugs that formed his bed Richard found that

for the first time a shaft of sunlight fell upon him as he knelt with his face to the opening of the cave. Its subtle warmth filled his body with the peace of the Lord, and yet he was still unsatisfied.

It was many months since he had made his confession and, even then, he had never revealed the real reason for his contagion. He worried that there could be no lasting forgiveness without confession and, although the Lord had opened the door of salvation to him, he knew that he was still unworthy and needed the blessing of a consecrated priest before he could begin to feel whole again.

He often watched the villagers answering the ringing of the bell from the square tower of the small stone church of St Mary Magdalene that summoned them to prayer on a Sunday morning with a longing that reduced him to tears of frustration and despair. Of all the rules that bound him it was the one that forbade him to enter any church that he found the hardest to keep. Yet, if Jesus could forgive the sins of Mary Magdalene herself, surely He could forgive what had taken place between him and Leila in Palestine.

The Dean had offered to hear his confession but he was reluctant to return to Wallei, not least because his stolen clothing might give away the kindness that Geoffrey had shown him. He did not want to make any trouble for the boy. But it wasn't just his guilt about the many things his young friend had acquired for him, it was a reluctance to confide in the Dean that also left him torn between his needs and his better judgement.

After the None bell he set out as usual. Richard was in the habit of walking around the hill each day after his washing and his prayers, with his cloak wrapped closely about him and his staff in his hand to assist his foothold on the tussocky grass. He paused, as he did every afternoon, when he reached a vantage point on the eastern side of the hill, near the gatehouse where the guards had at first watched him with suspicion but where their attention was now scornful. Geoffrey had assured him that although Sir Robert always spent the winter at Pontefract he would return to Cliderhou in the spring and Richard leaned on his staff and stared at the road that came from Yorkshire, trying to will the timely return of his grandmother's cousin.

As he watched he thought he saw a glint of distant metal flashing a reflection from the sun. Hoping that he was not deceiving himself into believing that this was the day on which two miracles could occur, he sat down and watched and waited as the sun hovered in the vivid blue sky.

Above him in the trees the rooks were squabbling noisily over their nests, stealing sticks from one another and squawking accusations and recriminations in a way that reminded Richard of the peasants at Halton when they had taken too much rich ale on a Holy Day.

As he waited, his eyes trained eastwards like a hawk's, he saw time and again the flashes of sunlight on harness as the procession drew nearer until at last he could make out the horsemen in their chainmail and surcoats of a golden yellow and purple, the livery of the de Lacy family. Two outriders passed him closely as they galloped up to the castle gates and horns were sounded from the castle walls to alert the villagers that their lord and master was on his way.

Soon he could hear the beat of the horses' hooves, the squeaks of damp leather and the jangling of the bits as the travellers approached and began the last climb towards the outer curtain wall of the castle.

Richard watched in anticipation as they drew near and stood up at their approach, checking that his hands were gloved and that his hood obscured his face completely. His vision was restricted but, as the sweating horses passed, the flecks of white foam from their panting mouths clouding the air, he saw the curtain of the litter lift and an elderly lady looked out at him. Behind her, riding a sturdy bay gelding, an equally aged man wearing a mantle lined with fur glanced at him as the procession paused for the huge castle gates to be scraped open. Richard raised a hand in greeting. The man regarded him for a moment before the horses moved on and trotted in through the gates and up the short incline to the castle keep. Sir Robert de Lacy had come home to Cliderhou. *And now*, thought Richard, *I can complete my mission*.

Impatient though he was, Richard knew that it would be ill-mannered to demand an audience with Sir Robert so soon after his arrival, so he returned to his cell and sat outside the entrance to bide his time with his face turned upwards towards the welcome sun. As it began its westward descent and the evening closed in Richard made his Vespers prayers and was preparing to break his fast with the bread from the village when he heard a rustling of the undergrowth below his cell and, taking his staff in his hand as a defence against an unwelcome intruder, he stepped to the edge of the cave and bent to see who was approaching.

He recognised one of the guards from the gatehouse who climbed reluctantly upwards, glancing about him like a stag that had caught the scent of pursuing hounds. Richard stepped forward, staff in hand, and the guard halted suddenly at his unexpected appearance, almost toppling backwards and grasping at the long grasses beside him to retain his balance.

After a moment, when he had regained his composure, he fixed Richard with an undisguised glare of contempt and called out, "You! Hermit! Sir Robert de Lacy commands that you come!"

"Wait there. I will be with you in a moment when I have donned my cloak and gloves," replied Richard, politely. Smiling to himself, he checked that he had his grandmother's letter safely stowed in the pouch at his belt before he followed the man down the track and around to the gatehouse. In response to the guard's knock a small door set into the larger one was opened and he was allowed to step through into the castle bailey.

The courtyard was still busy from the arrival of Sir Robert and the guard preceded Richard as they threaded their way between the throng of busy servants as belongings brought from Pontefract were unpacked from carts and ponies and carried inside.

The guard led him across an inner drawbridge and up the steps of the keep to the great hall. As the evening was growing darker, a servant was moving around with a taper to light candles, a page boy was laying cups and trenchers on the cloth covered trestle table that had been set up on the dais at the far end of the hall and two others were attempting to hang a tapestry. A charcoal brazier was glowing in the centre of the hall and the aroma of roasting meat wafted in through the open window from the kitchen.

The guard indicated with a dismissive wave of his hand that Richard should stand just inside the doorway and wait. Then, as if he had been waiting and watching from his adjoining chamber, the elderly man whom Richard had seen earlier came out from behind the screen on the far side of the dais to greet him.

"Good evening, Hermit."

"Good evening, my lord," replied Richard.

"So you *are* of Norman descent as I have been told," replied the man. "I am Robert de Lacy, lately returned from my castle at Pontefract, where I had already received news of the holy hermit who has taken up residence beneath my castle."

"Forgive my intrusion on your hospitality, my lord. It was, however, done with good reason and I would speak with you privately on a family matter if you would permit me."

"A family matter!" replied Sir Robert. "That is far from what I expected. Who are you, Hermit? Reveal yourself to me," he demanded.

"I do not think that the removal of my hood, or the revelation of my name is fitting here," said Richard with a brief indication of the servants whose ears were almost straining from their heads as they lingered at their tasks around the hall. "I crave a word in private if it pleases you, my lord. You need have no worry about my contagion. I am much improved," he added as he saw the hesitation on the older man's face.

"Come," he said and led the way back to the screen

and the private chamber beyond. He beckoned Richard to join him in the small solar where two wooden chairs, one bare and one padded with cushions flanked a blazing hearth. "Come and be seated and warm your hands at my fire."

Richard was aware that Sir Robert was studying him carefully as he sat down on the edge of the chair to the left of the fire and slowly peeled off the gloves to hold his hands out towards the flames. The skin that had been red raw and peeling was almost smooth now and as Richard spread his fingers and held them out to the glow of the heat he heard a slow breath of relief escape from his host.

Slowly Richard reached up and lifted back the hood from around his face.

"Forgive my unkempt appearance, my lord, but as you know I have been living as a hermit in a cave below." Richard lifted his face to the light and allowed Sir Robert to study him.

"I thought you were a leper."

"By prayer and fasting and the grace of God I have been granted a cure by washing in the holy well of St Mary Magdalene, whom Jesus forgave for her many sins," said Richard.

He waited as Sir Robert hesitated, still assessing him and no doubt wondering about his trustworthiness.

"I am Richard FitzEustace," he said.

"Richard FitzEustace? By God, I thought you were dead!"

"I am dead," replied Richard, "to all intents and purposes. I have been read the Mass of Separation and cannot claim my birthright or inherit. But I have a letter for you here from my grandmother, your cousin Albreda, that begs your consideration in the disposal of your lands after your death."

As Sir Robert stared, Richard put his gloves back on before removing the parchment from inside his pouch and holding it out.

"I have never touched it with bare hands," he said when Sir Robert did not reach forward immediately to receive it. "It is safe for you to touch."

Moving slowly as if the long journey had bruised all his bones, Sir Robert lowered himself to the cushioned seat and took the letter.

"Then Albreda is still alive?" he asked. "I had heard rumour that she was also dead."

"She is much alive," replied Richard with a wry smile. "It is true that my grandfather is dead and my father John died at Tyre last year. I have been cast out as a leper and the whereabouts of my brother Roger are unknown. Yet my grandmother lives and I have a mother and two sisters, so the FitzEustace family still remains and my grandmother begs that you do not disinherit her when your time comes."

Sir Robert was silent as he held the letter at arm's length to the light of a candle to read it. Richard watched him as he studied it. He must have been a good looking man when he was young and his face still had strength in the line of the jaw and there was an acute intelligence in the dark brown eyes under thick grey brows.

He took his time reading and re-reading the letter and studied the seal that Albreda had pressed into the wax. Meanwhile Richard sat and waited, acutely embarrassed by the audible growlings of his empty stomach. Then Sir Robert rolled up the letter and looked at Richard intently.

"I think that somewhere under all that hair I can detect a family resemblance," he said. "Have you eaten?"

"I was about to when your messenger came to me."

"Then you shall eat here – a proper meal tonight – you look as if you are in need of some nourishment."

"I have been fasting to gain redemption," Richard told him.

Sir Robert snorted. "That is all very well, but there is nothing to be gained by starving yourself to death. You can eat in the hall with us and tell me about yourself."

Sir Robert eased himself up from the chair and limped ahead of him back into the hall where the supper dishes were being brought in and set out on a side table. Richard's mouth watered at the sight and smell of the steaming mutton stew, fresh bread, nut tarts and jugs of wine, though the servants kept glancing suspiciously at his unhooded face as Sir Robert commanded one of them to set an extra place at the top table.

As they waited, the lady that Richard had seen in the litter came down the stone steps from an upper level with her maid. She came slowly across the hall as if she was very weary and her husband stepped towards her to take her hand raise it to his lips before leading her to her seat at the table.

"My wife, the Lady Isobel," he said and Richard bowed to her. "The hermit is a FitzEustace," Sir Robert explained to his wife. "He is Albreda's grandson."

Lady Isabel smiled up at him. "Then you are welcome," she told him as she indicated that he should be seated.

"Will you say a prayer before we begin?" asked Sir Robert. "My chaplain is not here." Richard said a blessing for the food but he restrained himself from touching it, the words of Father William echoing in his head. "Eat, eat," urged Sir Robert.

"I may not eat nor drink from any vessel that is not my own, and my cup and platter are in my cell," he explained. Sir Robert hesitated fleetingly before shaking his head.

"Eat and drink," he said again. "This bowl and cup can become your own."

Richard still delayed, wondering if God would forgive him for breaking his vows so soon. But once again his bodily desires took precedence over his better intentions and he wiped away a dribble of saliva on the back of his hand before tearing off a chunk of the bread and dipping it into the aromatic stew. He placed it on his tongue as a communion, closing his eyes to savour the sweet intense flavour of the meat. Today was truly a day of miracles, he thought, so let it be a feast day after all to the glory of God, and may God still forgive him his weaknesses.

"I presume you caught your disease whilst in the service of the king?" said Sir Robert after watching his guest quell the first urgent pangs of his hunger.

"Yes indeed. I was in Palestine with King Richard until last summer. After the death of my father in Tyre I took the cross and journeyed to join the king at Limassol on the island of Cyprus."

"I hear it was there the king took his wife. Is that so?"

"Yes. He was wed to Berengaria, the first born daughter

of the King of Navarre. They were married at the Chapel of St. George in May, not long before I arrived."

"So you were not there for the wedding?"

"No. But I met the queen briefly."

"Then let us hope that they are soon blessed with a son and heir. No one knows the disappointment of being denied a son more than myself and my wife," he said as he glanced at Lady Isabel with a tangible sadness that made Richard want to reach out and give him the comfort of his physical touch. "But tell me more about the Crusade. Were you at Acre?"

"Indeed. I helped to build the siege engines and trebuchets to bombard the city until it eventually fell to us on the twelfth of July. The whole army fell to their knees in triumphant prayer."

"What a sight it must have been. How I wish I could have been there."

"The life was hard. It was unbearably hot at times and there were flies and insects and all manner of creatures I have never seen before nor wish to see again. Food and water were short and many fell ill."

"Yourself included."

"Yes. As soon as it was seen that I had contracted a leprosy I was sent back home to put my family's affairs in order. My brother Roger has disappeared. No one had news of him and I can only presume he is dead like our father before him."

"I am sorry for your loss. I met your father once when he was a young man and I liked him. The longer I talk with you the more it is revealed to me that you are truly his son. He was a devout man and he gave his life in the service of the Lord, as you too have made your pilgrimage and your sacrifice."

"I am unworthy to be compared with him," said Richard, remembering how his father had embraced his mother before he left her for the last time. He remembered the tears in her eyes as she dabbed her face with a fine silk cloth and how his father had leaned down from his powerful war horse to cup her chin in his hand and kiss her one last farewell. He recalled how his father had reminded her that he was about the Lord's work and that the Lord would keep him safe and return him to her. But it had not been so. "The day the letter came that told of his death my mother fell to the floor and raged against God," he said. "She begged me not to go and swore that she could not continue to live if I was taken from her as well. She was on her knees before my horse when I rode away, having chosen my duty to God over honouring the wishes of my mother."

"A difficult decision."

"Indeed, almost impossible – and when I returned like this it was almost more than she could bear. I promised that I would remain nearby at the Leper House of St Giles. But here I am in Lancashire, deceiving her again, for the sake of the family inheritance and at the behest of my grandmother."

"Albreda never was a woman to be disobeyed," remarked Sir Robert in sympathy with Richard's plight. "And I will make certain that your journey was not for nothing."

"For that I am grateful, my lord."

"Then humour an old man and tell me more of the battle," he urged, his brown eyes alight with the anticipation of hearing at first hand the events of that day when the city of Acre surrendered to the Christian force.

Richard smiled at his enthusiasm and settled to describe as fully as he could everything that had happened; everything except his meetings with Leila.

It was late by the time the candles had burned down. Sir Robert's eyes were closing as his head began to nod forwards and beside him Lady Isobel stifled several yawns.

"You are both tired after your long journey," said Richard at last. "Let us talk some more tomorrow when you have rested."

"When will you return to the Leper Hospital?" asked Sir Robert as they stood up.

"I have no pressing plans," said Richard, recalling his grandmother's admonition that he should remain until a copy of Sir Robert's will naming her as heir was in his possession. "But if you would rather I went..."

"No, no!" cried Sir Robert, stretching out a hand towards his visitor. "I was hoping that you might stay longer. I have enjoyed our talk and would know you better."

"Then I will gladly stay and talk more of the Holy Land," promised Richard. "But for now, with your permission, I will return to my cell."

"And have you everything you need there?"

"I have sufficient for my needs, thank you, my lord."

"Then I will show you the way."

"No," replied Richard, gathering up his cloak and gloves. "Rest here and I will find my own way."

"I doubt it," laughed Sir Robert with a gleam in his eyes. "Come with me."

Intrigued, Richard followed him across the small hall

to where a narrow spiral of stone steps led down to the cellar. Sir Robert lifted a torch from one of the sconces that lit the stairwell and beckoned him to follow. Their footfalls rang around the silent space as they descended until they reached a stout wooden door cut into the wall half way down. Sir Robert fumbled at his belt and in silence produced a key, which he held up with a smile before turning it in the well oiled lock and swinging back the door to reveal a further flight of stone cut steps beyond.

"Do you know where you are?" he demanded conspiratorially, smiling like a boy.

"Indeed, I think I do," replied Richard.

"I will light your way," said Sir Robert holding the torch aloft to illuminate the steps as Richard descended. "Can you manage now?" he asked as Richard reached the bottom and the entrance to the narrow tunnel which led back to his cave.

"I know my way," he confirmed.

"Then I wish you a good night, Richard FitzEustace. Come to me again tomorrow and we will talk some more."

Then, as Richard reached out to touch the walls so as not to lose his bearings, the light retreated and as the blackness thickened he heard the door above him gently close and the key turn in the lock.

He edged his way along the tunnel until he reached the half light of the cave where an almost full moon nudged its light under the low entrance.

For the first time in many months, Richard felt that his life was worthy. His prayers were being answered one by one, his stomach was full and his mission, if not accomplished, was at least moved on one step further, and he knelt in the beam of moonlight to give thanks.

The following morning Richard once again approached the gatehouse and found that his reception was much changed. The door was opened for him and he made his way across the courtyard to the castle keep, sensing the curious glances of the servants from beneath his hood.

Perhaps Sir Robert had been watching out for him, for by the time he reached the top step he was already waiting at the door of the hall, looking younger and refreshed after a night's sleep – probably in a soft feather bed rather than on a hard floor, thought Richard, then silently begged pardon for his selfish thoughts.

"Come," said Sir Robert and led him into the hall where he motioned him to a chair beside the brazier. "Have you eaten?"

"My needs are met by the Lord, as are those of the birds of the air and the fishes of the sea," replied Richard. "In fact the peasants bring me bread each day. It seems to please them to do so."

Sir Robert nodded. "They are superstitious," he remarked. "I believe it is they who have named you the Holy Hermit. They are a simple people, these English, and probably believe that they are warding off some evil by feeding you."

"They are certainly warding off the evil of my starvation," laughed Richard, surprising himself at the unexpected return of his humour. How long had it been since he had last made a jest, he thought, and he wondered if making such quips was in keeping with his new vows.

"So is there anything I can do to make your stay more

agreeable?" asked Sir Robert. "I crave your company and your stories of the Holy Land. What can I do to ensure you stay close by?"

"I have all my needs," replied Richard as he looked into the lined face of Sir Robert and wondered if this elderly man was lonely. He had his wife of course, and his household knights, but perhaps not the companionship he desired, not here in this small castle. "Yet, there is one matter," he began, unsure how to continue, "if it is in your power." Looking up and meeting Sir Robert's indulgent brown eyes he found strength to explain his predicament. "It is many months since I made my confession to a priest and there is a matter which weighs heavily on my soul. Yet I am forbidden entry to the church."

Sir Robert nodded. "That I can remedy," he said. "I have a priest who will come to act as my chaplain and he will hear your confession."

"I am grateful, my lord, but there is one more indulgence I must beg of you. I would ask you not to reveal my identity to anyone as my grandmother believes that there are others who are plotting to steal her inheritance and I am unsure who is my friend and who is my enemy."

"My cousin Albreda need have no fears," replied Sir Robert. "The lands will pass to the FitzEustace family as she requests and my will and testament will be written to that effect."

"For that I am grateful," said Richard. "Now that I have completed the mission my grandmother set I am easier in my mind, but I would still ask that you do not reveal who I am. For truly I am dead and now the name of Hermit will suit me as well as any other."

"Your secret is safe with me," Sir Robert assured him. "Now, indulge me a little with more of your tales whilst I send a messenger to fetch the priest."

After an hour or so of storytelling Sir Robert insisted that Richard eat dinner with them in the hall. "I have told the servants to put the cup and bowl you used last night to one side for you to use again. They will be your own whilst you are here and there need be no worries about breaking your oath."

"I am grateful for your consideration, my lord," said Richard, warming to this kindly man who was taking such an interest in his wellbeing.

"I want to keep your companionship," confessed Sir Robert. "For whilst I must spend time here to administer my estates it is a lonely place and there is only you and the Dean of Wallei who can make decent conversation – and his conversation is at times rather dull," he observed.

"I met the Dean. He was kindly disposed to me when I first arrived and I am in his debt."

"Then tell him so as you make your confession, for I believe he will be with us soon."

The news rather dulled Richard's appetite and having eaten only a little bread he wondered if the sickly feeling in the pit of his stomach was caused by the unaccustomed surfeit of food or the thought that he had committed himself to revealing his worst secret to a man that he did not quite trust.

As the servants cleared away the trenchers there was a commotion outside as the main gates were dragged open and Sir Robert hurried to greet his guest. Richard remained, skulking in the shadows near the entrance, and watched as the Dean trotted up on his magnificent horse.

The animal, barely breathing heavily after the short ride, tossed its head and its bridle jingled and shone as the afternoon sun peeped through a gap in the black clouds that were threatening a heavy shower. In the daylight Richard could see that the animal was not in fact pure black but a very dark bay without even a patch of white about its coat. The Dean leapt from the horse with the grace of a striking hawk and tossed the reins to a stable boy before sweeping off his feathered hat and bowing a greeting to Sir Robert. Watching, Richard wondered at his ability to bow so low and yet not subjugate himself in any way to the man who was his master.

He ran up the outer steps and ushered Sir Robert back towards his own hall, smiling broadly and leaned towards him to make some conspiratorial comment, until, catching sight of Richard in the shadows, his face hardened momentarily.

"Good afternoon, my friend," he said nodding in Richard's direction. "I see that you have sought refuge with Sir Robert and he tells me that you are now ready to make your confession and receive the absolution I offered you when we last met." There was an edge to his voice beneath the friendly tone and Richard had the impression that he was both surprised and a little alarmed to see him on such intimate terms with Sir Robert. "How do you fare?" he asked.

"I have washed in the Holy Well and, by the grace of God, am much improved," said Richard.

"Praise be," replied the Dean. "I am glad to hear it. I

also hear that your washing and praying have made quite
an impression on the villagers and that they have named
you the Holy Hermit."

"Whilst Hermit I can answer to, I am not holy," replied
Richard as he watched the Dean twist his hat round and
around in his troubled fingers. Peering out from under his
hood his eyes locked with the Dean's and for a long moment
the two men contemplated each other like stags at bay.

"Let me offer you some wine after your ride," said Sir
Robert, gesturing a servant forward.

"Thank you no; maybe later," said the Dean. "I believe
our hermit is anxious to make his confession, so let us
proceed to the chapel."

Richard nodded briefly and detached himself from the
Dean's inquisitive blue gaze, knowing that by doing so he
conceded defeat on this occasion. He watched as the Dean
turned to Sir Robert with a fawning smile and wondered
whether this was the man that his grandmother had warned
him about.

"Come," he said, and summoned Richard to follow
with a gracefully long forefinger before preceding him
back down the stairs and striding with authority across
the courtyard towards the chapel of St Michael. Pausing
only to pull the hood further down around his face and
to tuck his hands into his sleeves Richard followed him,
admiring the lithe movement of the man and thinking that
from behind he could pass for a man still in his twenties.
It was only when he turned that the fine lines around his
shrewd eyes revealed that he was old enough to be the
father of a son himself almost ready for marriage.

The Dean unbuckled his fine black woollen cloak and

handed his outer garments to his servant who was waiting anxiously behind him. Beneath he wore the black cassock of a priest which accentuated the hint of red in his hair.

He paused to wash his hands in the small stone sink at the entrance to the chapel and indicated that Richard should do the same. Richard leaned his staff against the stone wall and stepped under the limestone arch, decorated around with the faces of the saints, before removing his gloves and tucking them into his belt. From under his hood he could see the Dean watching him as he stretched his now unblemished hands towards the water and cupped the cold clear liquid for a moment before touching a drop to his forehead and making the sign of the cross.

"Come, my friend," said the Dean. He gestured to the cold stone step upon which Richard should kneel.

"Father, forgive me, for I have sinned," began Richard, realising that that was the easy part. What he had to confess was painful and hard, but he knew it was the penance he must pay to be granted forgiveness and the sacrament of absolution. His legs and knees, devoid of any cushioning flesh from his long fasts, were already excruciatingly painful as he fumbled around his confused memory for the best place to begin.

"What manner of sin?" intoned the Dean.

"I have committed a sin of fornication," he replied, his head bowed and his eyes unfocussed on the ground.

"Fornication?" repeated the Dean with a mixture of surprise and admiration in his voice and Richard realised that he viewed him only as a semi-repulsive leper rather than the man he had once been.

As he struggled to form the words of his confession it was the images and the sensations of his stay in the Holy Land that formed themselves in his mind. He had been privileged enough to have his own tent within sight of the sea shore, where the cooling breeze had made the nights a little more bearable. In fact, sometimes the nights had been welcomingly chilly as an on-shore wind had flapped at the sides of his tent and rustled the rush mats that covered the sand.

He had grown used to hearing the comings and goings of the other Crusaders nearby, but on the night he had heard a woman screaming he had risen from his bed, pulled his surcoat over his undergarments and gone out under the starlit sky to see what the commotion was about.

In the light of a half moon he had seen one of the Crusader's servants with a woman in his grasp, holding her around the waist with one arm and with her long black hair twisted around the fist of the other so that she could not move her head. She kicked her bare feet at another man who baited her as if she was a tethered bear.

"What are you doing?" demanded Richard as he approached unseen in the darkness. The two men ceased their sport and turned to stare at him and, although Richard could not see their faces, he could sense their palpable resentment. As he came up to them he could smell the strong wine on their breath and knew from their aggressive stance that he would need to handle the situation delicately to prevent them turning on him too. "Who is she?" he asked, feeling the woman's terrified eyes on him.

"She's from the city," said the one who was still holding

her tightly. "We caught her creeping about the camp, *stealing*."

"Stealing what?" inquired Richard. Although both the men were subordinate to him they were older and very drunk, as well as being obviously determined to vent their frustrations on the girl who Richard could see was no more than sixteen or seventeen.

"Food," ventured the second man, holding up the flat, unleavened loaf that he had been waving just out of her reach.

"Let her go," he said.

"But she is an Infidel. A filthy, thieving whore!"

"Let her go!" repeated Richard, mustering as much authority as his voice would carry.

The second man unwrapped the girl's hair from his grasp and pushed her in Richard's direction causing her to stumble and fall on the sand as her knees gave way.

"One rule for us and another for them," he muttered to his friend as they broke the bread between them and lurched off into the night to see what other trouble they could cause.

Richard went to the girl and made to grasp her arm to help her up, but she screamed and scuttled away from him on all fours.

"I won't hurt you," he tried to reassure her, suddenly realising that she thought him no better than the other scoundrels and could not understand his explanations. She scrambled unsteadily to her feet and pulled her clothing tightly around her, reaching for her veil to cover her hair. Even in the darkness Richard could see that she was painfully thin. If he and the other Crusaders were hungry then it was obviously worse for those within the city walls as the siege progressed. "Come," he said, beckoning her to follow him.

Glancing at the two men who were watching from a distance and realising that she would soon be back within their grasp if she ran, she seemed to decide that obeying Richard was the better option and she followed at a distance as he returned to his tent and lit an oil lamp.

"Come," he said again as he saw her frightened eyes peering in through the open flap, and he broke off a piece of his bread ration and poured some wine into a cup and held both out towards her. Her hunger quickly overcame her fear and she took both from him and ate and drank eagerly where she stood. Richard saw how the bones of her wrists and hands stood out starkly from her dark skin and her eyes seemed huge in the hollows of her starving face.

Having eaten she smiled at him briefly and turned to go, to disappear into the night, but the raucous laughter of the drunken men made her hesitate as both she and Richard realised that they were still lying in wait for her.

"Stay," said Richard.

She turned and looked at him for a moment, then as the men's laughter disturbed the night once more she seemed to make a decision. He pointed to his bed but she quickly shook her head and made to leave again until he reassured her by making signs that he was only offering her a place to sleep. At last she agreed to stay and settled herself on the floor near the entrance to the tent. Content that she was safe for the time being at least, Richard took off his surcoat and returned to the straw mattress on which he had been lying.

When he woke the next morning she was gone and he wondered if he had dreamt her, except that his empty bread basket and cup betrayed her visit and meant that he had nothing left to eat. Going outside he saw the two men from the previous night still sleeping in the morning sun and decided to say no more about the incident. There were enemies enough in the city above; he did not need to make them within the camp as well.

The day was spent in another assault; organising the men loading the trebuchet with rocks that had been brought from the shoreline. As the heat of the sun bore down on him, cooking his head inside the metal helmet, and the sweat soaked into his padded gambeson until it was wet through he prayed that the siege would soon come to an end and that the Infidel would be routed. Yet the face of the girl, her thin starving face and pleading eyes, haunted him. She was a human being, just like him. She was suffering and it was at his hands and the hands of his fellow Crusaders and he felt guilty – then guiltier still for doubting his calling and the will of God.

That night, as he knelt exhausted in his tent and prayed about the events of the day, he was suddenly compelled to open his eyes and look up. Standing at the entrance to his tent, her hair covered and with a bruise clearly showing across her left cheek, was the girl. For a moment their eyes communed in silence until Richard got up from his prayers and beckoned to her.

She came forward, glancing away from him to the food and drink that stood on the small coffer by his bed. Richard followed her look. He had eaten earlier, although the ration was scarce, but had risked pilfering a little more bread and a jug of ale in some forlorn hope that she might come to him again.

"Come," he said quietly in the voice he often used to soothe his anxious horse and held out a hand to her. Coming forward with a rustle of silk she reached out and touched his hand. Her skin was darker than his and her hand much smaller and more delicate with neat round nails showing pale half moons like the one that was hanging low on the horizon outside. He met her dark eyes; long lashes brushed her cheeks as she glanced down under his scrutiny. She was no prostitute, he realised; she looked well born and her cloak of dark green, though a little torn, was made from fine cloth and fastened with a gold brooch. "Hungry?" he asked and offered her the bread. She took it and broke some off, eating quickly whilst watching him carefully. After a moment she paused, broke off another piece and offered it to him. Richard hesitated, then reached out and took the bread she offered, putting it into his own mouth. She smiled and nodded.

"Thank you," she whispered in accented French.

"I am Richard," he said, pointing to himself. After a moment her eyes suddenly cleared as she understood.

"Leila," she told him.

"Forgive me Father for I have sinned," said Richard, as the cold damp surroundings of the Lancashire springtime reasserted themselves on his senses. The pain in his legs and knees, forgotten as he relived his nights with Leila in Palestine, reasserted their agony and he was suddenly desperate to receive his Absolution and to stand. But the Dean, who seemed well aware of his discomfort, did not rush to end his penance and when Richard risked glancing up he saw him standing with the evening sun lighting his face and hair as he stared across the castle bailey towards the plains beyond. The look on his face was what Richard could only describe as self-satisfied and he wished that he could have made his confession to anyone but him.

"Fornication is indeed a grave sin," said the Dean. "and to fornicate with the Infidel requires a greater penance."

Chapter Five

It had been his growing regard for his grandmother's cousin, Sir Robert de Lacy, that had made Richard co-operate in the matter of his confession to the Dean of Wallei rather than insisting on another priest. Sir Robert spoke well of him. But although the Dean had eventually granted Richard his absolution and watched as he struggled, shriven yet numbed, to his feet, Richard was left feeling even more unsettled than he had been before.

The memories of what had happened with Leila, suppressed for so long, would no longer be so easily dismissed from his mind. During his prayers her face would come between him and his words to God and she would ask him what they had done that was so wrong. He knew that it was the devil who tempted him, but the temptation to believe that their love had been good and wholesome was one that he was finding it increasingly hard to resist.

Yet God did not send the plague upon him for a second time. His skin was almost healed, though he still wore the leper's garb and revealed his face to no one but Sir Robert. The two men grew closer as the spring warmed into summer. Richard enjoyed talking to Sir Robert in the way that he used to enjoy his father's company. And Sir Robert seemed happy to see him, telling him about the intertwining histories of their families and how they came to own the lands in the north of England.

"And what of the Dean?" asked Richard one evening as they sat talking in the private chamber.

"The Dean is a cousin of my wife Isabel," explained Sir Robert. "He has been my priest and my confidant here for many years and I rely on him to keep an eye on my affairs when I am away in Yorkshire."

"He has your trust then?"

"Of course," replied Sir Robert with a note of surprise. "Have you reason to think badly of him?"

"No. Indeed, the Dean has shown me nothing but kindness and his son Geoffrey has been more than good to me. But..."

"Yes?" urged Sir Robert leaning forward in his chair with a puzzled expression clouding his dark eyes.

"He... he makes me ill at ease," replied Richard, searching for a more rational explanation. "I get the impression that he does not like me."

Sir Robert nodded. "It could be true," he said. "The peasants have come to regard you as a holy figure and I think the Dean resents the challenge to his authority. But the peasants are superstitious and the apparent miracle of your cure appeals to them more than the Dean's sermons on chastity, poverty and self denial. Not that the Dean denies himself much," he laughed. "His hunt is one of the finest in the district."

"And his horse is a magnificent creature," added Richard.

"Bred in France," said Sir Robert with an appreciative nod.

Just then there was a gentle tapping at the door and Lady Isabel came in with more wine and honey cakes. She smiled shyly at Richard as she set the platters before them.

"Stay and eat with us," urged her husband, but she shook her head.

"I will leave you to talk men's talk," she said in her lilting voice, resting her hand on her husband's shoulder in a simple gesture of affection. He reached to pat it as he smiled up at her.

"Then we will talk later," he told her and turning to Richard as she left the chamber in a cloud of lavender scent he urged, "Eat, drink!" And their talk of the Dean was forgotten as they continued their discussion on well bred horses.

One sultry afternoon at the beginning of June, Richard was sitting on a rock outside his cell watching the distant thunderclouds gathering from the west. It had been hot for a couple of days and such heat almost always boiled over into a storm. The spectacle of thunder and lightning was one he had enjoyed as a boy, standing at a narrow window on the top floor of the castle at Halton and watching the forks of lightning dancing on the surface of the river as the booms of thunder had echoed around the mountains of Wales. But today he was hoping that the weather would stay dry, as he had discovered that torrential rain resulted in a stream of water running through his cell from the roof at the back and out over the lip of the entrance. There was dry ground enough for him to sleep on, but he found the noise of the constant dripping an irritant and it meant moving his few possessions well to the side of the cave and remembering not to turn in his sleep lest he accidentally roll into the water.

A rustle of grass, more than that caused by the freshening breeze, made him look up and he was surprised to see Sir Robert's steward climbing up the hill, sweating in the humidity. Richard rose to greet him as he drew nearer, wondering what news he brought and hoping that it was nothing bad. Sir Robert had been wheezing these past few days, the flying pollen from the long grasses irritated his lungs and made him sneeze and his eyes and nose watered incessantly. His physician had brewed up some foul smelling tincture from the local herbs that he swore would stop the fever but Richard was not convinced that his ministrations were doing any good and Sir Robert's attempts to drink the medicine down seemed only to result in his spewing it straight out again.

"Good day, Bertram. What brings you here?"

"Sir Robert is ailing," the steward told him, as he stood a few steps away breathing heavily. "He has sent me to ask you to come. My lord seems agitated and thinks that only you can help."

Richard nodded and reached into the cell to retrieve his cloak and gloves and staff. "I will come," he said, and followed the steward back around the hill to the main gatehouse where the sentry stood momentarily to attention as they passed through and approached the castle.

Bertram led the way up the steps and into the cool stone interior where, for once, the fire was unlit and a few grey ashes mingled with half burned charcoal in the hearth.

"This way," he said, leading Richard behind the screen to Sir Robert's solar where his bed had been brought down from the bedchamber above to save him having to climb the stairs. He paused and knocked on the door before lifting the latch.

"The Holy Hermit is here," he heard Bertram say before the man stepped back and opened the door wider to usher him in. "Go in, go in," he said. "Sir Robert is ready to receive you."

With a nod of thanks Richard entered the chamber where a shaft of sunlight from the unshuttered window cut across the floor. Sir Robert was half lying on the bed, propped on cushions, with a thin cover over him, struggling to breathe. The rasping in his chest was not unlike the death rattle Richard had heard on the battlefields and he stepped forward, pushing back his hood in instant concern.

"My lord, you are unwell," he said. "What can I do to help?"

"You can stop that damn' fool physician torturing me with his cures," wheezed Sir Robert.

"I am unsure that he will listen to me," remarked Richard, "as he believes there is no cure for my plague and will not believe the evidence of his own eyes when I show him how my skin has healed. He thinks that I am either a fraud and a trickster or some purveyor of magic who is somehow dangerous to him and challenges his authority. If you have taken notice you will have seen how he tries to avoid my presence and looks ill at ease when I am around."

"True, true," gasped Sir Robert, "but if the Lord can do away with your leprosy perhaps you could intercede on my behalf and beseech a cure for me also?"

"My lord, be assured that I pray for your welfare night and day and if it is in the Lord's power to make you well then it is not for lack of prayer that you are not cured."

"Richard, I don't doubt you for a moment," coughed Sir Robert, "and that is why I need your aid today."

"My lord?"

"You must recall what you asked of me when you first came to Cliderhou?"

"Indeed. I brought a letter from my grandmother Albreda imploring you to leave your lands in your will to your rightful heirs, the FitzEustace family."

"And it should have been done long since. I have waited too long to put these affairs in order, but I shall wait no longer. I am afraid that I am dying and I shall write my will."

"My lord," replied Richard moving forward and kneeling beside the bed. "It grieves me to hear you speak of your death when we have become such good friends."

As he knelt, with his face buried in the covers near Sir Robert, Richard felt the old man's hand upon his head.

"Bless you, son of my cousin's son. How I wish that you were not a leper and that it was you to whom my inheritance would pass, for nothing would give me greater joy than seeing my lands pass to you. I have come to regard you almost as my own these past months and you have brought companionship and great joy to me in these twilight days. Now, help me Richard. Bring me parchment and ink from the desk so that I can write. My lands will go to Albreda Lisours, my cousin, and to her heir, your brother Roger if he returns alive from the Holy Land which I pray he will."

"Then your prayers are added to mine," said Richard as he rose and fetched the writing materials. He pushed more pillows behind Sir Robert and brought a stool for him to use to rest the parchment on.

Sir Robert's hand shook as he took the quill and dipped it in the well of ink that Richard held. Then he began to write the document that would complete the task Albreda had set. Yet the thought of the death of this man, of whom he had become so fond in so short a time, cut his heart to the quick and Richard prayed that he would be spared a while yet.

"Now," said Sir Robert, at last, breathing hard as he leaned back, his words completed. "I have made two copies of this will and before I give them into your custody for safekeeping I want you to go to the door where Bertram should be waiting. I want both you and Bertram to witness this will, for I want no word of it to reach anyone else. I think the Dean of Wallei has expectations of me that I cannot fulfil and I do not want to see the reproachfulness in his eyes."

As Richard rose from beside the bed to return the ink to the desk and do as he was bid he heard the sound of horses in the bailey below and paused to glance out.

"The gentleman you mention is here," he said as he watched the Dean dismount from his prancing horse and hand the reins to a servant. "Word must have reached him of your illness."

"Then quickly do as I ask. I shall have this matter resolved before he is admitted."

Bertram quickly crossed the chamber and signed his name below Richard's with a light flourish on both copies and then the parchments were rolled and the hot wax dripped onto them before they were secured with Sir Robert's seal.

"Now," he said to Richard, "conceal these about your person before my visitor arrives."

Richard quickly hid them in his pouch, then lifted his hood over his face before turning to face the door just as Bertram ushered in the Dean.

"Sir Robert," said the Dean, sweeping off his feathered hat, "I hear you are ill and I have come to offer you my ministrations. But I see that the Hermit has once more arrived before me," he commented with a look of contempt in Richard's direction. "I pray, Sir Robert, that you do not consider me to be lax in my duties as your priest?"

"By no means," wheezed Sir Robert, holding out his hand to the Dean. "I value your visit and the Hermit was about to leave."

Richard nodded to Sir Robert and the Dean and retreated to the door where Bertram accompanied him down the stairs.

"Do not allow the Dean to overtire Sir Robert," he warned the steward. The look from the Dean's blue eyes was still piercing him and he wondered how the man always seemed to give him the impression that he knew far more than he revealed. From what he had discovered he now knew that the Dean was indeed the Englishman that his grandmother had warned him about and although he had ensured that the Dean could not be sure of his own identity he was aware that the man had his suspicions.

As he traversed the hill the first huge splodges of rain began to spot the ground making a patchwork of wet and dry on his cloak and he lengthened his stride and quickened his steps as the first flash of lightning split the sky and the thunder rolled in.

Back in his cell, just as the storm broke, Richard hid the two wills in different places, well out of reach of the water. One on a shelf near his food store and the other, further into the depths of the cavern near the entrance to the passageway that led to the door to the castle.

Then he returned to his cell and sat just inside the entrance to watch the storm. With the will written and his sores healed he felt for the first time in many months that he could consider the future, although he was unsure what it would hold. He had no intention of returning to St Giles as he had first planned. He would stay close by Sir Robert until his time came. He realised that might not be far off and he wondered how easily the terms of the will would be accepted by the Dean; he doubted that the man would let these lands pass to a woman without a fight.

Later, as the last of the storm rolled on over the hills towards the east, Richard heard a noise that he first thought was a remnant of the thunder. Then he realised it was coming not from outside but from behind him, inside the rock. He reached for his staff and flattened himself against the cold, wet rock face near the place where the fissure opened up into the passage to the castle. Someone was approaching from the house and Richard was afraid that the Dean had discovered the truth and was coming down to destroy the wills and maybe him as well. As the hesitant footsteps made their way towards him and the light of a candle cast strange shadows ahead of it, Richard lifted the staff above his head and asked God if there was a penalty for striking down a man of the cloth even if his intentions were set on the pursuit of an evil deed.

Holding his own breath, he could hear the anxious breathing of the interloper and he flexed his fingers on the shaft of the staff ready to strike the blow. But the face, grotesque in the candlelight that appeared from the passageway was that of Bertram and Richard quickly lowered the staff on catching sight of his terrified eyes as he squeezed through the gap and peered around.

"Bertram," he said, moving forward into the circle of light that visibly jumped at his voice. "I thought it was the devil rising up to greet me."

"Hermit," said Bertram, his voice shaking and the lantern in his hand casting a trembling light around the dark cell. "Sir Robert bids you come."

"And the Dean?"

"Just gone, after waiting for the storm to abate."

Richard propped the staff to one side against the wall. "Then light our way," he said, "and we shall not need to get wet, even though we own no feathered hat for the rain to spoil."

Walking ahead of him Bertram eased his bulky body back along the narrow passage and Richard followed until he stumbled into the cavern. Bertram lit his way as he climbed the steps before lifting the latch and letting them through into the gloomy castle were he doused the flame and set the lantern to the side of the door.

"I know the way," said Richard quietly and went to Sir

Robert's chamber where he found him grey and exhausted upon his bed.

"My lord, you are too tired for more talk tonight," he said.

Sir Robert shook his head and waved Richard nearer. "One thing," he panted, "you must do. You must take a copy of the will to Albreda for safekeeping. I am sure the Dean suspects what I have done. The man can read minds, I swear, and I fear I may have made an enemy today of my old friend. There is no one else I can send. No one will suspect if you go. They do not know who you are." He stopped to get his breath and Richard watched his laboured breathing as he coughed and began again. "You must go. I will ask Bertram to find you a good horse. He will bring you some clothes too. You will ride as a nobleman. Your face is clean. No one will know. Promise me, Richard, that it will be done and that Albreda will have proof of her inheritance."

Sir Robert stretched out his hand and kneeling by the bed Richard took it in his and kissed it. "It shall be as you desire, I promise," he said. "Can we trust Bertram to keep this secret?"

"With my life," said Sir Robert, and that was reassurance enough for Richard. If there was a traitor here, then it was not the steward. "Take this too," said Sir Robert, reaching under his bolster and taking out the key that Richard recognised as the one that unlocked the door to his cave. "Bertram will be waiting at the door with clothes for you just before first light in the morning. Ride out before the castle wakes and I will spread a rumour that the Holy Hermit has gone on a pilgrimage."

Richard nodded and clasped Sir Robert's hand between two of his. "It will be as you ask," he said. "I will return before you have even missed me and I pray that I will find you well."

"Bless you," said Sir Robert, stretching out his other hand and Richard bent his head to receive the benediction.

Without seeing anyone Richard had slipped back through the door, taking the lantern that Bertram had left, and returned to his cell where he tidied his few belongings and selected the items he might need on his journey. His leper's cloak and gloves he hid in the cave before lying sleeplessly on his bed, watching for the first sign of morning to penetrate the mouth of his cave.

When the melodious song of a blackbird alerted him to the coming day Richard forewent his ritual morning ablution for the first time since his arrival. Taking only one copy of the will and his purse of money he crept quietly to the door to the castle. The key turned the lock in silence and he eased open the well greased door. Bertram had thought of everything and, with a finger to his lips, he beckoned Richard towards a corner of the hall where a pile of fresh clothing, a basin of steaming water, cloths and shears were waiting.

"If you are to pass as a nobleman then I think the hair and beard of the hermit will have to be cut," he remarked, indicating a stool as he prepared to barber Richard's appearance back to respectability.

With hair and beard trimmed short Richard stripped off his grimy undergarments, washed and put on the fresh fine linen shirt and braies, the woollen tunic and hose. He pulled on the leather boots and picked up the cloak that he would only need to wear until the heat of the day took its hold. Richard suddenly felt like himself again rather the holy hermit he had become and he pulled back his shoulders and raised his head to look Bertram straight in the eye rather than adopting the stooping posture behind which he had been hiding for so long.

"Are you ready?" asked Bertram, his eyes wide with admiration for the transformation he had helped achieve.

"I am," said Richard, adjusting the belt around his tunic from which hung his purse and the pouch in which the will was safely stowed.

"Take these," said Bertram handing him a saddle bag packed with a blanket, food and a flask of ale. "Come."

Careful to prevent their booted footfalls ringing out from the stairs and across the bailey, the two men crept down to the courtyard where a grey palfrey was tethered.

The animal turned and snickered in recognition as Bertram approached it and gently fondled its ears.

"Edric, my own mount," he said. He is a good strong horse and will carry you well."

Richard reached up to pat the horse's neck and then ran a hand over its withers and down its short foreleg.

"He will do well," he said as Bertram strapped the bag behind the saddle and held the horse's head as he mounted.

Richard found the stirrups and gathered the reins. It felt good to be astride a horse again and, as the morning mist draped the summit of Penhull Hill to the east, Richard turned the horse to the south, and with a smile he headed home.

It was darkening at the end of a long day as the weary palfrey splashed across the Mersey, thankfully at low tide, and Richard paused on the far shore to look up at Halton Castle.

He felt a rising surge of emotion press on his throat as he gazed at the home he had thought he would never see again. A few of the servants were still moving around the outer bailey, rounding up the chickens for the night and closing and locking doors to secure them until morning. Richard slid down from the saddle and led the horse to a sheltered spot in the trees where he sat on a log and allowed Edric a long rein so that he could tear at the sparse grass whilst they waited for everyone to go to bed.

The darkness intensified but the night was still dark blue rather than black as Richard led the horse up to the gatehouse where a single sentry was dozing.

He recognised him as Jean and was pleased because he knew the man to be both honest and discreet. He reached out and gently roused him, putting his finger to his lips as the surprised sentry stared, obviously unsure if he was awake or still dreaming.

"Sh!" warned Richard. "Do not be alarmed. It is really me and not some vision come to greet you. Here, take this horse and feed and water him, and find me the key to the back door for I must speak with my grandmother."

"But, but..." began the man, seeking some explanation as he stared at Richard in the torchlight.

"Do not seek an explanation. Just do as I ask and speak of this to no one. If anyone asks about the horse tell them you found him wandering riderless and brought him in for safekeeping. I will attend to the rest. Now. The key?"

"Wait here," said Jean, and Richard watched as he led Edric away, his pale tail swishing in the starlight as his ears pricked forward in recognition of a place where he would find other horses and something good to eat.

As he waited, Richard counted the windows along the top floor until he came to his grandmother's and was pleased to see a light still burning.

Moments later Jean returned and pressed the large key to the door to the kitchens into the palm of his outstretched hand.

"It is good to see you looking so well, my lord," he said meeting Richard's eyes for a moment before looking down at the dark earth, faintly illuminated by a rising moon that was creeping skyward from behind the tower of the castle.

Richard patted the man briefly on the shoulder. "I will return the key to you before daybreak and will have gone before the sun is risen above the horizon. Speak of this to no one, you understand? No one; not even my grandmother – and I will see that you are rewarded for your loyalty."

The guard nodded briefly and Richard, enclosed in his dark cloak, passed as a shadow across the courtyard and in through the kitchen door.

It was black inside, but Richard knew his way well and barely had need of sight to find his way up the stairs until he stood, panting slightly with both exertion and nerves, outside his grandmother's door. He tapped gently, hoping that he would not alarm her too much, but refrained from calling out lest he should wake any other members of the household.

"Who's there?" whispered his grandmother after a moment, her voice quavering a little more than usual with the anxiety of finding someone at her door in the depths of the night.

"It is Richard," he whispered and almost immediately the door was drawn back and Albreda pulled him inside.

"Richard," she said, holding up a candle and studying his face. "You are well?"

"Indeed I am Grandmama. I have prayed and fasted and bathed in the holy water at Cliderhou, and the Lord has heard my prayers and looked kindly upon me."

"Your face..." Albreda reached up and Richard felt the warm and gentle touch of her fingers caress his cheek. The tears welled in his eyes as he covered her hand with his and relished the contact that he had missed for such a long time.

"The Lord has looked benevolently upon me," he said.

"Then let me add my meagre blessing to that of our forgiving God," she said and in the light of the candle Richard saw that her eyes also shone with the tears of joy. "Come," she said, "and sit beside the embers of my fire for the night has turned chilly. Have you eaten? Do you need to drink?" she asked reaching for a flagon of wine from the stool beside her bed. "How have you come? On foot or do you have a horse? How did you get into the castle?"

"Hush, hush!" laughed Richard, holding up his hand. "So many questions and not a moment between to answer them." He sat down and uncovered the fire and poked at it, re-kindling a reluctant flame from the ashes as she sat on the edge of her bed and watched him.

"Did you see Robert de Lacy?" she asked.

"Yes," Richard reassured her, knowing that this was the one question that needed to be answered straight away. "And I have brought you a copy of his will that names you as his heir." He unfastened the cloak and draped it over the bottom of the bed before taking the parchment from his pouch and handing it to her.

With a glance she broke the seal and unrolled the will to read its contents.

"And how is my cousin?" she asked, re-rolling the paper.

"Ailing," replied Richard. "I do not think he has long left in this world."

"And the Englishman?"

"I met him," said Richard. "His name is Robert, Dean of Wallei, and he is related to Robert de Lacy's wife. He... he is an ambitious man; although he showed me kindness when we first met and his son Geoffrey is as good a boy as any man would be proud to call a son." Albreda nodded and Richard continued. "I left Robert de Lacy on his bed with an affliction of his breathing. He fears that he has made an enemy of the Dean."

"What will you do now?" asked Albreda.

"I will return to Cliderhou, at least until Sir Robert dies. I feel I owe him that much."

"And your mother?"

"Need she know of this visit?"

"You do not want to see her?"

Richard sighed and poked the dying fire again as he tried to make sense of his own emotions.

"I want nothing more than to come home and take my mother in my arms again," he said. He looked up and met his grandmother's perceptive gaze. "But I have pledged myself to God in return for my cure. I am no longer a leper. But neither can I come home and reclaim my inheritance. I am torn," he said, "between my duties and my loyalties and my promises to those I love."

Albreda came to him and ran a hand across his hair, as she used to when he had been a small and puzzled boy, in a gesture of reassurance that was overwhelmingly familiar to him. He took her frail and fragile hand and raised it to his lips and kissed it.

"What shall I do?" he asked.

"There is something you can do that will help us all," she replied.

"What is that?"

"Take your sister Johanna back to Cliderhou with you."

Richard watched in silence as his grandmother sat down again and searched for the right words to tell him what had happened since he went away.

"Johanna is presently kept locked, alone, in the bedchamber by your mother," she told him. "Twice she has run away and reduced your mother to tears and despair and sorely tried my patience."

"But why?"

"She is afraid that she will be sent to Nottingham to be married."

"Nottingham?"

"Your brother Roger has returned from the Crusade to hold Nottingham Castle for the king and Maud has gone to join him. Your mother is planning to send Johanna there so that she can be married."

For a few moments Richard stared at his grandmother in stunned silence.

"I feel as if I have been away for a lifetime rather than just half a year," he said at last, trying to make sense of what he had been told.

"Johanna first ran away shortly after you left. She rode to St Giles to look for you and found you absent. Then she tried to ride north but thanks to the quick thinking of the ferryman, who sent his son with a message, Dutton found her before she forded the river and he brought her home. The second time she was well into Lancashire before she was brought back."

"Why Lancashire? Does she know?"

"Your sister is not a stupid girl," observed Albreda. "Whilst I managed to persuade your mother that you had taken a longer route to the leper house, Johanna is not so easily convinced and having heard my stories of my cousin in the north I think she decided to take refuge there. But, I sympathise with her. You know how it stands with her and Roger and I do not want her to be unhappy."

"But how can we achieve this?" asked Richard. "Must we confide in my mother?"

"Not necessarily. I have another key," said Albreda indicating the iron ring that she usually wore on a belt around her waist. "If you are willing, you can take your sister north disguised as your page boy."

"And what will you tell Mama?"

"I will tell her the truth. But not until it is too late for her to stop us, for I fear she will object to this plan. Her heart is set on sending Johanna to live under the care of Roger, whom she says will tame her."

"She never would think badly of him, despite the evidence," said Richard. "But I remember well how he plagued and bullied Johanna when we were children and I love my sister too much to see her placed under his jurisdiction. So, if it can be arranged, I will take her back with me. She can stay at the castle and help to nurse Sir Robert. I'm sure that Lady Isabel will be glad of her companionship."

"Then rest here awhile whilst I make the arrangements," said Albreda, pulling her brown cloak more firmly around her shoulders. "You must ride out before dawn if you are not to be discovered."

Chapter Six

Johanna was chasing a wild boar through a thickly wooded forest. She could smell the rotting leaves in the damp undergrowth and hear the pounding of Etiole's hooves on the earth when she suddenly jolted in the saddle, woke in her bed and realised that she had been dreaming.

Raising her head as the sight and sound of the hunt faded from her memory she realised that she was in her bedchamber at Halton Castle and that it was months since she had been allowed outside, let alone down to the stables to even visit her mare. After her second attempt to run away, when she and Etoile had fled in the night and had even crossed the ford at low tide and clambered the far bank as the sun rose before Dutton caught up with them, her screaming mother had pushed her into the bedchamber, locked the door and vowed that she would only be released when Roger came from Nottingham to fetch her.

She pushed the bedclothes from her hot body and turned to lie on her back and stare towards the ceiling. She sighed as she reviewed the hopelessness of her situation and it wasn't until the gentle tapping came for the second time that she realised it was not a part of her dream.

"Who is it?" she shouted only to be met by gentle

shushing noises from outside and the sound of a key being turned in the lock. Suddenly afraid that her mother had come to fetch her in the middle of the night, Johanna leapt up from her bed and snatching down her cloak from the peg on the wall she pulled it defensively around her. She glanced out of the high window and imagined the ground far below, wondering if she could squeeze through the narrow gap and if she had the courage to jump, and whether slamming into the hard courtyard would be a better solution than being forced into the care of her cruel brother.

Standing with her arms folded across her chest and within one stride of the window she watched in anticipation as the door swung slowly back and a lighted candle swayed into the room carried by her grandmother, with a finger to her lips warning her to remain silent until the door was gently closed.

"What is it?" asked Johanna. "Is something wrong?"

"Pack some clothes," whispered her grandmother. "You are leaving."

"I'm not going to Nottingham. I'm not going to live with him!" Johanna glanced anxiously from the window to the dark drop below. "I thought you were on my side," she accused her grandmother, her vision blurred with angry and frightened tears as she glared at the old woman in the candlelight.

"Hush," warned Albreda. "Do you want to wake your mother? You're not going to Nottingham. You're going with Richard."

"Richard? How can that be..." she began. And then her suspicions began to be confirmed. She remembered Richard

walking north after the Mass of Separation; she recalled
how the priest at the leper house told her he wasn't there.
"Richard never went to St Giles, did he?" she whispered.
"He went to Cliderhou. Didn't he? Has he come back?
Why?"

Her grandmother shook her head. Then, as she heard
a door slam somewhere in the castle, she raised a quivering finger to her lips.

"This is not the time for questions," she said urgently.
"Do you still have any of the boys' clothes that you
borrowed?"

"I have some hidden," said Johanna, thinking that poor
Will had probably been left with nothing much of his own
to wear since she had demanded a second tunic from him.
Still, she knew that the shy young stable boy was in love
with her and she salved her conscience by thinking of the
pleasure it would give him to imagine her wearing his
clothes.

"Then dress yourself in them and pack a small bundle,"
instructed her grandmother. "Quickly now," she added.
"There is no time to delay."

With mounting excitement, Johanna threw her cloak
down on the bed and opened the heavy wooden coffer
where she kept her clothing. Beneath the soft kirtles and
gowns her hands felt for the stouter material of the woollen
stockings and tunic. She pulled them out with no regard
for the other contents and dressed with shaking hands
and pounding heart whilst her grandmother stood with
an ear to the closed door. She made a small pack with
two linen chemises, her favourite green gown, a plain
white wimple and a pair of pointed leather shoes.

"Carry the boots," said her grandmother as Johanna fastened up her hair into a net and having covered it with a hood retrieved her cloak from the rumpled bed.

Albreda opened the door cautiously and beckoned for her to follow. Johanna paused for a last glance around the bedchamber that had been her sleeping place and her refuge for the past fourteen years: the soft feather bed with its slightly faded red hangings, the rushes spread across the floor, the scented pomanders, the oak coffer with its lid still open spilling out an assortment of clothing, the jug and basin where she washed, the wooden stool by the bed, and the narrow window with its wooden shutters and the view towards the river. Too many tears had been shed here, she decided, and she smiled with satisfaction to be leaving it all behind. With her boots in one hand and her pack in the other she turned with a sweep of the night blue cloak and tiptoed out of the room and down the cold stairs. She had to restrain herself from laughing and singing out loud as she followed her grandmother who walked much too slowly through the kitchen to the heavy back door.

Johanna walked into a wall of warmth as she stepped out of the stone walled castle into the barely dark night. Already there was an early bird singing from the branch of a nearby apple tree and as she glanced up at the fading constellation shaped like a plough she realised that it would soon be dawn and understood her grandmother's urgency.

She heard the familiar creak of leather and turned as a shadowy figure stepped towards them with two horses, one of which was her beloved mare. Dropping her things on the ground she ran forward and slipped her arms around

Etiole's muscular neck and buried her face in the springy hair of her mane.

"Oh how I have missed you," she said, lifting her face only to kiss the star between the horse's eyes as it nuzzled her affectionately.

"Come quickly," urged a familiar voice behind her and she turned in delight as she realised that the other person was her brother.

"Richard!" she exclaimed.

"Hush!" he warned, picking up her pack from where she had dropped it and fastening it behind Etoile's saddle. "Put on your boots!"

Johanna glanced down and saw that the feet of her hose were soaked with early morning dew from the ground. Fumbling with anticipation she struggled into the boots and took the reins from Richard's hand. Without needing to be told she crooked her leg backwards so that he could grasp her shin and leg her up onto the horse. She caught the swift smile that passed his almost perpetually serious lips as he watched her settle astride the mare with accustomed ease.

Johanna watched as he mounted a sturdy grey that she did not recognise. They would struggle to keep up with Etoile she noted with delight as he urged the palfrey forwards.

She circled the prancing mare and leant precariously from her saddle to kiss her grandmother.

"I love you," she whispered. "You have saved my life."

"Go now," said Albreda. "May God go with you," she added as she raised her hand in farewell, and with a wave Johanna held back Etoile to keep pace with the grey as they trotted briskly out of the castle bailey and, as the sun foretold its coming with a smear of pink in the east, they took the well worn track down towards the river, towards Lancashire, towards freedom.

Johanna followed her brother in silence. The only sound was the steady beat of the horses' hooves and the burgeoning birdsong of the dawn chorus, as if every bird on every branch was serenading her escape. She laughed out loud with joy as she looked back to see the castle retreating behind them and wondered if she would ever return there.

Turning to look at Richard she could see in the half light that he was no longer dressed as a leper, but once again wore the clothes of a nobleman.

"Are we headed for Cliderhou?" she called. He held up a hand to silence her and reined in his horse on a wider part of the track that led down to the river so that she could draw level.

"Hush, sister. Let us not trouble the ferryman from his bed," he warned. "The fewer people who see us pass then the fewer lips there are to spread gossip."

They walked the horses down the steep slope and Johanna raised herself in her stirrups for a glimpse of the water. "The tide is out I think, we can cross without waiting."

"Yes, but the tide will turn soon so we must not delay," he said. "I would like to be across before our mother wakes. I do not think she will be pleased to find you gone."

"Grandmama is bold enough to manage it," remarked Johanna. She glanced at her brother's face which was no longer hidden by the leper's hood. "You look almost normal," she remarked. "I looked for you at St Giles, you know. But you never went there, did you?"

"No. I went to Cliderhou to see Sir Robert de Lacy."

"Why?"

"Grandmama asked me to go and request that he bequeaths his lands to her. I rode back yesterday to deliver her a copy of his will. I fear Sir Robert is dying, though I pray that the Lord will spare him until my return so that I can assure him my task is complete."

"Then what will you do? Will you return home?"

Richard shook his head. "There is no return for me," he said.

"And what about me? What will I do?" she asked.

"I'm sure Sir Robert and his wife Lady Isabel will take you into their household. Lady Isabel is childless, though a kindly lady, and I know that she will welcome your company and your help in nursing her husband."

"I will do whatever she asks," said Johanna with uncharacteristic meekness. She saw Richard glance at her to judge her sincerity. She looked him straight in the eye. "Anything is better than being sent to Nottingham into the care of Roger," she told him.

"What? Even a nunnery?" he teased.

"Yes! Even a nunnery!"

The sun was breaching the horizon as the horses splashed into the shallows, disturbing some sleeping wildfowl from their rest. The birds flew away, low over the water, calling angrily. Johanna's face began to ache slightly from the unfamiliar smile that had settled on her features. The water splashed up and made dark spots on her boots as Etoile danced across the river, following the staid grey whose name Richard had told her was Edric. Johanna reached forward and stroked the mare's neck to calm her. She was brimming with energy after her long confinement in the stables and Johanna struggled for a moment to keep her under control.

"Can you manage?" asked Richard. "We can change horses," he offered.

"You just want a well bred mount instead of that gelding," laughed Johanna.

"Edric is a good horse," he told her, turning in his saddle. "Besides, people will comment if a servant rides a better horse than his master."

"Then let them talk," responded Johanna, tasting the salt water on her lips as they plunged ahead into the tide. She saw Richard smile indulgently as she overtook him and headed towards the bank on the Lancashire side. Her new life lay ahead of her and after so long locked in her cold, dark chamber she was anxious to discover what her future held.

They made good time northwards, stopping once to eat the bread and mutton that Albreda had cut and wrapped for them. They sat in a secluded grove and ate as the horses munched at the summer grass with eager tearing sounds and Johanna was able to study her brother's face more closely.

"Your skin is clear. The leprosy has gone. How can that be?" she asked.

"I have washed in the Holy Well and prayed night and day and the Lord has been good to me. The Lord has healed me and I have dedicated my life to Him," he told her. She met and held his hazel eyes for a moment and saw that he was serious.

"Then you mean to remain outside society? Why not ask the priest to declare you cleansed? You could take your rightful place again. You could marry."

"Let us ride on," said Richard, getting up suddenly and brushing crumbs from his tunic. "We still have far to go."

The shadows that filtered down through the canopy lengthened as the sun passed its zenith and began to fall to the west. They left the depths of the forest behind as the landscape changed and the track became steeper.

"Look at that hill," said Johanna as a huge mound seemed to grow before them, like a sleeping hound, curled up in the stable.

"That is Penhull Hill," said Richard. "We are nearly at Cliderhou."

Johanna watched as the sun set behind the walls of a small grey castle.

"Is that it?" she asked, disappointed at its size. This castle was nowhere near as large or as grand as Halton. As they approached the gatehouse a guard came forward and challenged Richard, who bent from his saddle and spoke quietly to the man who stepped back with a look of bewilderment before giving the signal for the wooden gate to be heaved open. It squeaked and dragged along the ground until it was wide enough to admit them and Johanna followed Richard through and up the sharp incline to the castle keep.

A man hurried forward and took Edric's reins as Richard dismounted. Etoile, tired and weary, snorted at the prospect of food and rest and Johanna sympathised. After she leaned forward and eased herself from the saddle she felt her numbed legs crumble a little as they thudded to the hard ground and she clutched at the saddle to steady herself. Richard took her pack from the saddle, then held her arm to support her as she stumbled.

"Look after the horses well, Bertram," he said, before helping her up the steep steps into the castle.

The day had turned chilly with a blustery wind from the west and Johanna was glad to see that there was a welcoming fire inside the hall. She was about to sink onto a stool before it to warm her face and hands when she saw Richard shake his head and indicate that she should stand behind him. Although dog tired, she saw that some of the servants were staring at them curiously as if they were complete strangers, and she could not understand why none of them acknowledged her brother who had been living there for the last six months. That was if anything he had told her were true, she thought, as her attention was caught by an elderly lady dressed in a dove grey gown, with long sleeves lined in the palest pink, who came forward, ushering away the servants.

"My Lady Isabel," said Richard, with a gracious bow. "I have returned with a guest. Beneath this disguise is my sister, Johanna."

The lady looked at her intently as if seeking her real identity.

Johanna curtseyed and smiled slightly and unsurely under the scrutiny. Lady Isabel was beautiful, she thought. Her face was framed by a plain white wimple fastened with a silver brooch; and although her eyes and mouth were touched by the passing years her pale skin still had a lustrous radiance and the whites of her pale blue eyes were clear and free of any redness. Lady Isabel smiled warmly in return and offered a small delicate hand which Johanna took, envious of its softness and embarrassed by her own red and sore fingers, badly bitten around the cuticles where the skin was dried and peeling.

"You are welcome to our home at Cliderhou," she said in a lilting accent that was unfamiliar to Johanna. "But why is your sister dressed as a servant boy?" she asked Richard with a puzzled frown.

"The story is long and complex," he told her. "I will relate it later at leisure, but meanwhile I must beg your forgiveness for bringing an uninvited guest and trust that your continuing goodness will extend to sheltering my sister for a while at least."

"Of course," replied Lady Isabel. "It will be our pleasure. Come with me," she said to Johanna. "We will allow your brother to go and speak with my husband – he has been anxiously awaiting his return – and I will ask the servants to prepare a bed for you and bring some hot water so that you can wash off the dirt of your journey. Do you have clothes to change into?" she asked, as she led Johanna up the narrow stone staircase.

"I have a gown," said Johanna, momentarily raising the small bundle she held. "We left in a hurry," she added as Lady Isabel tutted softly at the inadequacy.

"I will see that you are properly clothed," she said. "I do not know what your brother was thinking of to bring you in this manner."

"I am sorry..."

"No, no," protested Lady Isabel. "I did not mean that

you are not welcome, only that you have come clad in curious garb and unprepared to stay with us."

"We left in a hurry," Johanna repeated as Lady Isabel paused and opened a door.

"Go in," she said ushering Johanna ahead of her into a small guest chamber with a view across towards Penhull Hill. "I am afraid it is only small, but I will ask Martha to bring fresh linen for the bed and make some room for your clothes, though I think that storage of your belongings will not cause us a problem."

"It is very kind of you," said Johanna, glancing around at the plain white walls and the bed, with a wooden coffer at its foot.

"Here is a peg for your cloak," she said as Johanna set down her bundle. She took the mantle from her and Johanna noticed the sweet scent of lavender that wafted about her as she hung it up. "You say you have a gown?" she said, looking at the small pack Johanna had placed on the bed.

"Yes." Johanna opened it and shook out the green garment which was creased and folded from its imprisonment and laid it on the bed. Then she took out the shoes and placed them on the floor by the coffer.

"Those are pretty," said Lady Isabel. "But are they all you have brought?"

"I have some clean undergarments," said Johanna. Lady Isabel shook her head.

"Why did you have to leave like this?" she asked, her gentle face becoming concerned.

"If I had stayed, I was to be sent to Nottingham into the care of my other brother Roger, but he is a fearsome and cruel man. I did not want to go so I ran away. Twice. My grandmother thought I would be happier in the care of Richard and asked him to bring me here. I apologise if we have caused you trouble."

Johanna hadn't given much thought to her welcome as they had ridden north but now she realised that arriving at Cliderhou uninvited and *expecting* to be made welcome was ill-mannered and she was ashamed and embarrassed as she stood, dressed in dirty boys' clothes, before this lady. But Lady Isabel smiled and touched her cheek gently.

"You look like a peasant child," she said. "Wash and change into your gown and then come to my solar. We will have some wine and you can tell me all about it."

Moments later a plain looking girl with plump face carried in a basin and a jug of steaming, scented water and some fresh linen cloths. She asked if Johanna needed assistance but she waved her away with a smile of thanks and closed the door behind both her and Lady Isabel. Then, in the chilly breeze from the open window, she pulled off the boots, the tunic and hose and the greasy underclothes and stood naked to wash away the sweat and dirt of the long ride. She unfastened her hair and brushed it out, enjoying the way it swung down her back, soft and slightly ticklish against her bare skin. Then once she was satisfied that she was clean she put on a fresh chemise and slipped the green gown over her head, smoothing it down as best she could. She slipped soft stockings onto her feet, fastening them up with garters just below her knees and put on the shoes; they felt fairy light after the heavy boots and she twirled around the small chamber as if dancing, feeling her hair fly free as she spun. She had escaped, and here she was at Cliderhou with no one to tell her what to do except Lady Isabel who seemed kind and well disposed towards her despite her sudden and unexpected appearance.

She took up her hairbrush and braided her long dark hair over her left shoulder before going to the door which opened smoothly without a sound. Outside she managed to retrace her way down the steps to the lower level where she found Lady Isabel by the fire in her solar with a jug of wine.

"Sit with me," she smiled, indicating a stool with a soft red cushion. "Come and take a drink and allow me to know you better."

Johanna realised that she was both hungry and thirsty and took up a cup without the need for any more encouragement. She was about to thank Lady Isabel again when she heard footsteps and Richard came to stand in the doorway.

"Sir Robert seems a little better," he said.

"He is much better," said Lady Isabel. "I had feared that the Lord would take him, but it seems that his time is not yet come and he has been spared to remain with us a while longer."

"Praise be, for we have prayed hard for this," replied Richard.

"Stay and eat supper with us," said Lady Isabel. Johanna watched as her brother's face clouded with seriousness.

"Forgive me if I do not, my lady. But know that I am grateful, and especially grateful for the welcome you have extended to my sister." He turned to Johanna and watched her for a moment. "You have turned into a beautiful woman in my absence," he remarked. "I'm sure there will be many more suitors for your hand in marriage."

Johanna smiled back at him. She loved Richard the most of all her family, apart perhaps from her grandmother, and she was happy to see him restored to health in this place, amongst family again, albeit distant family. It was even more than she had implored God for in her prayers and she was overwhelmed with pleasure that so many of them had been answered in spite of her doubts.

"But you can protect me from them now," she said, thinking of the likes of William FitzNigel.

"Your protection must come from Sir Robert," he told her. "He has asked to see you and I have promised that you will go to him shortly, but do not stay too long or overtire him. He is still a sickly man. I must withdraw now..." he began and Johanna suddenly realised that he was making his farewells.

"But you cannot leave me!" she said, jumping up in alarm and catching hold of her brother's ungloved hand, which Richard pulled quickly away.

"I must withdraw," he said, "and leave you in the care of Lady Isabel." Then, with a nod towards them both, he turned his back and went down the stone steps. A moment later an unseen door closed quietly, although it was clearly heard by both Johanna and Lady Isabel as they sat in silence.

Suddenly Johanna felt completely abandoned in this strange place with people she did not know and although only moments before she had felt blissful at her escape from Halton Castle she was now unexpectedly overwhelmed by homesickness. As tears flowed Johanna felt a soft hand take hers. "He is not far away," said Lady Isabel gently, "and meanwhile you are safe here with Sir Robert and me." Johanna watched as her hot tears splashed onto the creased green cloth of her gown. She felt Lady Isabel squeeze her hand. "You are safe here," she repeated. "We will care for you."

After a few moments Johanna began to bring her sobbing under control. Was life nothing but weeping she wondered as Lady Isabel pressed a square of linen into her hand for her to wipe her eyes and nose.

"I apologise," she said again, wondering if she was condemned to utter the phrase over and over forevermore.

"You are tired and distressed and far from home," said Lady Isabel kindly. "When you have eaten something you will feel better. Afterwards we will visit Sir Robert and then you must go off to bed. After a good night's sleep you will feel happier in the morning," she assured her.

Johanna looked up into the gentle blue eyes and found that she could still manage a smile. "Thank you," she said. "You are kinder to me than I have a right to expect."

As they ate supper in the hall, Johanna was struck by how few people there were in the castle. Sir Robert was in his bed in the chamber beyond the hall, too ill to come to table. Apart from Martha, who had attended her, Lady Isabel was alone. She had no retinue of ladies to keep her company and Johanna thought how lonely this castle must be for her and how worse it would be if her husband should die.

"My brother told me that Sir Robert has been very ill," she said.

"Yes. He sometimes has trouble breathing, but the physician has treated him with medicines and with our prayers he is much improved. We will go to see him soon," she said. "He will be pleased to meet you."

As the servants cleared away the platters, Lady Isabel took Johanna behind the screen to where a door stood partly open.

"My lord," she said as she slipped inside. "I have brought Richard's sister Johanna to see you. Come in," she said, turning and beckoning Johanna to enter.

Johanna noticed a sickly sweet smell as she entered the chamber and the heavy hangings made it so gloomy that it took a moment for her eyes to focus on the frail man sitting propped up by cushions in the bed.

"Come," he croaked in a hoarse whisper as he waved her forward. "Let me see you."

She tiptoed across the room, frightened of disturbing the scene too much and curtseyed low in front of him before looking up to study Sir Robert with curiosity. It was his thick grey eyebrows she noticed first, like unkempt bird's wings flying from his face at angles. Below them his dark brown eyes watched her with amusement.

"Do not be afraid," he said. "I may look a fright, but I promise not to expire in front of you." Johanna smiled a cautious smile and his face was suddenly transformed as he smiled in return and she saw a glimpse of the handsome man that his illness concealed. "Come and sit beside me," he said, pointing to the small stool, "and tell me about yourself. Your brother Richard says you are a wilful girl who runs away. I hope you do not plan to run away from us." He coughed a little with the effort of conversation and Lady Isabel passed him a cloth to wipe his mouth. He took it from her with an affectionate smile. "She resembles her brother, do you not think?" he asked his wife.

"She is prettier than Richard," remarked Lady Isabel.

"But can you see a family likeness?"

"She certainly has the de Lacy blood," said Lady Isabel. "You only have to look at her nose and jawline to see that."

"Yes, she does remind me of my cousin Albreda, although it is many years since we met."

"People say I am like my grandmother," Johanna told them, feeling relief and pleasure that Sir Robert should accept her as one of his family.

"In character as well as appearance," laughed Sir Robert. "But you are tired after your long journey," he said as he saw Johanna stifle a yawn. "Go to your bed and we will talk again tomorrow – so long as you do not decide to flee in the night," he teased.

"I will not run away from here, my lord," she promised him. "You must know how grateful I am to you for taking me in."

"You are welcome, more than welcome," he reassured her, patting her hand with his. "Stay as long as you like. My wife and I will be glad of your company to brighten this dull castle."

Johanna smiled again and bade him goodnight with another curtsey. Then Lady Isabel led her back to the bedchamber that had been prepared for her. Smooth clean sheets and warm blankets covered the bed, candles had been lit and the floor had been strewn with freshly scented herbs that broke underfoot and released their perfume into the night air. Lady Isabel drew the curtains around the bed against the draughts. "Sleep well," she said. "Goodnight."

"Goodnight, my lady," replied Johanna as the door closed gently behind her. She sat down on the edge of the bed and eased her aching feet from her shoes and, as tiredness engulfed her, it was as much as she could do to take off her gown and hang it on a peg before sinking into the fragrant bed and sleeping a deep and dreamless sleep.

Chapter Seven

Richard locked the secret door behind him. Lights flashed in his eyes as his sight tried to accustom itself to the complete blackness and for a moment he was completely bewildered. Afraid of falling he sat down and felt for the steps with his feet, going down one at a time as he vaguely remembered doing as a small child. No moon shone through the crevice from his cell tonight and after a moment's panic, when he thought that the gap which led to the cave had somehow been sealed up in his absence, he inched his way along the passage like a mole in a tunnel, progressing by touch and the slight draught from the chilly evening breeze that quickened as he reached the opening into the cavern.

Water was still dripping from the roof after the storm and he went to check that his copy of the will and his other meagre possessions had remained dry on their shelf. He had been away for only two days, yet it seemed an eternity since he left and the cave had the feel of a once familiar place revisited after a long time, at once well-known and yet strangely alien.

Reluctantly he took off the clothes that he was wearing and placed them in the bag with the chainmail and

FitzEustace surcoat that he had taken from his old bedchamber at Halton. Then he replaced their softness with the coarse and scratching material of the leper's garb before kneeling to offer his evening prayers to God, giving special thanks for the deliverance from evil of his sister, Johanna.

With a loud amen he made the sign of the cross and immediate felt guilty that he had given God the impression that he considered his brother Roger to be the evil from which Johanna had been delivered. He knelt once more on the cold, hard stone and tried to explain himself, hoping that the Lord would understand and that it was indeed part of His plan that Johanna should be brought to Cliderhou Castle, though to what purpose he was so far unsure.

The harsh fabric of his habit rubbed at his skin and he found himself scratching at his back once again. He thought of the soft undershirt and tunic that were neatly folded nearby and was tempted to put them back on. Then he recalled again the temptations of Jesus and realised that the devil was also intent on constantly tempting him in some manner.

At least wear the linen undershirt to keep the coarse cloth away from your delicate skin, goaded the voice of Satan. Irritated by the harassment Richard stood up, sharply catching his skull on a jagged rock and, touching the wound, he felt blood on his hand.

"See," he said out loud, displaying his sticky fingers, "are you satisfied now that you have my blood? Get away from me with your wilful suggestions and know that I am a holy man."

Angrily he sat back down and began to think about Johanna. Bringing her to Cliderhou was only a short term solution, he realised. What would happen to her when Sir Robert died – as he surely would before many more seasons passed? Would Lady Isabel take her back to Pontefract? Or would she be returned to Halton and then to Nottingham into the care of Roger? It was a problem to which he needed to find a solution he thought, realising that although he had been declared as dead to his family, they were still the most important concern in his life. Dedicated to God as he was, he could not turn his back on them and not until all their futures were secure could he consecrate his life completely to the Lord.

Eventually tiredness overtook his meditations and although he did not remember lying down to sleep it was well past dawn when he was woken by a noise outside his cave.

Grasping the staff he crawled to the entrance and gazed out as the woman from the village looked back. For a moment their eyes held and he raised a hand in acknowledgement before she turned and ran down the path. Half a loaf of freshly baked bread and some sheep's cheese waited on the customary rock near the entrance to the cell and Richard smiled as he bent to pick them up and place them on his food shelf.

It was later than his usual time to wash at the well, but he picked up his bucket anyway and headed down the hill, aware of the villagers watching him as he stripped off his clothes, lowered the bucket into the stinking water and then poured it over his head. No longer did his hair and beard stick to his skin and as he ran his fingers through the shorn hair on his head he could feel the eyes of the villagers watching him. He re-dressed himself and filled his bucket to take back to his cell. He could hear their whispering voices as they discussed yet another change in his appearance and wondered what stories they would create to explain what they saw.

As he prepared to return to the cave he heard hooves in the distance and saw the Dean of Wallei, in his fine feathered hat, riding on his stallion towards the castle. Behind him came Geoffrey riding an unfamiliar chestnut with four white socks. He heard the castle gate scrape open to admit them without delay and he wondered who amongst the villagers supplied the Dean with his information.

Richard waited until mid-afternoon. Then he donned cloak and hood, picked up his staff in his gloved hands and made his way to the castle gate. Bertram came down to meet him and took him across the courtyard and up the stairs to Sir Robert. As they crossed the hall Richard glanced around, but saw no sign of Johanna and surmised that she must be with Lady Isabel in her solar.

Sir Robert was sitting up in a chair when Richard went in.

"Ah, Richard," he said with pleasure. "Bertram, bring us some wine to quench our thirst in this oppressive heat. I think it could thunder again," he said. "Take off your cloak," he added, waving his hand at Richard, "and give me the news you promised me last night."

Richard peeled off his gloves and after folding his cloak and placing it on a low coffer he laid the gloves and his staff on top before sitting opposite Sir Robert.

"My grandmother told me that my brother Roger was not in the Holy Land but is returned from the camp in Sicily. He has been instructed by the king to guard the castles at Nottingham and Tickhill. He sent to Halton for his wife Maud to join him at Nottingham and her child is due to be born there soon. Your lands will pass to Roger now after your cousin Albreda's death and then on to his son should the child be born a boy," said Richard.

"And this pleases you?" asked Sir Robert.

"It does," he said. "But I wish all the affairs of my family could be resolved so easily."

"You worry for your sister Johanna." Richard nodded. "Despite her objections she needs a husband," observed Sir Robert.

"Indeed," replied Richard. "Yet I am in no position to influence the outcome," he said, indicating the leper's cloak and gloves on the coffer. "I do not want to send her to Nottingham any more than my grandmother does, but I wonder what the alternative might me."

"She is welcome here."

"But when..."

"When I am dead," said Sir Robert, acknowledging the problem, "then your brother will come to claim the land and his sister."

"Yes," sighed Richard.

"Then let us hope I can manage to live until a solution is found," said Sir Robert.

"I pray you will live long."

"I had a visit from the Dean this morning," said Sir Robert, changing the subject.

"I know. I saw him riding up to the castle as I was washing at the well. What did he want?"

"Who can ever tell what the Dean wants? His conversations take circuitous routes that only he can fathom. He asked after you."

"Does he know about Johanna?"

"Could such a thing be kept from him?"

Richard laughed wryly. "The Dean seems to have both the ear and the confidence of God, or else his spies are many."

"I think the second more likely," said Sir Robert. "Remember that he holds the confidences of his parishioners and, whilst it is his priestly duty not to divulge that which he hears in the confessional, the knowledge does give him a certain leverage over the peasants."

"It is a sobering thought. Does he know who Johanna is?"

"My wife introduced her as a cousin of mine – a member of the FitzEustace family, but his enquiries after the whereabouts of the Hermit these past two days have left me in no doubt that he at least suspects the truth."

"I think he has had suspicions since the first time we met. The man seems able to read souls," said Richard. "But what do you think he will do?"

"What can he do?" asked Sir Robert. "He is too wily to ask about his inheritance outright, but we both know that he will not cede these lands without a fight."

"But the will is witnessed and sealed and my grandmother has a copy as well as mine. Surely that is enough?"

"You would think so; for I know no other steps we can take. Yet still I find myself waking troubled in the night. I have recently grown to distrust the man, Richard. I know that is a monstrous thing to say about a priest, and one who has been a good friend to me for many years, but I do not trust him over this. Promise me that when I am gone you will stay and make sure my wishes are carried out."

"I promise," said Richard, thinking that this place must be his home now; that this was his destiny. "But there is other work to be done before your demise," he added.

"Ah, yes, Johanna," said Sir Robert, "though I'm afraid that suitable husbands are not easily found in the wilds of Lancashire.

Richard nodded, inclined to agree.

Chapter Eight

The same morning, Johanna had woken to the sound of ewes calling to their lambs as the shepherd drove them out to the pasture. She had thought momentarily that she was at home until she opened her eyes to the unfamiliar surroundings. Roused from a deep sleep it took her a few seconds to make sense of what she saw and remember where she was.

Then, when she did, she felt a creeping sensation of pleasure and contentment spread until it filled her whole being. She sighed out loud and stretched her legs and arms across the clean, comfortable bed as she thought about how kind Sir Robert and Lady Isabel had been to her.

Below her window she could hear voices coming up from the courtyard and, as the sun looked well risen, she surmised that she had slept late and that it was time she was up and dressed.

She washed in the now cold water and, having no choice, put on her green gown and shoes before venturing down to the hall. She could see that there were visitors arriving and for a moment her heart beat quickly as she feared a party had been sent from Halton to bring her home. But as the man beneath heard her steps and looked up, she saw that he was a stranger.

"And who is this, pray?" he asked Lady Isabel, as he appraised her.

Johanna paused on the last step, under the stranger's piercing blue gaze, and watched as he twirled his feathered hat in his hands, giving away a nervousness that was not betrayed in his unflinching expression. His hair had once been red but was now faded to a dark auburn, swept back from his face and longer than was fashionable amongst the Norman nobles. She guessed that he was of English blood, though he seemed very sure of himself and she surmised that he must hold some position of rank, as the servants as well as Lady Isabel seemed slightly in awe of him. They were almost afraid, thought Johanna, although she couldn't understand why this should be so, except that the man carried an air of authority that even she recognised and her first impression was that he was not a man to cross without inviting danger.

"This is the cousin of my husband who has come to stay with us, Johanna FitzEustace," said Lady Isabel, and Johanna watched with interest as a slight frown momentarily crossed the man's face at the mention of her name.

"Demoiselle FitzEustace," he said, bowing with a sweep of his hat across the floor. "I am very pleased to make your acquaintance." Johanna smiled nervously and looked to Lady Isabel who motioned her to come down.

She curtseyed briefly to the man, who was taller than she had first realised now that she had stepped down into the hall.

"This is the Dean of Wallei," said Lady Isabel. "He has come to visit Sir Robert."

"Indeed I have. For I hear that our prayers have not been in vain and that by our intercession the Lord has heard our supplication and your husband is much improved."

Johanna watched as the man turned, the ornate buckle of his dark cloak catching the light and the movement revealing the fine fabric of his tunic above kidskin boots. A priest he might be, she thought, but not clothed in the conservative fashion of Father William; this man was finer even than a Norman lord; wealthy, assured and slightly threatening. He was not a man she would like to trust with her confession, she thought, as he turned his knowing smile back to her.

"I hope that we can come to know one another soon," he told her, "but for now I must tend to Sir Robert and, as his priest, I must minister to him, though..." he hesitated and turned again to face Lady Isabel, "I hear that the Hermit is returned."

"Yes. I have also heard that the Hermit has come back to his cell," she replied.

"And where has the wanderer been these past two days, I wonder," he said, now sweeping Johanna into his observations. "You come from Halton, to the south?" he asked her.

"Yes, my lord," she said, unsure where his questioning was leading. She was about to mention her brother Richard when she caught Lady Isabel's warning look from behind the Dean. She let out the breath she had taken to speak and stayed silent under his inquisitive gaze, feeling her heart beat a little faster as he held her eye a moment longer than was comfortable.

Then he smiled and nodded both to her and Lady Isabel before brushing past her on his way through the hall.

"I will go to Sir Robert," he said. "Come!"

Released from his scrutiny Johanna now looked at his companion who had been lurking in the shadows by the door. As he stepped forward she felt a contraction in her stomach, as if Etoile had taken a high jump and they were plummeting down on the far side. She saw that he was his father's son, with similar reddish hair, but there was a warmth and kindness in his dark brown eyes that was lacking in his father's icy gaze. He glanced apologetically at her with a shy smile, seemingly embarrassed by his father's behaviour. But instead of returning the smile she merely stared at him in a confusion of emotions as he passed her by, near enough for her to catch a slight scent of the meadowsweet in which his clothes had been stored. She felt a yearning that she was at a loss to explain and could only stare after him, hoping that he did not think she was a dumbfounded fool.

She turned to meet Lady Isabel's worried eyes. "Be very wary of that man and think hard before you tell him anything," she warned. "He is dangerous. And so is his son," she added. "Now, come and eat, and later we will see what we can do about clothes for you to wear. I have some gowns that I do not need that may fit you if the seams are resewn and when we have the chance we will buy more cloth to make you new ones."

After eating some bread dipped in honey Johanna found her way to the stables to check on Etoile. The stable boys were busy with the visitors' horses and were still discussing how fast the Dean's stallion could gallop and whether they knew of any other horse that could outrun it. But she saw that her mare was well cared for with fresh straw, clean water and hay in a manger. Etoile snickered a welcome when she saw her and Johanna rubbed the star between the horse's eyes as she listened to the boys decide that the Dean's stallion was probably the fastest they had ever seen. They smiled politely at her but treated her with a distant respect and Johanna yearned for the stables at home where the grooms treated her as one of them and included her in their talk. She wanted to ask them more about the stallion and the chestnut tied beside it, but mostly she wanted to ask them about the Dean's son. She had discovered from Lady Isabel that his name was Geoffrey but she would not be drawn on the topic, only telling Johanna to keep away from the Dean and his family. But Geoffrey's dark eyes and sympathetic smile were imprinted on her inner eye and she could not stop thinking about him.

If someone had asked her the day before if she believed that she could fall in love at the first sight of a man she would have scorned them and told them that no such thing was possible. But now she wondered if it could be so. Father William often said that God moved in a mysterious way and Johanna wondered if God had brought her here to meet Geoffrey de Wallei. Yet she was warned to stay away from him, when her mother and grandmother had been inclined to marry her off to any ugly old man who showed up at the castle gate. It was incomprehensible, she decided. She wished that she could talk to Richard about it, but she had no idea where he was. After a day in his company she missed him more than ever.

It was mid afternoon when Martha came to find her and said that Lady Isabel had woken from her nap and wanted Johanna to look at some gowns. Johanna had been sitting in the window embrasure, dreaming of meeting Geoffrey again and she paused to pull her clothing straight and tidy her hair before going up to Lady Isabel's solar. As she did so, she heard the outer door to the hall open and saw Sir Robert's steward, Bertram, come inside and stand back for someone to follow him in. Instantly afraid that it might be Dutton come to take her home again she looked around quickly for a place to hide and slipped silently behind the long tapestry depicting hunting scenes, thinking how much she had in common with the deer that was pictured concealing itself in the undergrowth as the hunters closed in.

The hooded visitor seemed not to be a stranger. He walked across the hall to warm himself at the fire that burned there despite the heat outside that never penetrated the thick walls of the castle. Johanna wondered why he felt so cold until she saw that the hands he held out to the flames remained gloved and the hood and cloak covering him completely belonged to a leper. So, she thought, this must be the Hermit that the Dean of Wallei had spoken about.

The visitor and Bertram spoke together in low voices until Bertram turned to lead the way to Sir Robert's chamber. But before he followed him the hermit looked across to where Johanna was standing and she would have taken a step back if she had not already been pressed close to the cold stone of the wall. As she watched she saw something familiar about the man. The way he held himself had not the bearing of a sickly man but rather reminded her of her brother's stance, and Johanna, holding her breath as he turned away, wondered if the covered figure could possibly be her brother.

As the echoes of their footsteps faded across the hall Johanna slipped from her hiding place and ran to Lady Isabel's solar where, breathlessly, she tapped on the door and danced from one foot to the other in agitation as she awaited the call to enter.

Lady Isabel was holding up a dark red gown to the light and she looked across with interest as Johanna almost leapt into the room and closed the door firmly behind her.

"You look a little startled," she observed as she laid the dress down with several others on the bed. "Have you seen a ghost in our castle?" she asked as she fingered the cloth thoughtfully.

"Not exactly, my lady," confessed Johanna, "but I have just seen a visitor arrive."

Lady Isabel looked up sharply. "Bring us some wine," she said to Martha. Though it was at Johanna she looked, holding her eyes in a silent warning to say nothing until they were alone. "Now," said Lady Isabel, as she motioned her to the bench at the fireside. "Tell me what you saw."

"I have just seen Bertram admit a leper into the castle. Is this the Hermit that the Dean spoke of?" she asked.

"Yes," said Lady Isabel. "The Hermit comes to visit Sir Robert. He is his confessor and his companion."

"Is the Hermit my brother Richard?" she asked directly, remembering that he had told her that he had intended to remain with Sir Robert until his death.

Lady Isabel hesitated. "Yes," she said after a moment. "But only you and I, Sir Robert and Bertram know the real identity of the Hermit – and if your brother had wanted you to know he would have told you himself."

"There are many things my brother did not tell me but I guessed them all. I knew he hadn't gone to the leper house. I knew he had come here to Cliderhou. I know he has secured the inheritance of Sir Robert's lands for the FitzEustace family. So why not tell me this as well?"

"He is trying to protect you and keep you safe," said Lady Isabel. "The inheritance is not as straightforward as you may think. Even now there are others who think it is rightly theirs and will stop at nothing to claim it."

"The Dean of Wallei?" asked Johanna, as everything that she knew suddenly fell into place. "Is he the Englishman that my grandmother speaks of? The one who is determined to take our lands?"

"He is a cousin of mine," explained Lady Isabel, "and as such believes that his claim is valid. He does have some legitimate claim, of course, but it is up to Sir Robert to decide who should inherit and, yes, he has chosen the FitzEustace family. The land will pass to your grandmother and then to your brother Roger."

"But Richard is the eldest. He could still inherit if a priest declares him clean. I have seen him and beneath the leper's cloak he is cured. There is no sign of disease, so why does he continue to wear it?"

Lady Isabel shook her head. "I cannot pretend to know the minds of my husband and your brother," she said. "But I know that they do not trust the Dean and for the time being it is safer for your brother to conceal his identity. You must not reveal what you know to anyone. Not to anyone," she warned again.

Johanna nodded. "I can stay silent. But my other brother Roger..." said Johanna, suddenly realising the danger. "He is cruel and intolerant and I hate him. When he inherits the de Lacy lands he will be sure to arrange a marriage for me to some equally cruel and ugly old man just to keep me under his control. If Richard remains a hermit he cannot protect me from him, and if he comes here looking for me I shall run away again!" she threatened.

"Then let us hope that Sir Robert lives for many years yet, for I would hate to lose your company when you are only so lately come," said Lady Isabel and Johanna realised that she was being gently teased.

"But I do hate him," she repeated as Lady Isabel picked up the red gown again.

"Well let us at least find you some decent clothes," she said, "so that if you do run away you can at least pass for a lady rather than a peasant." She looked up as Martha came in with a jug of wine and some honeyed cakes. "Fetch your needles and threads," she said to her, "and let us try to make these tunics fit this girl."

Later, when she had been dressed and undressed and admired and measured and sighed over, Johanna left Martha and Lady Isabel busy with their needles after they had both become exasperated by her ineptitude.

"I'll take these down to the kitchen then," she'd said, picking up the cups and jug and carrying them down the steep stone steps whilst trying not to trip over her skirts. She was thinking how much simpler life was for boys with their sensible clothing and the expectations that they should be good at riding and hawking and hunting rather than embroidery and needlework, when she stopped suddenly and took a step back as she heard a door being unlocked and opened below. Peering cautiously around the turn of the stairs she saw Bertram disappear through a small door half way down. He carried a lamp and a parcel wrapped in cloth that was steaming slightly. Moments later he returned, put out the lamp and concealed a key on a length of twine beneath his tunic. As if he was aware of being watched he glanced up. Caught spying, Johanna came down the steps as innocently as she knew how.

"Lady Isabel asked me to return these to the kitchen."

"Give them to me," said Bertram, taking the jug and cups from her hands. "You can go back upstairs now."

Johanna nodded at his brief dismissal. She turned away and went slowly back up to her own bedchamber. It was still only mid-afternoon and the strong summer sun was penetrating the narrow windows, making stripes on the floor. It was too pleasant a day to be inside. No one could complain if she went for a walk, she decided. Returning to the hall she pulled open the outer door just wide enough to allow her to slip through and closed it behind her as gently as she could before lifting her skirts in her hands to run down the steps.

In the bailey there were a few people busy at their tasks: a woman was sweeping with a stiff broom and the black-smith was sweating over a roaring fire, heating a metal shoe whilst one of the stable boys held the head of a patient horse. Johanna strolled across to the gatehouse trying to look unconcerned but with a quickly beating heart. The guard at the entrance nodded his head briefly and pulled open the small wooden door for her to pass through.

"Thank you," said Johanna as she passed and stepped out of the castle grounds and onto the road that led down to the village. No one questioned her. No one asked where she was going and, with a glance around to make sure that she was not observed, Johanna turned off the road and followed a path that led around and beneath the high stone wall.

She knew that castles were built with secret passages below them to allow escape in case of an attack or siege. At Halton there was a passage that led underground to the banks of the Mersey and she was certain that there was a passage here too and that it was the door to the secret way out that Bertram had locked so carefully. The steaming parcel she surmised was food and she guessed that when Lady Isabel had told her that her brother Richard would never be far away she was speaking the truth. Johanna was sure that her brother was concealing himself somewhere close by.

In the woodlands below the castle walls the birds were busy finding insects for their flapping, demanding babies. Johanna took a path that began to lead upwards and became narrower and more overgrown as she climbed. The brambles and thorns plucked at her skirts, but she was determined to follow it to its end. At last, panting, she emerged from the bushes onto a rocky ledge from where she could see the white walled houses and the stone church of Cliderhou far below her and a vast plain of flat land to the west that ended in a ridge of hills that seemed to go on forever. To the east was Penhull Hill and above her the almost vertical escarpment on which the castle was built.

Having paused a moment to regain her breath she was moving slowly towards the rock face when she felt a swift, sudden movement behind her and strong arms quickly encircled her, pinning her arms to her sides and lifting her from her feet. Before she could scream a hand covered her mouth and a voice, breathing hot in her ear said, "Where are you going?"

Writhing and kicking backwards with all her strength Johanna struggled against her assailant. He was stronger and held her firmly until she stopped squirming, but as she felt his grip relax slightly she opened her mouth and bit his finger as hard as she could until she tasted blood. With a curse he pulled his hand away and she took the opportunity to pull free from his grasp before spitting his blood from her mouth and turning to face her enemy.

Geoffrey de Wallei stood and glared at her before examining the wound to his hand.

"You little vixen!" he exploded and for a moment she thought he was going to slap her, but he merely caught her by the wrist to prevent her running away. "What are you doing up here?" he demanded.

"And what business is that of yours?" she asked, thinking that this meeting was nothing like the encounters she had dreamed of.

"This is no place for you. You should be inside the castle walls."

"Who says?" she asked, pulling her arm back from him and wishing that she was taller so that she could have faced him directly rather than having to look up. "Who says? Your priestly father?"

He took another step towards her and she took one back, realising a moment too late that she was standing on the edge of a drop. As she gasped and momentarily tried to regain her balance she felt him grasp her shoulders with both hands and pull her towards him.

"You see, it is dangerous," he whispered in her ear before placing her back on the path behind him. "Go back to the castle before you are hurt."

Shaken, she almost obeyed, but a movement from behind Geoffrey caught her eye and, stopping to look again, she saw that hidden behind some shrubs was a low break in the rock that seemed to be an entrance to a cave. She sensed another movement and, holding out a hand to bid Geoffrey to be still, she said, "Shh! There's something there."

He turned and looked and as he did a figure dressed in black moved away from the rock face and came towards them. As he approached, the leper lifted back his hood.

"Well it didn't take you long to find me," said Richard. "I should have known better than to think that I could hide anything from you. This," he said to Geoffrey, "is my sister Johanna. I had hoped to keep my secret from her and I thank you for your brave attempt to keep inquisitive visitors from my cell, but my sister is not as biddable as most women and should have been born a boy – or a wolf," he said as saw Geoffrey's finger, still dripping with blood. "I have some water from the Holy Well that you can use to wash that. You had both better come inside before we attract too much attention."

Johanna bent down under the jagged lip of the cave and stepped into her brother's home. A small fire burned at the back to give some light and there was an unlit torch beside it. Some horse blankets were neatly folded against the wall with a staff laid across them and, on a natural shelf of rock, sat the parcel she had seen Bertram take though the secret door. Though it no longer steamed, she could smell the freshly baked oatcakes contained within.

On the other side of the cave, near a roughly fashioned altar on which her brother had placed a wooden cross, was a bucket filled with water and the leper's ladle, cup and platter.

"Hold out your hand," said Richard to Geoffrey and he took some of the water in the ladle and poured it over the wound.

"I thought he was a thief," said Johanna in her own defence, "or some peasant intent on taking my honour." She scowled at Geoffrey in the gloom. Their second meeting had not been as she had expected and she wondered if her first impression of him had been mistaken. "I did not know he was your friend. I thought the Dean and his family were our enemies."

"Sit down, Johanna," said Richard, tossing her one of the blankets. "I should have told you where I was, but I thought that the less you knew the safer you would be – especially where the Dean is concerned."

She looked around for a dry and smooth spot and put the blanket down before sitting on it and hugging her arms around her knees as she watched her brother help Geoffrey bind a clean rag around his finger. She felt a little guilty, but consoled herself with the thought that creeping up behind her had been an ill-advised thing to do and that the fault was partly his own.

As she wiped her tongue across the back of her hand to try to get rid of the taste of his blood she looked up to find him watching her with a half smile playing across his lips.

"Among some heathens the exchange of blood would bind a couple together as if married," he told her.

"Then I am lucky that no blood of mine was drawn," she replied.

"Then perhaps I should have let you fall."

"I would not have fallen," she told him.

"If you believe so, my lady."

"Children!" interrupted Richard. "Neither of you should be here. It is too dangerous. You need to go, and neither of you is to come again."

"But..." they both began at once and Richard held up a hand to silence them.

"Geoffrey, you know that I am in your debt for the help you have given me, but Bertram is attending to my needs now and there is no need for you to risk your father's displeasure by being caught visiting me. Johanna, I told you nothing so that when you are asked about me you can answer truthfully that you do not know where I am. There may be those who suspect that the Holy Hermit and Richard FitzEustace are one and the same person but without proof there is nothing they can do or say. What I do not want is anyone following either of you to this cave. This is the last time you will come here – either of you – do you understand? Do you both give me your promises?"

Johanna nodded sulkily and saw Geoffrey do the same.

"You must both leave here now. Geoffrey first and then you, Johanna. Both of you go straight home and do not speak to anyone or to each other about this. Do you understand?" he asked again.

"Yes, my lord," said Geoffrey. "But you know that my father suspects you of some collusion with Sir Robert. He will not be satisfied until he has Sir Robert's promise that the de Lacy lands will be his."

"The lands will go to the FitzEustace family," Richard told him. "My grandmother has Sir Robert's will and I also have a copy here. I am sorry, Geoffrey, but your family will not inherit." Richard laid an arm across the boy's shoulders. "I would like to see you rewarded for your kindness and I will do whatever I can to make it so, but your father will be disappointed. He will not inherit. Go home now. Go with my blessing," said Richard as he made the sign of the cross on the boy's forehead before ushering him out under the overhanging rock. Geoffrey went without a backward glance at her and Johanna listened, a little disappointed, as the sound of his footfalls faded away down the hill.

"Stay away from the Dean and his family," said Richard turning back to face her.

"You sound like Lady Isabel."

"Lady Isabel is astute, and she is right. Listen to her and allow her to protect you. Forget that you have seen me here today. Go back to the castle and when the Dean and his son come to visit stay in your chamber. Do not allow your heart to lead you into danger. Geoffrey is a good boy, but this is one friendship that it would be too dangerous to allow."

"He is not my friend!" replied Johanna. "Look what he did. He attacked me. I despise him!" She looked up to see her elder brother smiling down at her in the firelight.

"I see what I see," he said, "and I have known you long enough to see that you find him attractive. But we cannot always have the things we want. I cannot have my inheritance and you cannot have him. We will both have to pray for the strength and resolve to accept the fate that God has decreed for us. Besides," he said, "love only leads to heartbreak."

"How would you know?" she asked. "You have never been in love." But as she watched him Johanna saw that she was wrong. "Who?" she asked him. "When?"

He shook his head, the way he always did when he didn't want to discuss something, but then he changed his mind and taking one of the blankets from the pile he came and sat beside her.

"I am only telling you this as a warning and because I may never see you again," he began.

"No, do not say that..." she replied reaching out and taking his hand and raising it to her lips.

"Listen," he went on, interrupting her, but not pulling his hand away. "When I was in the Holy Land I met a girl. Her name was Leila. She was an Infidel, but that was not important at the time because I fell in love with her. I rescued her from two drunken soldiers and shared my food with her. We were all hungry but she was almost starving. I thought that I was doing a good thing, but it was the devil who tempted me and I succumbed. I allowed myself to fall in love with her and we lay together and this is my punishment," he said simply. "Now, go back to the castle and forget that you have seen me. And forget any notion of a romance with Geoffrey de Wallei."

Chapter Nine

Life in the castle went on in its regular rhythm as the summer days lengthened and the peasants rounded up the sheep into wooden pens and separated the frantic mothers from their bleating yet full grown lambs so that they could be sheared of their wool.

Johanna relished the freedom that Cliderhou afforded her. True to her word she kept away from Richard, realising that if she did so he would have no opportunity to criticise her behaviour, and as Sir Robert and Lady Isabel indulged her every whim in their efforts to ensure that she was happy she felt the separation less keenly.

She was allowed to ride Etoile at will across the pastures, exploring the woods and the river banks, and she was already breaking into the circle of friendship of the stable boys who were impressed by her knowledge and skill with the horses. She had mentioned training her own hawk to Sir Robert a couple of times and he had not dismissed the idea, saying that he would have to see and Johanna had every confidence that she could charm him into a yes before the summer was out.

The Dean was still a regular visitor, but when she saw him coming she would take herself up to her bedchamber or down to the kitchen or out to the stables. The only place she could not avoid him was at Mass in the chapel, but during that time she kept her eyes downcast in prayer, and when the time came to make her confession she professed to live such a blameless life that she told him little besides her temptation to eat a second helping of frumenty at dinnertime or her extravagant longing for a new pair of shoes – neither of which could draw too much censure from the well-fed and well-shod priest.

There had been no need to heed her brother's advice about avoiding Geoffrey as they had not met again, though he sometimes accompanied his father on visits to the castle. But if she caught a glimpse of him Johanna's heart would leap with pleasure and she would be in a happy mood for the remainder of the day until she was forced to acknowledge that any relationship with him seemed impossible, at which moment her feelings would sink again and she would rage in frustration.

One morning after she had experienced a day and night of the swooping highs and lows of such emotions – like an eagle in flight – she woke early and, seeing that the sky was already cloudless and the temperature rising, she slipped into the boyish riding clothes that she had persuaded one of the laundresses to wash and secretly return to her. In the kitchen there was already bread on the scrubbed table and she paused to break off a portion to eat. Not realising how hot it was she felt it burn her tongue as she closed her lips and too ladylike to spit it back out she tried to breathe in cold air until Wynn, the cook, passed her some cool milk to take out the heat.

"Serves you right to be such a glutton and not wait to

eat at table," she reprimanded her, wiping her floury hands on her course apron. "I suppose you're off riding that beast of yours again."

Johanna nodded as she swallowed down the bread and milk mixture. "It's such a beautiful morning."

"For those without a care in the world, who have no work to do, I suppose 'tis. Here," said Wynn handing her another slice of bread, spread thickly with honey, "make the most of your freedom before some young knight comes to claim you for his wife. You'll be busy enough when you have a babe or two in the cradle and a household of your own to tend to."

Johanna bit the soft bread and savoured the taste of the sweet and sticky honey as it melted in her mouth. "I shall never marry," she vowed.

"Well I can't see you headed for the nunnery, my lady," said Wynn as she began to chop some leeks for later in the day. "You're not one to do as you're bid. But then perhaps that's a good reason not to marry too. You'll change your mind though when the right man comes along."

Johanna smiled and licked her fingers. "Perchance," she said, her thoughts turning unbidden to Geoffrey de Wallei and the feel of his arms around her as he had held her fast outside the hermit's cave. The bread in her mouth seemed to take on the taste of his blood as she relived the encounter once more and she drank down the rest of the milk in an attempt to dispel the feelings that plagued her day and night. She wished that she could put him from her mind and close the lid on the open coffer of feelings that he excited in her: strange feelings that stirred her body in ways that she could not quite explain or understand. Banging down the cup with a force that caused Wynn to raise her eyebrows, Johanna hurried out into the morning air, determined to saddle Etoile as quickly as she could and gallop and gallop until her emotions were safely back under her own control.

The rush of air against her face swept back her hair and the feel of the mare's lithe body between her legs lifted her spirits as Johanna turned Etoile's head towards the river and a place she had found that was concealed from prying eyes. Reaching the turn on the steeply wooded path that led down to where whirlpools frothed and eddied in the water, she slid from the saddle and pulled the reins over the horse's head, pausing only to free one as it caught behind Etoile's furry ear. The mare shook her head and followed Johanna with a soft snickering sound. It was a place they both delighted in. Johanna knew that there were some flat topped boulders where she could sit and dangle her bare feet in the fast flowing water and the horse knew that she would be free to graze the sharp unspoiled grass along the riverbank.

Johanna took off the saddle and bridle, knowing that she could trust Etoile to come to her call, and let the mare roam free. Then, having placed the harness at the base of a wide tree trunk she stepped across the rocks and sat down to pull off her boots and woollen stockings. She gasped as her feet plunged into the cold water, feeling the current tugging at her toes, but the water seemed to warm with the rising of the sun in the sky and she sighed as she lay back and let the warmth soak into her body.

Thinking that she must have either fallen into a doze

or that the roaring of the river must have masked any sound, Johanna was suddenly aware that a shadow had fallen across her face. She jumped and sat up sharply, jerking her dripping feet from the water.

"I could have cut your throat," remarked Geoffrey de Wallei with a smile as he stood over her.

"Do you mean to make a habit of creeping up on defenceless women?" she accused him, aware that the pounding of her heart in her ears was louder than the crashing water. "Are you determined to terrify me?"

He looked at her in amusement for a moment longer before sitting down, so close that their shoulders were almost touching.

"What are you doing out here alone if you are so afraid?" he asked.

Embarrassed to be found unclothed she shifted away from him and plunged her feet back into the cold water so that he would not see her bare flesh.

"What are you doing here?" she asked. "Have you been following me, despite my brother's warnings?"

No," he said. "I often come here early in the morning, if I can give my father the slip. Up until now I have found it a pleasant and secluded place to have some peace."

"Well I have been coming here for a long time," she accused him, disturbed that her secret place had been discovered.

"You have only come here lately," he laughed, looking around and rummaging through the loose pebbles with his long fingers until he found one smooth enough to skim across the water. He stood up and sent it flying through the air, bouncing once, twice, thrice, four times on the surface of the water before it sank. "I have been coming here for years."

Johanna stared at his back, noticing how his shoulders were beginning to broaden and strain under the fine cloth of his tunic. She saw how the sun highlighted the paler threads of red in his hair and made him look as if his head were surrounded by a halo like the saints painted on the church walls. The strands that were just beginning to curl as they grew long below his ears fascinated her and she raised one wet foot from the river, kicking it in his direction and showering him with droplets like precious gems.

"Hey," he shouted, shaking himself like a dog and turning to seize her bare ankle.

She felt the strength in his grasp and tried desperately to claw at the thin grass that sprang from between the rocks as she felt herself being dragged forward. The smooth surface of the boulder was as slippery as ice in winter as she felt herself drawn across it.

"No!" she screamed, thinking that he intended to plunge her into the river, but he turned at her shriek with a slight smile plying his lips and his eyes bright with laughter. Her stomach contracted as he suddenly reminded her of his father and she was momentarily afraid that he too might be capable of some understated cruelty, like kennel boys who sometimes tormented the dogs for their own perverse pleasure.

Geoffrey laughed and let her foot fall with a thud to the rocks.

"Ow!" she complained, sitting up to rub at her heel. "That hurt."

"Did it?" he asked, kneeling down at her feet and taking the bruised foot into his hand. His palms were warm and slightly roughened, though not as calloused as a peasant's. Then raising his eyes to meet hers he asked, "Shall I kiss it better?"

Johanna pulled her foot away and scrambled out of his reach.

"It's time I went back," she told him.

"Are you afraid?" he asked, turning to skim another stone across the river.

"Of what?"

"Of meeting me here again?" he said, turning to hold her in his gaze.

"No."

"Then when will you come again?"

"I do not know," she replied, reluctant to seem too eager, yet aching and happy that he wanted to see her again; longing for his touch yet knowing that it was forbidden.

"I try to come here whenever I can," he said.

Johanna shrugged. "I do not know when I can come again. I cannot raise suspicions. Both my brother Richard and Lady Isabel have told me to have no dealings with you, or your father."

"Yet you take the consecrated bread from his hand into your mouth at Mass," commented Geoffrey, watching her as she pulled on her boots. Eventually his gaze compelled her to look up and meet his eyes – brown eyes not blue eyes she reminded herself. They must be like his mother's eyes. He raised his brows quizzically as he awaited her reply.

"I will come when I can," she said at last, knowing that she would count the hours until she could see him again.

"If I have been here I will leave a sign," he said. "See this stone? If it is here on this rock then I have been and gone. If you come, replace it with this one," he said, indicating a slightly smaller, pink coloured rock. Johanna nodded and stood up, her damp feet feeling strange and slightly sticky. She smoothed down her clothes and picking up her bridle called to Etoile, who raised her head with ears pricked and came obediently to her mistress's call.

Johanna slipped the bridle onto the mare's willing face and, as she tossed the reins over the horse's head, she felt Geoffrey beside her, lifting the saddle onto Etoile's grass-stained back where she had been rolling in the damp dewy grass. He tightened the girth, his arm brushing against hers.

"Here," he said, bending to cup her shin in his hand to lift her onto the mare's back. "I will see you soon?"

"Yes," she said, smiling down at him as he stood beside her, a hand on the horse's rein to prevent her riding away. Then he nodded and stepped back and Johanna urged Etoile up the slope away from the river bank and up to the pasture where she gave the horse her head and laughed out loud as they galloped flat out through the summer morning.

Bursting into the great hall from the bright sunlight Johanna was blinded by the sudden gloom and did not see Lady Isabel straight away.

"Where have you been?" she asked.

"I've been riding. It grows too hot later in the day," she replied, suddenly realising that she would have to take care not to alert other people to her meetings with Geoffrey.

"Go and wash your hands and face and change your clothing," advised Lady Isabel as she studied her with pursed lips. "I do not like you to wear those clothes. It is not seemly."

"Yes, my lady," she said meekly, realising that Lady Isabel would be horrified if she knew what had taken place by the river. But once upstairs Johanna lay on her bed with her eyes closed and re-lived the events of the morning over and over in her mind. She knew that the next day she would rise early and go to meet Geoffrey again.

Johanna slept fitfully, tossing and turning and throwing off her covers in the heat, hoping that a breeze from the narrow window might cool her feverish body and her excited imagination as she thought about Geoffrey and his warm hand clasping her ankle. But the night was still and humid and the air did not stir until dawn when she eventually fell into a deeper sleep. By the time she woke she could hear people moving around in the courtyard below and she knew that it was later than she would have wished.

She jumped quickly from her bed, feeling a little light-headed and pulled on a chemise and a loose yellow gown that had been altered to fit her. Lady Isabel had insisted that the boys' clothes were taken away again, but Johanna had managed to keep back the linen braies that made riding astride Etoile more comfortable. She fastened the cord around her hips, then pulled down her skirts over them and went down the stairs, hoping to slip, unseen, out to the stables.

She was too late to help herself to fresh bread and as she ran to saddle Etoile she already doubted that Geoffrey would still be waiting for her. Once out of the castle walls she urged the mare on, counting every pace as the ground thudded beneath her hooves. When she reached the path to the river she slid from the saddle and ran, stumbling over tree roots, towards the water, leaving the horse to slip down behind her at a distance.

She couldn't see anyone but, as she approached the race of water, she refused to abandon the hope that he would be there. Panting as she neared the spot she could imagine him standing there; but the only sign of him – that he had been and gone – was the rock, sitting isolated on the top of the stone where he had knelt before her yesterday and offered to kiss her foot.

She reached down and picked it up, turning it over and over in her hands, knowing that he had touched it before her, and trying to feel some connection with him. Etoile came up behind her and Johanna turned to see the horse watching her with solemn eyes.

"We've missed him," said Johanna, holding out the stone to show her. Then, as the horse lowered her head to nuzzle her sympathetically, she grasped a handful of the springy mane in her hand and used it to cover her tears as she clutched the stone close to her heart with the other hand.

Suddenly realising how late it had become, Johanna put the stone safely behind the rock and retrieved the pink one to show that she had been there. She raised it to her lips and held it there for a moment before placing it with reverence. Then she took Etoile's reins and led the horse to the top of the path before mounting and trotting disconsolately home.

Back at the castle, as she took Etoile into the stable, she saw the Dean's dark stallion being fussed over by the stable boys. She quickly looked down the row of stalls to see if Geoffrey's horse was there and her stomach lurched as she recognised the chestnut with four white socks, drinking noisily from a bucket of water.

"Will you tend to Etoile?" she asked Harry who had become her friend. He took the reins from her and after patting the horse's neck and telling her that she would come back to see her later, Johanna ran across the courtyard and into the castle keep.

She was aware of the momentary silence as all eyes turned in her direction as she burst in through the doorway. The Dean remained seated by the hearth as he looked her over and she suddenly remembered that her hair was uncovered.

"Johanna," said Lady Isabel, softly. "I see that you have been out riding. Perhaps you should go and tidy your appearance."

"Yes, of course," said Johanna as her eyes locked onto Geoffrey's. For a second their gaze held, though he made no acknowledgement of her, and then she fled up the stone steps before her smile could give her away.

After she had washed her face and hands and fastened her hair neatly under a veil, she was about to return to the hall when she heard the sound of horses below and realised that they were already leaving. She watched from the window, hoping to see them ride away, but she could only hear them leave and had to imagine the sight.

Tomorrow, she vowed, she would rise early and make sure that she was at the river in good time.

In fact Johanna hardly dared to sleep at all and almost as soon as the first rays of the sun peeped over the summit of Penhull Hill she was up from her bed. She carefully braided her hair, threading a ribbon through it as she wove the strands. Then she cast an eye over the gowns that were folded carefully in the coffer. For a moment her fingers lingered on a fine silken one, but then she dismissed it in favour of the plainer one she had worn the day before. For one thing it would get spoiled if she wore it to ride and for another she was determined not to look as if she had made any effort to impress him.

The early morning was chilly and a slight mist had gathered over the river creating ghostly wraiths amongst the trees. Etoile pricked her ears and whinnied and an echoing whinny told Johanna that Geoffrey's horse had heard it. The mare quickened her pace without any urging and they wove their way through the trees until they reached a small clearing where the chestnut had been left to graze. Leaving the horses to rub their soft muzzles together Johanna made her way down the steep slope to the river bank. Geoffrey looked around as he heard her coming and without a word he stretched out his arm to take her hand firmly in his to help her jump across to the flat topped rock. As she landed their shoulders nudged together and he smiled down at her.

"I see you came yesterday," he said indicating the pink rock.

"I was too late; you had been and gone," she replied. He reached out to tuck a loose strand of her hair back into place and, for a moment, she thought he was going to bend and kiss her, but his arm fell to his side and he looked back at the river.

"Let us sit down," he said. "I think I should like to dip my feet in the water today."

Johanna laughed as he pulled off his shoes and hose and plunged his feet into the fast flowing river. His bare legs were well muscled and covered in hair that was the same reddish shade as that on his head. But, aware of how improper her behaviour had been the last time they were here, she kept herself modestly covered.

"I went to see your brother," said Geoffrey, after a while, "to try to persuade him that there is no harm in us being friends."

"And what did he say?"

"That I could not keep it from my father. He said that he would discover it and then expect me to tell him the true identity of the hermit and who Sir Robert is planning to leave his lands to."

"But you wouldn't tell him anything."

"No. As I pointed out to your brother I've been helping him – bringing him food and clothes since he first arrived last year – and my father has no idea."

"But he seems to know things – your father, I mean. He looks at you with those sharp blue eyes of his and it's like he can read your thoughts."

"It's all an act," said Geoffrey, standing up to skim a stone across the surface of the water and leaving perfectly formed wet footprints on the rock beside her. "He terrifies the peasants with talk of hellfire and makes them reveal all their secrets and then uses what he knows to control them. He used to be able to make Sir Robert do anything he wanted but, since your brother came, he has lost a lot of his influence over him and that makes him feel afraid."

"You do not like him, do you?"

"The priestly man that people see is very different from the person he is at home," said Geoffrey. "He likes to control everyone and his interests always have to come first. He pretends to care about me, having me accompany him everywhere and training me to be a priest like him, but really he does it so that people will admire him and say how good he is and what a fine and caring father. But he knows nothing about me. He has never stopped to ask what I want or what I think."

"He makes me afraid," said Johanna.

"I am not afraid of my father," said Geoffrey. "I see his weaknesses." He paused to skim another stone then sat down again beside her. "So," he asked, "is it true that your brother brought you here as a punishment because you had run away from your home?"

"My mother had lined up a succession of ugly old men for me to marry and when I refused them all she threatened to send me to live with my other brother, Roger, in Nottingham. I hate him. He really *is* a bully. Far worse than your father, believe me. So I ran away. Twice," she told him proudly.

"But they caught you?"

"Bad luck," she commented.

"And now?"

She shrugged. "I don't know. I suppose I shall stay with Sir Robert and Lady Isabel."

"But you will have to marry eventually."

"Better than the nunnery I suppose," she agreed. "As long as he does not have a whiskery wart on his cheek like one who came to Halton." She looked at Geoffrey and saw that his skin was smooth and clear. For a moment he held her glance then leaned across to brush his lips fleetingly over hers.

"I must go," she said, jumping up quickly, "before I am missed."

He picked up the pink rock and placed it where she had been sitting.

"You were here," he said. "And you will come again."

She called Etoile before answering. "Yes," she replied, "I will come again." But as she turned to lead her mare back to the path she caught a movement in the corner of her eye.

"What was that?"

"What?"

"I thought I saw someone."

Geoffrey shook his head. "It was probably a hare. These woods are full of them."

Johanna wakened the next morning to the sound of rain pouring from the battlements and with a groan she turned over, thumping her bolster in anger and wondering when she would be able to see Geoffrey again. All day she watched the dark rain clouds from various windows around the castle until Lady Isabel became frustrated with her incessant wandering.

"For goodness' sake, child, find yourself some useful employment instead of sighing around and turning the cream sour. The horse will wait until tomorrow. Come and help us sew these cloths," she said, handing her a needle and a square of white linen.

Johanna sat down on a stool near some of the servants whose heads were bent to their tasks. She watched Lady Isobel's needle as it burrowed its way along her neat hemming.

"Do you think the Hermit's cell stays dry in the rain?" she asked.

"Are you concerned about the Hermit?" asked Lady Isabel without pausing in her work.

"Of course."

"I am sure that all is well with him."

"Do you think someone should check?"

"Has the Hermit asked you to visit him?"

"No. I have been told to stay away," she said.

"Then you have your answer." Lady Isabel put her sewing on a side table and reached across to lay her gentle hand on Johanna's. It was small and soft and cool; so unlike Geoffrey's. "Do not concern yourself about the Hermit," she said. "He is cared for. Why not go and keep Sir Robert company for a while? You know that he likes to hear you read to him."

Johanna eagerly escaped from the needlework and went down the stairs, pausing at each window to survey the blackened skies and wondering where the birds went for shelter on days like these. It was a pity, she thought, that you could not open the door and invite them in to sit on the rafters until they were dry.

She knew there was little chance of a visit from the Dean in this weather, so she was surprised to hear the low exchange of conservation coming from Sir Robert's chamber as she approached the half open door.

She knocked gently and there was a sudden silence beyond the door before Sir Robert called out, "Who's there?"

"It is Johanna," she replied.

There was a pause before he called her in and as she entered she saw why. Her brother Richard was sitting beside the bed. His leper's cloak and his shoes were put aside to dry near a fire burning in the hearth and his hair looked tousled and damp.

"Richard," she said.

"Johanna," he replied. "How are you?"

"I am well."

"No riding today?" he said, looking at her meaningfully. "As I have said my prayers each morning I've seen that you have been exercising Etoile early these past few days."

"The mornings have been cooler," she replied, "and the days so hot."

He nodded, but held her gaze for a moment. "Remember what I told you," he warned.

She slumped down on the foot of the bed as Sir Robert's shrewd eyes flickered between them.

"I know," she muttered. "I must stay away from the Dean and his family."

"I think that is good advice," Sir Robert told her.

"So why am I not excused Mass?"

"I would not want your soul to be in danger also," Richard said. "You must heed me in this, Johanna."

"I might as well have stayed at Halton and been locked in the bedchamber, or even sent to Nottingham!" she complained, leaping to her feet in sudden temper. "Am I not even allowed to ride my horse?" she demanded, then looked down at the floor where she moved the strewn herbs about with her toe, releasing the powerful scents of basil and meadowsweet.

She had known as soon as she saw Richard's face that he was aware of her secret meetings with Geoffrey. How he knew she could not say; except that he knew her too well for her to keep anything from him. Sir Robert and Lady Isabel she could fool, but she had overlooked the fact that her brother could watch her comings and goings from his cell and from under the concealing hood of his leper's cloak.

"Johanna," said Sir Robert gently, "sit down." He patted the bed with his hand and she went and sat beside him. He took her hand in his; the skin was thin and dry, almost like parchment, and the veins stood out blue, raised like the roots of the trees on the path to the river. "The Dean is a ... a manipulative man – and we must be careful if my true wishes are to be fulfilled. He has had an expectation these past years that my lands will be bequeathed to him – and although I have never made him any promises I suppose that I am guilty of having allowed him to believe that the inheritance will be his." Sir Robert paused to cough a little and catch his breath before continuing. "The truth is that I have been reluctant to admit that I will not dwell here on earth forever and that my earthly affairs needed to be put in order before I pass on –"

"No," she interrupted, stroking his hand, "do not speak like this."

"But you must understand, Johanna. Until your brother came I had turned away from this question of inheritance as if it did not exist. Yet it is right and proper that the de Lacy lands should pass to your grandmother. She is a de Lacy by birth. But..." he coughed again and Richard passed him a cup from which he took a short drink before wiping his mouth and continuing, "the Dean believes that he is being cheated. He believes that a woman should not inherit and that the lands are rightly his and have been promised to him. He suspects that the Hermit has turned me against him. He is very angry and will stop at nothing to get his own way. You must understand this."

"We are not telling you to stay away from Geoffrey de Wallei to be cruel and unkind," explained Richard. "But the Dean will surely discover if you two become friends and he will use that knowledge. You will say things to Geoffrey in unguarded moments that would be better left unsaid. Such intimacy encourages confidences that are better left unspoken. And even though you will convince yourself that you have said nothing that can be used against us, you will surely let a word slip that the Dean will extract from his son. I know that Geoffrey is a good and honourable boy," he went on as Johanna stared at Sir Robert's hand, "and it is for his sake as well as yours that this friendship must not continue."

"You do not know that we are friends," she said, sulkily.

"Johanna, I am neither blind nor stupid," replied her brother, "and you must obey me in this or I will have no choice but to return you to our mother at Halton."

Chapter Ten

Richard watched his sister leave them and sighed out loud.

"Am I doing the right thing?" he asked Sir Robert. "I promised my grandmother that I would bring her here to save her from heartbreak and sorrow."

"It's a difficult thing to be young and in love," replied Sir Robert. "Do not tell me that even a Holy Hermit like you has not had his heart wrenched by a woman?"

Richard turned away so that Sir Robert wouldn't see the guilt in his eyes. "Such things are sent by the devil to tempt us and must be resisted," he said, picking up the cloak which was now more or less dry and shaking it impatiently. "I have done what I can here and I had best return to my cell to pray."

He put on the shoes and lifted the cloak around him but, before pulling up the hood to conceal his face, he glanced back at Sir Robert who was breathing more easily as the rain dampened down the pollen from the grasses outside. "We will all be judged eventually by a greater power," he remarked. "Just let us pray that we will not be judged too harshly for our sins."

The look on his sister's face as he had explained to her as gently as he could why she must not see Geoffrey de

Wallei again still haunted him as he slipped the key into the door beyond the great hall. Johanna's expression had mirrored Geoffrey's as he had sat rebelliously in the cell the previous day having failed to convince him that he had sharper wits than his father in this matter.

Was it so wrong, he wondered as he lit a torch to light his way down the steep steps. He held the flame aloft and surveyed the dripping cavern walls and thought of what his life could have been like if he had remained celibate, as he had vowed he would to Father William before he left for Palestine.

Richard squeezed down the narrow passageway into his cave and used the flame from the torch to kindle the grasses he had brought in to dry earlier in the day. Sweet scented smoke rose up and, after a moment or two, the twigs he had arranged over them in the small hearth began to burn and he extinguished the torch and put it up on its place on the shelf. Then he reached for one of the blankets to make a seat and pushed back his hood as he stretched out his hands to the meagre flames that would at least deter any wolves that might be prowling.

Though the rain outside had more or less stopped there was still a steady and persistent dripping all around him from the rocks. He shivered, and for a moment wished that he was safe in his bedchamber at Halton Castle. As the first born son he had grown up believing that one day the castle would be his domain. He had imagined living there, taking a wife and raising children to follow him, but none of that would happen now. Clad as he was in leper's robes, no woman would look at him except with fear and revulsion as she covered her mouth and nose and passed him by as widely as possible. Never again would a woman come willingly to his bed as Leila had done.

Like the birds his mother tamed in her garden at Halton, Leila had returned for food. Richard was filthy when he returned to his tent at dusk after a day in which he had supervised his men throwing stones and fire bombs into the city. With the noise of the day's battle still reverberating in his ears he gratefully eased off his chainmail and sent his squires away. After eating part of his already meagre ration and saving some for Leila, he drank and then filled a small basin to wash. He peeled off his grimed and stained underclothes and plunged his aching face into the cold water and held it there for a moment before standing upright to ease the tension at the back of his neck, wiping his wet hands across his face and running his dripping fingers through his matted hair.

A movement behind him had him reaching for his dagger before he was aware of what he was doing and he found himself holding the point at Leila's neck as she gasped and drew back.

"No. Come," he said, dropping the weapon and beckoning her to come forward. "Come," he repeated. "Hungry?"

"Yes. Hungry," she said and he smiled, pleased at how quickly she had learned to speak with him.

"Here." He handed her the food and pulled forward a small canvas stool. "Sit."

He smiled down at her as she ate quickly, a strand of her long hair escaping from the dark cloak that covered her from head to toe, and he imagined how she must have been cowering somewhere all day long, waiting for the noise and the fighting to stop so that she could creep out, like a night animal, and squeeze through some small hole to come to him.

It was not until she had finished eating, ensuring that no last morsel had been missed, that she raised her dark eyes and seemed surprised to find him standing virtually unclothed in front of her. He had been too engrossed in watching her delicate movements to remember that he had removed his clothes and, suddenly embarrassed by his near nakedness, he reached for a grubby shirt, but she rose elegantly from the stool and laid a hand on his arm.

"No," she said, then removed her hand to unfasten her own cloak and folding it once she laid it aside before stepping up to the basin of water and wringing out the cloth. "You sit," she said, pointing to the stool that was still warm from her own slight body. In the twilight, with the warm breeze of her breath on his shoulders, Richard allowed her to gently wipe away the dried blood from a graze to his cheek, surrendering himself to the stinging pain.

Back in his cell at Cliderhou, Richard knew that he ought to be on his knees offering up his evening prayers, but tonight he seemed to have too many questions for God and he doubted that he would receive a satisfactory answer. He wished that he could talk to Father William about what troubled him. The old priest was wise and kind and understood that sometimes even the most faithful soul could have doubts that prayer alone could not answer.

Richard sighed and stood up, his legs aching with tension. He paced the cave restlessly like a caged animal, bending every now and then to see if there was a moon rising that would give him enough light to walk outside without the risk of falling and being injured. But there were only glimpses of faint stars every now and again as the clouds raced unseen across the sky. What was out there beyond that sky, he wondered. Was it heaven – that place of reward and sweet peace that was promised to those who repented and followed the one true God? He fervently hoped so, for a reward in heaven was the best that he could hope for now, having failed so miserably to make the best of this life on earth.

Eventually he dropped to his knees facing the wooden cross he had carved with his knife and placed on the two flat stones that he had dragged inside the cave to serve as an altar. Gazing eastwards, towards the Holy Land, through the low entrance to the cave he prayed at last: "Show me how best to serve You," he pleaded. "I will put all thought of earthly love behind me in return for your pity on my transgressions. But what of Johanna? Guide me in my dealings with my sister so that her heart may not be broken too. That's all I ask," he said. "May Your will be done," he added and made the sign of the cross before stumbling up from the unforgiving floor to see that there was indeed now a moon rising beyond Penhull Hill.

Taking his staff, Richard picked his way down the rocky slope in the darkness until he reached the village. All was quiet except for the snuffling and munching of the animals and faint sounds of sleeping folk from inside the huts. He walked past the houses and out onto the path that led up the hill. On he walked until the path became steep. At first the ground was sodden and muddy with the day's rain, but as Richard climbed it become drier and the rising moon lit his way. Panting and slipping on the wet grass, sometimes even falling to his knees – not in prayer, but to grasp handfuls of prickly gorse and heather to prevent himself sliding back down from whence he had come, Richard at last reached the summit and, breathless but joyful, he dropped the staff and raised both arms high into the air, as if from here he could reach out and touch heaven.

"This shall be ours," he vowed as at last the clouds were chased westwards by a freshening wind and the moonlight draped his tired body like a blessing and revealed the vastness of the lands he had promised his grandmother would be passed from blood relative to blood relative.

The dawn seemed to come early as a yellow-pink smudge on the horizon long before the sun itself actually rose. And as soon as Richard could see his way he stumbled down the hill, slipping on the dewy grass until he came to the holy well. As was his ritual he discarded his cloak and tunic and drew the cold, sulphurous water to wash. Then he returned, uphill, to his cell to pray again.

Tired from his sleepless night and hungry too, though knowing that he had no food and would not in any case eat until darkness fell once more, he stumbled as he crouched to enter under the low stone entrance. A movement from within made him jump and he heard the crack as his head connected sharply with the low stone roof, making him momentarily dizzy.

"Richard!" For a brief moment he thought that the voice was Leila's until his senses returned and his eyes accustomed themselves to the gloom.

His sister Johanna came forward to take his arm and

guide him to a seat near the ashes that had been his fire.

"What are you doing here?" he asked impatiently. "I told you not to come here again." He had been hoping to pray and then to sleep a little if the pangs of his hunger allowed, and if they had not he would have lain awake and meditated on his past sins.

"I need to talk to you," she said, standing out of his reach, her dark cloak pulled tightly around her.

"Sit down," he said, trying to sound more gentle. He knew that she was going to raise the subject of her friendship with Geoffrey de Wallei once again and he knew that this morning he would find it difficult to resist her arguments.

She settled near him on a small rock covered with a blanket and, as a low beam of sunlight illuminated her, he watched as she raised her sore and scabbed fingers to her mouth and began to bite at them. He stretched out and took her nearest hand in his. "Don't," he said. "Tell me what troubles you."

"You know what troubles me," she replied, looking him steadily in the eye with her green gaze. "I do not know if I can find it in my soul to obey you."

"Johanna," he began, "you must know that I only act in your best interests."

"Do I know that?" she asked with a sudden flash of anger. "It often seems that no one cares about my interests!"

"I could have left you at Halton," he reminded her. "Or persuaded Grandmama that Roger was the better brother to care for you." He watched as she looked down, fiddling with edges of her cloak. "You may well have been in his care at Nottingham by now."

"And been miserable."

"You are miserable here."

A silence fell between them and Richard turned away from her to fix his gaze on the view beyond the cave.

"If love is so wrong then why does God allow us the capacity to love another person?" she asked. Richard glanced back at her, surprised at her question.

"Sometimes," he explained, finding it difficult to choose the right words to discuss this matter with his young sister, "sometimes we mistake love for the cravings of the flesh. That is the temptation of the devil. We must learn to discern the difference between the two."

"And what about you?" she asked him. Her hood had fallen back and her eyes sparkled with anger under her dark hair. "What about the woman you met when you were on Crusade? Was she just a temptation of the flesh?"

Richard wanted to answer with a resounding yes, but he hesitated and saw a flicker of triumph pass over Johanna's face.

"So you do know what it feels like to be in love," she said.

"Yes," he replied with a brief nod, acknowledging that this answer was at least truthful. "But we cannot always have what we want."

"But you loved her?" she asked.

"I thought I loved her," he said.

"And you believe it was a sin?"

"I believed that the leprosy was my punishment from God for lying with an Infidel woman."

"Believed?" said Johanna and he suddenly realised what he said – that he had spoken as if his belief no longer existed.

"I have prayed and washed and been forgiven. I have dedicated my life to God and I will spend the rest of it in fasting and prayer to His glory."

"But have you forgiven yourself?" asked Johanna. He looked down, away from her penetrating eyes and, picking up a stick, he began to stir the remnants of the ashes in the hearth, though there was no flame left to kindle there.

"No," he admitted. "I cannot forgive myself. I should not have touched her, for when I had to leave her it broke her heart and I do not even know now whether she is alive or dead."

He felt his sister's hand on his shoulder as she moved closer to him.

"Oh Richard," she said. "What else could you have done?"

"I could have brought her back to England with me."

"To live in a foreign land with an outcast leper for a husband?"

"She wanted to come," he said. "But I told her that I did not love her – that I had merely used her – because I thought that it would be better for her to remain with her own people. I thought that she would soon forget me. I thought I would forget her."

"And have you?"

"No," he said, drawing the outline of a crescent moon in the ashes. "How can I forget her when I still love her?"

"And how can you ask me to forget Geoffrey?" asked Johanna.

Richard threw down the stick and looked once more at his sister. She had grown up whilst he had been away on Crusade, and since he had got back he had scarcely had time to reacquaint himself with this young woman who used to be his little sister. But he suddenly realised that, young though she still was, she was probably the only other person in the world who really knew him.

"I am trying to protect you," he said. "I am trying to protect you from the Dean, but mostly I am trying to protect you from the suffering that I have endured these past few months. Not the leprosy," he added, "but the torment of being parted from Leila and the memory of when I left her."

He remembered how he had put off telling her that he was going home time and time again, knowing that it would be the hardest thing he would ever have to do in his life.

Despite the sores that pervaded the whole of his once smooth and soft body, Leila had continued to come to him every night and had bathed him in special oils that she brought – oils that reminded him of the incense that Father William burned during the Mass.

"What sorcery is this?" he had asked her as she smoothed the oil across his shoulders with her warm, gentle hands, massaging the muscles that were tired and taut from yet another day of bombardment.

"It will stop the itching and help you sleep," she said.

"And what if sleep is not my interest," he had asked reaching up to trap one of her hands under his as it moved across his shoulder.

"Whatever you want," she promised and he knew that despite his ravaged appearance she would still kiss every inch of him.

"Does this disease of mine not repel you?" he asked.

"It is the man I love, not his looks," she replied.

Richard closed his eyes and for a moment gave himself up to her touch. "Leila," he said, without looking at her. "I have to go back to England."

The soothing sensation of her fingers paused and then her touch was gone.

"And me?" she asked.

"You will stay here."

"I will come."

"No. You would be unhappy in England. You must stay here, with your own people. Go now," he said and stood, pulling on his shirt and staring at the side of his tent, flapping in the wind.

"But you love me?"

"No," he said. "This was not love. This was just fornication."

Behind him he heard her gather her things. He didn't hear her leave, but when he turned, his eyes blurred with tears, to tell her that he was sorry, that of course he loved her and that she must come back to England with him, she was already gone. The only trace of her was the scent of her oils and a few scattered footprints in the sand.

He looked up to find Johanna watching him with concern.

"Geoffrey and I love one another," she told him. "Is that wrong?"

"No," he said. "It is not wrong. And yes, Johanna, I do know what it is like to be in love. But I do not want you to suffer this pain that I feel daily. It plagues me more than the itching of my sores ever did and it is too deep to be relieved by scratching its surface."

"But I already feel such pain at every moment Geoffrey and I are apart."

Richard looked into her eyes and saw that her feelings were sincere. He saw that her love for Geoffrey de Wallei was sincere and he knew that he himself could never have chosen a kinder or better husband for her.

"There is too much risk," he said, in an effort to convince himself that his forbiddance of their relationship was the right thing to do.

"I am old enough now to take some risks," she replied and Richard saw that this too was true.

"We must be careful," he said at last. "The Dean must not discover it."

"Then we will meet here," smiled Johanna. "This is one place the Dean will never come."

Chapter Eleven

As the hot summer days cooled and the squirrels buried nuts under the trees for their winter larder, the feast of Michaelmas came and went and the villagers gathered and stored their winter crops. The barns and storerooms under the castle began to fill and after All Hallows, when Wynn began to salt meat for the cold months ahead, Johanna and Geoffrey found it more difficult to meet without arousing suspicion.

Whilst riding out to the river in the summertime had provided them with an ideal place for a tryst, the darker mornings made an early ride more remarkable. Their occasional meetings under the watchful eye of Richard were tame affairs, where they each sat on a horse blanket on a separate rock and talked politely about the weather and the state of Sir Robert's health. When Geoffrey reached for her hand or began to tease her, Johanna could feel the tension rise and she was too wary in the presence of her brother to allow anything more than insignificant conversation. But, she acknowledged, it was better than nothing. At least she could look into Geoffrey's dark eyes and watch the smile that played around his mischievous mouth. She could admire the way his hair curled and beg him not to have it cut short as his father was constantly asking. And she was grateful to Richard for giving them some time together and she hoped that it would not distress him too much by reminding him of the love he had left behind.

But the Dean was keeping his son busy collecting the tithes from the harvest and Geoffrey was unable to get away as often as he would have liked.

"My father is also teaching me to say the Masses," he told her one afternoon after he had seen her walking in the castle grounds and given the call of a wood pigeon that they had arranged as a signal to meet at Richard's cell. For once they were alone, but knew that Richard could return at any time. "He says that soon I will be able to assist him."

"And will you become a priest?"

"Yes, the Deanery will pass to me after my father's death, along with the lands he owns. They are not many, but I will not be a pauper. I will be able to support a wife."

Johanna stared at her bare and bitten fingers and wondered if he was planning to speak of marriage. Her heart was beating quickly in anticipation and she looked up to find him standing, tracing an imaginary figure in the rock of the cave wall.

"My father has a girl he wants me to meet," he confessed. "Her name is Alys and she is the only child of a land-owning family in Yorkshire."

"What will you do?" asked Johanna, hearing her voice shake as she spoke. She watched his back as he shrugged his shoulders without turning to face her.

"You know my father," he said. "He gets what he wants."

"But what about me?" she asked and then regretted the selfishness of her outburst. "What about you? What if you do not want to marry her? What if you do not love her?"

"Marriages do not often have anything to do with love. They are political: the joining of estates; the paying of dues; the fulfilling of a duty. Before long your brother, Roger, will find you and arrange a marriage for you and you will have to obey him. What we have had here has been a dalliance... a pastime... it can never be anything more."

"Do you not want to meet with me again?" she asked in a small voice, wondering whether it would have been better to have heeded her brother's warnings about heart-break and to have stopped this months ago.

Geoffrey turned and came across and knelt before her. He reached out to cup her face in both his hands and drew her slowly to him, fixing his gaze on her until she felt his soft lips meet hers. As he kissed her gently she closed her eyes and believed that the world had stopped turning and all that mattered was the moment.

Slowly he drew back from her and as she opened her eyes their gazes reconnected.

"I love you, Johanna," he admitted. "You are the only woman I want to be with, but how can we fight our destiny?"

"I have fought it so far," she told him, reaching out to hold his face in the same way that he held hers. "We cannot retreat now."

At the sound of footsteps outside they both let their

hands fall and Geoffrey stood up as Richard came in, leaning on his staff and panting a little after the steep climb.

"I should go," he said. "My father will be looking for me."

"But you will come again?" said Johanna, getting up and catching hold of his arm.

"Yes," he said. "I will come when I can, but it can only get more difficult."

Johanna bit her quivering lip and wiped away a tear that strayed down her cheek as she watched him go. She was determined that neither of them should see her cry, but Richard's hand on her shoulder proved too much and she turned and buried her face in the leper's cloak and sobbed whilst he stroked her hair and waited for her to tell him what was wrong.

As Geoffrey had predicted, their meetings became less frequent and on a day that Johanna even caught a glimpse of him she was filled with a mixture of happiness and anticipation, tempered with despair. About the girl Alys she heard no more, but she spent many miserable nights imagining Geoffrey wed in secret, rendering him lost to her forever.

Early one damp and misty morning Johanna heard the familiar clattering of horses' hooves entering the outer courtyard of the castle and she leapt up from one such morbid daydream and went to a window to try to catch a glimpse of the visitors. But she could not see who had come and, anxious to know, she pushed her feet into her shoes and fastened them around her slim ankles. Then she quickly braided her tangled hair, fixed her veil and hurried down the steps to the hall in the hope of at least catching sight of Geoffrey.

"Demoiselle Johanna," said the Dean as he caught sight of her at the turn of the stairs. He swept off his hat, upon which the feathers looked distinctly limp, in a gesture that could easily have been interpreted as patronising. "This is a pleasant surprise. I only seem to see you in the chapel and converse with you at your confession," he remarked looking up at her.

She dropped a small curtsey in his direction, her eyes anxiously searching behind him for any sign of Geoffrey. Then her eyes were drawn back to his spellbinding gaze.

"I am alone today," he said in a tone that conveyed to her that he had his suspicions and that they did not please him, and Johanna realised that her brother was right when he warned her that it was not easy to keep secrets from this man. "My lady," he continued as Lady Isabel came out to greet him, "I hope that Sir Robert is well this day. I have momentous news from Palestine that will cheer him greatly. King Richard has made peace with the Infidel, Saladin."

"Then the Crusade is won? Praise be to God," exclaimed Lady Isabel making the sign of the cross. "Come, you must tell Sir Robert and then we must make haste to the chapel to light candles to the glory of God for the salvation of Jerusalem."

"It may not be so simple, my lady," explained the Dean. "The news is indeed good, but not entirely what I had hoped to hear. The king has not reclaimed the holy city entirely, but has come to an agreement with Saladin that unarmed Christian pilgrims may enter. Jerusalem still remains under the control of the Infidels and we must accept that for the present time, although it may not please us."

"But it is good news?"

"Yes, indeed," smiled the Dean. "And I will go to tell Sir Robert, if I may? I am sure it will rally his spirits." He made a small bow towards her. "Lady Isabel." Then turning his attention back to Johanna he said: "I am sure that you will be pleased to hear that the war is over and that you will be able to return home into the care of your brother." And as he disappeared around the back of the screen, his cloak swinging behind him, Johanna was suddenly struck with an icy terror. Would Roger really now come and fetch her to Nottingham?

As the castle buzzed with excitement and Sir Robert ordered a boar to be killed for a celebratory feast, Johanna climbed the narrow twisting steps to the battlements in order to think. How much longer would she be allowed to remain here, she wondered. Sir Robert would not live forever. Geoffrey might soon be the husband of another woman and she could not rely on a leper for protection. The only alternative was her brother Roger and his choice of a husband for her. It was an unpromising outlook all round.

As she stood, staring into the distance, she began to make out the figure of a rider on horseback approaching the castle from the south and she reached out to grasp at the wall as her legs suddenly felt that they themselves had turned to stone and her stomach was turned to rock. She raised a hand to stroke at the lump she could feel in her throat, convinced now that the horseman was Roger, coming to take her away.

Then she made a conscious effort to be sensible. Of course Roger would not come alone; he would come with men-at-arms and horses and banners. But this could be an advance messenger. She glanced across the low fertile land to the west and thought of Etoile in the stables. But where would she run to? And if Geoffrey was to be wed to this woman his father had chosen then what was the point? Her life was over and she may as well either give herself up to her brother's will or end it right now.

She leaned over the edge and looked at the white jagged rocks below as the sound of hoofbeats now thudded across the still air. The rider came closer, approaching the last rise to the castle gates and she could see that he wore the familiar red and gold quarters and black diagonal stripe of the livery of the FitzEustace family.

"Mistress Johanna!" called Martha's voice. "Lady Isabel bids you come inside before you catch cold. Whatever is the matter?" she asked, looking shocked as Johanna turned towards her. "You look as if you've seen a spectre. Come child, you're as pale as snow. Come inside and get warm instead of standing out here without a cloak. I do not want to have to nurse you as well as Sir Robert."

"There is a messenger," she whispered, pointing down, and Martha studied the horse and rider as the gate was scraped open to admit him.

"Perhaps he also brings news of the king," she said.

Martha took her gently by the hand and led her inside and they followed Lady Isabel down to the hall where Bertram had already brought the messenger in to stand by the fire and drink a cup of ale.

The aroma of the feast being prepared in the kitchen

was already seeping through the castle, though Johanna found she had little appetite for the food as the exhausted man fell to one knee as he saw them come in.

"Arise, arise," Lady Isabel told him. "You look as if you have ridden a long way."

"I have ridden from Nottingham Castle," he said and Johanna heard herself give out a tiny uncontrolled squeal that made them all pause and look in her direction. "But my journey began at Halton Castle, my lady," he continued as he handed her a rolled parchment with the FitzEustace seal attached. "I bring news of the king."

"Sit down," Lady Isabel enjoined him as she moved forward towards the fire, gently pulling Johanna to join her. The man reluctant, though obviously grateful, sank to the bench and Lady Isabel sat opposite and gestured for Johanna to join her. "We have already had news of the king, but are anxious to hear more," she told him.

Although the heat from the fire burned on her face, Johanna could not control the tremors that shook her and even the touch of Lady Isabel's hand on hers did little to soothe her.

"Bring a little heated wine for Johanna," she said to Bertram. "She has been standing outside in the cold air and seems chilled. And make sure that a place at the feast and somewhere to sleep is prepared for this man who has taken such trouble to reach us with his news."

"My lady," said the messenger. "I fear that you may not have already heard the news I bring. I believe your feast is in celebration of the peace that the king has made with Saladin. But news now comes that on his way home the king was shipwrecked."

"Dear Lord!" gasped Lady Isabel, raising both hands to her mouth. "How can this be? How can we tell this to Sir Robert? It will surely set him back when he seemed to be recovering so well."

"The king lives," went on the messenger, "but has been taken prisoner. At Acre he made an enemy of Duke Leopold of Austria when he had his colours taken down from the city walls and replaced with his own. And now, crossing Italy disguised as a pilgrim, his identity was revealed and the Duke has taken him and demands a ransom of a hundred and fifty thousand marks. My lady, I am also instructed by my lord, Roger FitzEustace, to discover the whereabouts of his sister and escort her back to Nottingham."

"No!" cried Johanna, looking at the thick-set man whose mud-splattered face and several days' growth of beard now seemed terrifying to her. "No," she repeated, looking up into Lady Isabel's troubled face. "Do not let him take me. Please do not let him take me." She felt her heart race as her whole body shook with fear.

"Hush, hush," soothed Lady Isabel, and the feel of her hand stroking her arm was the only thing that prevented Johanna from jumping up from the bench and fleeing the castle straight away. "We will discuss this later," she told the messenger. "But first I must speak with my husband. Bertram!" she called. "Take this man and show him where he can wash and eat. There is grave news of the king that I will relate to Sir Robert myself. Is the Dean still with him?"

"Yes, my lady."

"Then he shall hear of it too. And Bertram," she added, glancing at Johanna, "bring up the Hermit."

The messenger rose and made an awkward bow to Lady Isabel. Johanna sat and stared at the leaping flames of the fire as she listened to his boots tramping down the steps towards the kitchen. She sniffed back the impending tears and wiped her face with the back of her hand, almost resigned to the fact that she would have to pack her few belongings and set out on Etoile with this stranger at sunrise. She wondered if she would be able to give him the slip. Although the horse he had arrived on looked sturdy enough she doubted that it could out-gallop her mare – and she had the added advantage of knowing the countryside around Cliderhou fairly well now. The peasants believed that there were magic beings who lived on Penhull Hill and Johanna wondered if she could appeal to them to work their charms on her behalf – or maybe the villagers themselves would shelter her, after all she knew that they had been good to Richard.

"Johanna?" Lady Isabel's voice cut across her wild plans and she looked up to find her staring down at her in concern, as if it was not the first time she had said her name. "Come," she said. "We must go to Sir Robert. You must be brave. Wipe away your tears now."

Johanna nodded and did as she was bid before following Lady Isabel to Sir Robert's chamber. The smell of the sickroom crept out and met them as they approached. The murmur of voices paused as Lady Isabel tapped gently on the door before going in. Johanna followed at a distance, remaining near the door and well away from the Dean who rose from the stool by the bed as they entered.

"A messenger has come with grave news," she told them without preamble. "The king has been taken prisoner on his way home." Both men stared at her for a moment without reply, though the Dean was the first to recover his senses.

"From where has this messenger come?" he asked, glancing briefly at Johanna.

"From Nottingham."

"Nottingham!" he repeated in surprise.

"From Johanna's brother, Roger FitzEustace."

"FitzEustace? In Nottingham?" repeated the Dean, the news of the king momentarily overshadowed. He looked again at Johanna, who found herself held in his inquisitive gaze until it was transferred to a place behind her and she turned to see the robed and hooded figure of her brother slip into the chamber.

"Ah, Hermit," wheezed Sir Robert, as Lady Isabel helped him to shift to a more upright position on his cushions. "This is sorry news indeed."

"News?"

"The king has been taken prisoner and is held for ransom by Duke Leopold," said Lady Isabel. "A messenger arrived not half an hour ago, sent by Roger FitzEustace from Nottingham. He travelled via Halton Castle."

"It's a bad business," remarked Sir Robert, coughing as he settled himself once more. "What is to be done do you think?" he asked the Dean.

"We must pray that the Lord's will be done," remarked the Dean evasively.

"Indeed, we must pray," said Sir Robert. "But what about the feast? Should we cancel it?" he asked Lady Isabel who had seated herself beside him on the bed and was stroking his hand.

"I think not," she said. "For the boar is almost roasted and the servants and villagers would be disappointed."

He nodded. "Then let them feast. Let them celebrate tonight, for tomorrow is soon enough to share bad news."

"Then I will bid you farewell," said the Dean.

"You're not staying for the feast?"

"Indeed no. I thank you for your offer of hospitality, but I have affairs which concern me now," he said as he reached for his cloak and hat. "Good day Sir Robert, Lady Isabel, Johanna, *Hermit*." And Johanna caught the tenor of contempt in his voice as he passed by her brother and out into the hall, calling for Bertram to bring his horse immediately.

When he was gone, Richard lifted back the hood from his cloak and seeing his sister's face asked immediately: "What is wrong? What other news has this messenger brought from Nottingham?"

"He has been sent to take me back to Roger," whispered Johanna, her voice audibly shaking as she spoke. "Oh, Richard, please don't let him take me away. Let me stay here with you."

She felt herself begin to tremble violently once again and her legs seemed to buckle beneath her like an over-stretched horse after a long chase. As she stumbled, she clutched at Richard's cloak and he stepped quickly forward to catch her in his arms and carry her to the stool by the bed where he put her down on the seat that was still warm from the Dean's body.

"I think we should have this messenger come up and tell us all he knows," said Sir Robert, "now that the Dean has gone."

"But I have sent him to wash and eat," said Lady Isabel.

"He will have time for that later," said Richard. "I will go myself to fetch the man, for there are several questions of my own I would like him to answer."

"But with care!" warned Sir Robert. "Do not give yourself away. Remember that your brother thinks you are safe in the leper house and at this time it may be wise to allow him to continue to think so."

Richard nodded and raised his hood. "It is surprising what confessions are made to a Holy Hermit," he remarked.

"Now, Johanna," said Sir Robert, reaching out and patting her cold hand with his papery claw. "Do not be distressed. You know that the Lady Isabel and I have grown as fond of you as if you were a daughter of our own. Is not that true, my lady? And we are not going to let you be taken away from us just yet." Johanna tried to smile as Sir Robert's kindly dark eyes peered out from under his forested brows, looking for a change in her expression. "Besides," he said, "it will soon be time for us to return to Pontefract Castle for the winter and you will accompany us there. We shan't let you go off with some unknown varlet of a messenger. It is unseemly and I do not know what this brother of yours is thinking of to send for you in such a manner. I shall write him a stern letter," he went on, turning to Lady Isabel. "It just won't do..." His angry outburst ended in a coughing fit and, as Lady Isabel rubbed his back and Johanna brought the dish that caught the phlegm and blood, they didn't hear the approaching footfalls.

When Sir Robert was comfortable once more Johanna visibly jumped as she turned and saw the messenger standing just inside the door, with Richard, concealed under the leper's hood, waiting near the window.

"Now, my good man," began Sir Robert, still a little breathless. "What is this news you bring?"

The messenger repeated what he knew of the capture of the king and insisted that he had been ordered to find Johanna and return with her to Nottingham.

"My lord's wife has given birth to a son and the lady Johanna is required at the castle," he said.

"An heir!" said Richard and the man turned to stare at the covered leper.

"And the lady Maud? Is she well?" asked Johanna. For although they had never been close she was fond of her sister-in-law and hoped that the rigours of childbirth had not been too painful for her.

"Yes, indeed. The lady Maud is well and so is her child."

"And what have they named him?" asked Richard.

"His name is John."

"After his grandfather who died in the Holy Land."

"Yes, indeed," said the messenger, with a slightly puzzled expression.

"Praise the Lord!" said Richard. "This is good news that you have brought us."

"Yes," said Sir Robert with a warning frown in the direction of the Hermit, "but what of this girl?"

From her seat by the bed Johanna looked from one to the other as they surveyed her and she was reminded of the occasions when her mother had brought her before her father for the meting out of some punishment for a misdemeanour. The silence was dense, broken only after a moment by the ringing of the Compline bell from the

church below, signalling that it was time for the peasants
to gather in the castle bailey, around the roasting hog for
the feast of celebration.

"I dare not return to Nottingham without her," said
the messenger, and Johanna recognised the fear in his voice
that betrayed the hold her brother had over all those who
were under his power.

"I will send you with a letter," said Sir Robert, "that
will reprimand your lord, Roger FitzEustace, for sending
for his sister in such a shameful way and telling him that
when he furnishes a litter and some ladies to attend to her
needs then I may be more inclined to return her to him."

Johanna watched as the man swallowed hard, feeling
a sudden sympathy for him.

"My lord, he will have my head," he replied. "I have
been instructed on pain of death to return her to
Nottingham Castle."

"Nonsense!" said Sir Robert, with a dismissive wave of
his hand. "Go and enjoy your feast and then stay here a
day or two until the letter is written. Go now!" he repeated
and with a stiff bow the messenger inched backwards,
from the chamber looking only half the man he had been
when he first came in.

In the doorway he paused and looking across to Richard
said, "Pray for my soul, Hermit."

"My brother is not someone to be dallied with,"
remarked Richard as he stared after the man. "I think that
it may be better to send a message with a servant of your
own that you have already left for Pontefract and that
this good man is following you there. My brother may at
least spare the life of another man's messenger."

"And is this the fool who will inherit my lands?" burst out Sir Robert. "I wonder if I have made the right decision after all. The Dean may have his faults, but summary executions to spite those who do not allow him his desires are not, to my knowledge, his code of conduct!"

"Hush, hush..." soothed Lady Isabel as the outburst brought on another coughing fit. "Do not distress yourself with this."

"Lady Isabel is right. You must trust my judgment in this matter," advised Richard.

Wiping his mouth on the cloth that was already bloodied and stained, Sir Robert slumped back on his cushions as if defeated. "Then it shall be done as you suggest. And tomorrow we will make preparations to travel. You will see to it, won't you Isabel?" asked Sir Robert, kissing his wife's hand to his cracked lips. "For I feel suddenly very tired."

"Then I will leave you to rest," said Richard. "Come Johanna, let us speak privately whilst the servants are engaged in their feasting."

She followed him out, trying to catch at his cloak and make him stop to reassure her.

"Richard, don't let them send me to him," she begged when he eventually paused before the fire in the great hall.

"Johanna," he said, turning to hold her gently, "you know that I have always tried to protect you from Roger, and you know that I will do everything in my power to keep you safe. But it is not so easy now. As a leper I do not have the authority that was naturally mine as our father's first born son. That authority is Roger's now. But he is your brother too and be assured that although his manner may be bold at times he will do nothing that will harm you."

"If I am taken to Nottingham and forced into marriage with some unbearable old man then I will run away!" she threatened, shaking herself free from Richard's hands and turning away.

"Johanna, life's problems cannot always be solved by running away," he replied and she glanced back at the change in his tone. "Perhaps," he went on, "it is time for my little sister to grow up."

"You do not need to bid me grow up!" she shouted, lifting a hand to strike out at him. But he caught her wrist and held her fast.

"Listen to me!" he said. "There may be a way to solve this, but you must trust me. In the meantime we will tell Roger that you have gone to Pontefract Castle, though I think it's doubtful that Sir Robert will ever see Yorkshire again this side of heaven."

Johanna pictured Sir Robert in his bed and suddenly realised that Richard was right. He was too ill to travel and it looked as if they would remain at Cliderhou during the dark cold winter months after all. But she still felt very afraid as she imagined what Roger's reaction would be when he discovered that he had been tricked.

Chapter Twelve

As the winter closed in it became obvious that the plans made to travel to Pontefract Castle would never reach fruition. Richard watched as Sir Robert grew frailer with the shortening of the days, as if the failing of the sun was taking his life with it, and he knew that the old man would not survive the journey.

Throughout the damp November days his breathing had become more laboured and, though the tidings from the Holy Land that the war was over had lifted his spirits for a few short hours, the news of the king's capture and the deception over Johanna's whereabouts had cast him down further. On most days he was only able to get out of his bed and sit in the chair by the fire for a few short hours, and on some days he was too weak for even that.

A messenger had been sent to Nottingham to say that the de Lacys, along with Johanna, had left for Pontefract Castle. He returned, safe, but no one at Cliderhou was surprised that the original messenger from Nottingham had disappeared without a word.

Richard spent most of his afternoons sitting with Sir Robert as he talked more and more of his childhood, sometimes even seeming to forget that his life had passed and imagining that he was still a young man.

Christmas approached as the weather settled into a damp and misty calm, where the air around the trees and the castle hung without a movement and even the birds were silent and hidden. Coming up from his cave in the last week of Advent, Richard found Bertram supervising some of the men from the village as they brought in a huge Yule log to burn in the hearth and bunches of holly, thick with red berries and other greenery from the woodlands to decorate the great hall. The smell of the foliage, mixed with the aromas of spiced meats being cooked in the kitchens, brought a sudden and vivid memory of Christmases at Halton Castle, when his father had invited all the villagers into the great hall to feast on roasted boar, minced meat pies, special breads and autumn gathered fruits. He remembered how the minstrels would sing the Christmas songs as they ate and afterwards they would all dance to the carols and there would be shouting and laughter as the games and joking began. He turned away as he realised that he would never see such a sight or join such a celebration again. And his legs seemed leaden and tired as he walked to sit with Sir Robert in the dank candlelit chamber.

"I fear that we will not be able to celebrate as I would have liked," said Sir Robert sadly in one of his more lucid moments. "Bertram is trying his best and tells me that the greenery has been gathered, but there are no minstrels to sing at the feast."

"We will make it a good Christmas," Richard reassured him. "For you are with family and those who love you and that is what is important in any celebration."

"You are right," wheezed Sir Robert, "although I would have liked to see one more Christmas in Yorkshire before I died."

"What nonsense is this you talk?" said Richard brightly in an attempt to cheer the frail old man who sat opposite him.

"Don't!" he replied, with a vestige of his old forceful self. "I know that my days are numbered and I am happy that God will take me as and when He deems fit. I do not need you to speak to me as if I were a child to be cajoled into better spirits."

"I am sorry," said Richard, realising that this was just what he was guilty of. "But Bertram and the others are working hard to make your Christmas memorable."

"And I appreciate it. And I appreciate you coming to sit with me, Richard. I value your friendship and your company; and the gift of your time."

"I have little else to do, but watch and pray," remarked Richard in a rare moment of self-pity.

"Your part is not yet over," observed Sir Robert. "Care for your sister. She too has become very dear to me these past months. I would like to see her happy before I die."

As Christmas approached Johanna felt her spirits lift with the excitement. The afternoon sewing sessions were forgotten as she and Martha and Lady Isabel joined Wynn and some of the other village women in the kitchen to prepare the food for the celebration.

"We've never had the Lord and Lady here at Christmas before," said Wynn as she minced and spiced the meat for the pies. "We usually have celebrations in the village, but we're all looking forward to eating our Christmas dinner in the great hall this year."

"Yes. At Halton Castle we have the most lavish celebrations," said Johanna, her sleeves pushed up to her elbows as she kneaded at the pastry dough on the wooden table. "Or at least we did," she added, recalling with sadness that she would never again watch as her father handed out small gifts to the village children, smiling his encouragement as they were pushed fearfully forwards by their mothers to receive them.

On Christmas morning itself, Johanna woke and gave thanks, as she had every morning since she had arrived at Cliderhou, that she was still safe from Roger. She pushed back her covers and tiptoed to the window to see if any snow had fallen, but a mist still shrouded Penhull Hill. Shivering, she pulled a blanket around herself as she tried to re-kindle the fire in her brazier whilst she waited for Martha to bring her hot water to wash. Hanging on a peg was the red gown that Lady Isabel had helped to sew for her to wear and beneath it the new soft leather shoes that had been bought from the market in Wallei. Johanna ran her hands over their soft texture, afraid of what would happen to her in the future and wishing that Sir Robert had been well enough to travel.

Lady Isabel had decided that they should go down to St Mary's in the village to join in with the Mass. It was something that she thought would be a kindly gesture before the villagers came up to the castle for their celebratory feast.

Sir Robert was determined that he too should go down

to the church, but Johanna doubted whether he would even be fit to be carried into the hall to sit at the top table during dinner. The Dean had offered to come to the chapel and conduct the office there, but Lady Isabel told him that it was more likely that he would have to say the Mass at Sir Robert's bedside.

Wearing her new gown and a cloak lined with fur, but leaving the new shoes by her bed to put on when she got back, Johanna went down the stairs to join Lady Isabel for the short walk to the village. Outside the door a fierce wind that had suddenly whipped up from the west blew strands of her hair across her cheeks and tugged at her hood. With a smile, she followed the others out of the castle gate and down the hill towards the church, where candles burned in the windows and the bell rang out to greet the Christmas morning.

Later, they and the villagers would return to the castle for their Christmas feast. The Dean would be there and Sir Robert had been insistent that his wife and Geoffrey should attend too. Johanna had never met Geoffrey's mother and she was looking forward to seeing what she was like. Geoffrey said that she was quiet and kind and rather in awe of his father. Johanna could believe that; she thought that all Geoffrey's best qualities must surely come from her.

She followed Lady Isabel under the carved archway of the door as Bertram and Martha stood aside to let them pass. They dipped their hands into the holy water and made the sign of the cross before moving forward. The church was packed with people in their best clothes, their breath hanging like the mist often did over the hill. They parted to allow her and Lady Isabel to move to the front near to the chancel where the Dean would perform the Mass.

An expectant hush fell over the adults and excited children behind them as the Dean appeared in his black robes, his hair brushed back and shining in the candlelight. He began to intone the Latin words of the Christ's Mass and Johanna felt tears choke her throat as she was suddenly and unexpectedly homesick for the chapel at Halton Castle and the soothing voice of Father William.

As Christmas Eve had turned to Christmas Day, Richard had prayed the words of the Angel's Mass. The Latin flowing from him without hesitation as he knelt, looking to the east, sorry that the misty sky obscured the bright evening star. Afterwards he slept a little, shivering under the damp horse blankets, but roused himself again as day dawned for the Shepherd's Mass.

He did not walk down to the well on Christmas morning but watched from the entrance to his cave as the villagers below woke and re-kindled their fires; the excited voices of the children who ran from house to house betraying that this was a special day of celebration.

He wondered what his mother and grandmother were doing now. He wondered if the villagers there at Halton would gather in the great hall for a feast as had always been the tradition. He imagined his grandmother, holding his mother's arm as they walked along the gravelled path to the chapel to hear Father William say the Christ's Mass. He wondered if the minstrels would come and play as the family and their guests ate and the thought of roast boar, brought steaming to the table with fruits and breads made him salivate in hunger.

When his father had been alive there had always been games to follow. He recalled how he and Roger and Helen and Johanna had mixed with the village children to play. There had been no formalities at Christmas and on the Twelfth Night one of the village children was always chosen as king or queen for the day and allowed to choose what game would be played next.

The adults would look on and laugh indulgently at the antics, filled to the brim with good food and strong wine – and later there would be singing and dancing and he recalled how the singing would often go on late into the night as he lay in bed and listened as the villagers eventually made their way unsteadily back to their houses.

Now he could see the people making their way to St Mary's and it was his banishment from the church that hurt him the most. He could manage without the feasting, the singing and the games, but his heart and soul longed to step inside the candle-lit church, to smell the scent of the incense on the air and hear the words of the Mass that celebrated the birth of Christ, so long ago in Bethlehem, in the Holy Land that he had fought so hard to keep from the hands of the Infidel.

He listened to the ringing of the bell until it fell silent to indicate that the Mass had begun. Then he knelt before his makeshift altar and followed the words in his mind, praying that his soul if not his body could take part.

Johanna almost ran ahead of the party as they walked back to the castle. The appetising smell of meat and spices coming from the kitchen was filling the bailey as she hurried in through the wide gates, welcoming rather than discouraging visitors on this very special day of the year.

Inside, the fire was blazing and crackling in the hearth and it seemed that every space had been decked out with greenery, transforming the great hall into a garden for the twelve days of Christmas. The holly was thick with red berries and she smiled as she heard an anxious mother behind her explaining to a small child that they were poisonous and must not be touched. She wondered if a similar scene was being enacted at Halton Castle; though she had quickly recovered from her moment of homesickness in the church she still missed her grandmother and hoped that there would be another Christmas that they could celebrate together.

She turned as a gusty cheer went up and the villagers clapped their hands together at the sight of Sir Robert being carried to his rightful place at the centre of the top table. Smiling, she joined in with the applause as she moved to take her own place, but before sitting down next to Lady Isabel she went to Sir Robert and kissed his cold, smooth cheek.

"Merry Christmas!" she said, pleased that he looked so well today in his fine new clothes, his face washed and shaved by Bertram who had brushed his hair to a snowy sheen and even tamed his magnificent eyebrows a little for the occasion.

He squeezed her hand in his and whispered, "Merry Christmas, my sweet Johanna. What a picture of radiance you look today. Is she not beautiful?" he asked Lady Isabel. Then added with a wink: "Almost as beautiful as you."

It could have been the heat from the brazier behind them, but Johanna watched as a pink glow rose to Lady Isabel's cheek as she bent and kissed her husband. These two elderly people, she realised, were still very much in love with each other after all these years and she knew that when it was time to make the Christmas wish, she would wish that she too would have a long and happy marriage with a man she loved. As she took her place at the table she glanced along the faces to the right of Sir Robert, passing by the Dean until she saw Geoffrey. He was wearing a tunic of midnight blue that made him look more comely than ever and as their eyes met he smiled at her amid the revelry, and the sight of him made Johanna's Christmas complete.

After their hands had been washed a huge roasted boar was carried in and there was an appreciative gasp as it was placed before Sir Robert for him to carve. Johanna watched as he struggled shakily to his feet and wielded the sharp knife but, as his hands were unsteady and he seemed on the verge of a coughing fit, Lady Isabel allowed only one slice to be cut before asking the Dean to take on the task of carving meat to place on her platter.

A couple of the villagers who played musical instruments had volunteered to accompany the eating; they would receive their laden platters later as a reward and as she raised her first handful to her mouth and looked around at the laughing, happy faces, Johanna suddenly wondered if anyone had thought of Richard.

"Bertram!" she called urgently as he passed her by with a jug of wine in his hand. "The Hermit?" she whispered as he bent to hear her above the jollity.

"I will make sure that plenty is saved for him," he nodded reassuringly and only then, when she knew that her brother would not go hungry in his dark cave below, did Johanna allow herself to eat.

The sound of the celebrations seemed to seep through the walls and down to his cell, though Richard, sitting and stirring his meagre fire, acknowledged that the sound could have been in his imagination. He wondered if Sir Robert had been well enough to come downstairs, and he hoped he had, as it was fairly certain that the old man would not see another earthly Christmas.

After the feast was cleared away and the dancing and games began, Sir Robert was taken back to the relative peace of his small chamber. Having seen him settled before the fire, with cushions to support his tired body and with Lady Isabel and the Dean's quiet wife to keep him company, Johanna slipped away and threaded her way through the gathering to a bench at the side of the hall. It was the place she had last seen Geoffrey lingering and she hoped that he might still be there.

With a hundred Merry Christmases exchanged along the way she eventually slipped out of the crowd and her heart leapt as she saw him sitting on the narrow seat under a window.

"Merry Christmas, my lady Johanna," he said with a mischievous smile.

"What are you hiding behind your back?" she asked as she approached him. His smile widened as she grasped his wrist, pulling it out from behind him. He laughed and held out an empty hand, palm up. Johanna slapped it playfully and reached for his other arm. He did not resist but let her see the small bunch of pale green leaves and white berries that he held.

"Mistletoe!" she gasped.

"Believed by the pagans to be a symbol of fertility!" he told her. "Come here." He moved to one side as she squeezed her body onto the seat next to his. The warmth of his thigh set hers on fire as they touched and, holding the bunch of mistletoe high in the air above them, he drew her to him with his other arm and gently pressed his lips to hers. "A kiss under the mistletoe at Christmastime will seal our fate," he whispered as he gently stroked her face. "I have thought about what you had to say and I have told my father that I will not marry Alys." She took a breath to speak but he placed his finger firmly across her lips. "Wait," he said, "hear me out before you make an answer. Johanna FitzEustace," he said. "Will you marry me?"

She saw that her stunned silence was interpreted by him as reluctance and as she saw the shadow of doubt cross his face Johanna reached out and put her hands first onto his shoulders and then his cheeks.

"Do not look so unsure," she said. "Surely you know that my answer will be yes? Yes, I love you Geoffrey. Yes, I will marry you. But..." she hesitated and shrugged her shoulders, looking around at the castle walls and hearing the noise of the merry-making just a heartbeat away. "How can it be so?" she asked him.

"I will find a way," he told her and raising her hand to his lips kissed it lightly.

Johanna looked up guiltily as a shadow fell across them.

"Geoffrey," said the Dean of Wallei, "your mother is asking for you. And," he said, turning his eyes on Johanna, "Lady Isabel is looking for you. Perhaps," he suggested with a knowing smile, "you would both like to join us rather than hiding yourselves away."

Like naughty children they slunk past him as he stood motionless before them and wove their separate ways through the dancing to Sir Robert's chamber. Glancing back Johanna saw the Dean pick up the bunch of mistletoe from where Geoffrey had discarded it on the bench and she turned quickly away as she felt his eyes track her across the hall.

As the first villagers began to make their way home, fathers carrying small sleeping children in their arms, Richard heard the faint shuffling of someone negotiating the narrow passageway at the back of his cave. He lit a torch from the fire and went to see who it was, hoping that Bertram had remembered his promise to save him some of the food. As he held the light aloft he saw that the figure was too small and slight for Bertram and after a moment recognised Johanna in a fine new gown, struggling to carry both a bundle and a lantern and to pick her way along the uneven ground.

"Merry Christmas!" she called as she looked up and saw him. Then she ran the last few paces and reached up on tiptoe to kiss him. Her breath smelt of wine and spices. "I have brought you some good things to eat," she said handing him the pleasingly large bundle and picking her way to his fireside before putting down the lantern and smiling up at him. "Eat," she told him. "Today is a feast day. You have had plenty of time to say your prayers and I know that you are hungry."

He returned her smile, pleased that she looked so radiantly happy for once, and he joined her by the fire where she sat and watched as he unwrapped the cloth and ate without hesitation.

"Have you enjoyed your Christmas Day?" he asked as the urgent pangs of his hunger subsided.

"Indeed I have." He looked up and smiled as her voice bubbled like the source of some small stream and he knew that she had a secret that she would share with him before long. He supposed that it was to do with Geoffrey and he suspected what she was going to tell him before it burst from her like the torrent of a river in spate. "Geoffrey has asked me to marry him and I have said yes."

Richard nodded as he chewed, his mouth full and she gazed at him in anticipation, obviously expecting a more enthusiastic response.

"Oh Johanna," he said, reaching out his hand to squeeze hers. "Of course I am pleased, but remember not to put too much of your heart into this. Marriages are agreed by families, not individuals, and whilst we would marry for love in a perfect world, you must know that an agreement between you and Geoffrey is not a binding one unless both Roger and the Dean of Wallei agree."

"And such an agreement is... is unlikely." She sighed as her radiant face gave way to sudden tears and Richard put his food aside to gather her into his arms.

"I am sorry," he said, kissing the top of her soft head with gentle lips. "I am sorry. This was unkind and thoughtless. I could at least have given you one day of hope and happiness," he told her as he cursed himself for his insensitivity and wondered if there was any way that he could give his sister the happiness that was lost to him; the happiness that she craved and deserved, for he could think of no one whom he would rather see her marry than Geoffrey de Wallei.

Chapter Thirteen

The twelve days of Christmas seemed long ago to Johanna as the cold strengthened after the Feast of the Epiphany and the villagers returned to work to plough the fields in readiness for the spring planting.

Sir Robert seemed weakened by his exertions on Christmas Day and it was decided that, as neither the physician's remedies nor the Dean's prayers were having much effect, another physician must be sent for from Pontefract to give a second opinion on the imbalance in Sir Robert's health.

One day, towards the end of January when the hoar frost laden on the bare branches never melted in the weak sun, both Lady Isabel and Johanna remained beside Sir Robert's bed all day, tending his fire and keeping him covered with a thick pile of blankets and furs. But he still shivered and his skeletal body was shaken incessantly with coughing fits that produced streams of vivid red blood.

Anxious that the physician had still not arrived as daylight failed, Lady Isabel seemed unable to keep still and Johanna began to fear for her health too as she walked restlessly from the bed to the window, to the outside stairs that led down from the hall and back again, calling out to Martha and to Bertram to check that the guards were keeping watch for the expected guest.

"Come and sit down," said Johanna, taking Lady Isabel's thin hand and leading her back to the chair by the fire. "You will surely make yourself ill with distress. I am sure the physician will be here soon and that Bertram will bring him straight to us."

"I know, I know," said Lady Isabel, repeatedly pleating and smoothing the fabric of her gown as she sat on the edge of the chair, ready to hurry across to her husband and hold cloths and basin to his mouth should he wake and begin another coughing fit. "But I feel that every hour that passes is a chance lost for a cure. I cannot lose him," she said, suddenly, turning with childlike helplessness to Johanna. "I am nothing without him."

"I know," she soothed, her arms around Lady Isabel's fragile shoulders as she knelt beside her. "I know," she repeated, thinking of Geoffrey. The last time she had seen him was as he rode away on Christmas Night. The departure of the Dean and his family had been almost discourteously early, but the Dean had explained that his wife had a headache and she had not contradicted him. Standing by the door as they left, Johanna had felt Geoffrey's hand briefly brush the back of her own as he passed her, though he had not looked at her nor said a word but followed the Dean, whose dark scowl had been blacker than the moonless night.

As she had watched the horses slip down the icy hill on the road to Wallei, Johanna had been confident that Geoffrey would soon find a way to visit her again. Despite what Richard had said, she believed that he would come and take her off to a safe place where they could be married. But as the days passed she had begun to worry. Neither Geoffrey nor the Dean had been back to the castle and Johanna had an uneasy feeling that something was not quite right.

Now, as she gently rubbed Lady Isabel's arms to comfort her, she understood thoroughly what she meant.

"We will not lose him yet," she said. "The physician will come soon and a cure will be found."

"I have heard that there is a woman in the village who makes potions and that the people go to her when they are ill. Martha tells me that she works magic and can ward off the evil spirits that cause disease. She says that she will bring her to the castle, and I have thought of consulting her," admitted Lady Isabel.

"The villagers must make do with superstition, for they cannot afford a skilled physician," said Johanna.

"Am I selfish?" asked Lady Isabel suddenly, looking across at her husband. "Is it just for me that I want to keep him here?" She stood up slowly and went to the bed where Sir Robert was sleeping, each new breath rattling his chest. "If it is God's will that his time has come, is it wicked of me not to submit to the will of God, but to fight it with herbs and cures?"

"Surely it is God who gives the physicians their skill?" said Johanna.

"But no one can prolong this earthly life forever. I fear that I may have to bid my husband farewell."

"But only until you meet again in heaven," said Johanna. "Have strength, and trust in God, my lady," she advised, realising that she had now taken on the role of the parent and that, rather than Lady Isabel and Sir Robert protecting her, she must now become strong enough to support them both through the difficult weeks and months ahead.

For a moment Johanna thought that Sir Robert's breathing was becoming worse and her heartbeat quickened in fear for his life until she realised that the sound she heard was that of the castle gates being opened.

"The physician!" she exclaimed in relief and gathering her skirts ran out to the hall in time to see Bertram pull open the outer door. But into the hall stepped the unmistakeable figure of the Dean of Wallei, his hat in his hand and his cloak sweeping closely around his imposing shoulders.

"Good evening, Johanna," he said, his voice as cold as the frosty air. "I hear that Sir Robert has sent to Pontefract for a new physician?"

"Indeed," said Johanna, feeling as if she was physically shrinking under his gaze. "We expect him at any moment."

"I passed no one on the road," said the Dean. "Where is Lady Isabel?"

"She is at Sir Robert's bedside. I will fetch her."

"No," he said. "I will go in." And he turned to the chamber, his cloak catching her hand as he passed her without another word and his cold eyes freezing her soul as she felt his intense displeasure.

She knew, of course, that he had seen Geoffrey kiss her on Christmas Day and she hoped that he had not chastised Geoffrey too much about it. She was anxious to speak to him, to make sure that he was all right and to reassure him that her promise to marry him still held, despite the difficulties that they would face. But she also knew that the Dean would try to keep them apart, and that he had come alone today.

She imagined Geoffrey back in Wallei watching his father ride away and knowing that he was on his way to Cliderhou and would see her. And although she was longing to see him again this seemingly insignificant connection helped her in a small way.

Reluctant to spend time in the Dean's censorious company, but more reluctant to leave Lady Isabel alone with him she turned and walked slowly back across the hall. Muted voices came from Sir Robert's chamber as the Dean and Lady Isabel spoke. Their tone sounded displeased on both sides and they fell silent as she entered. The Dean turned away to warm his hands at the fire and Lady Isabel cast her a sympathetic glance. Sir Robert was still sleeping uneasily and Johanna had the feeling that she had been the subject of their discussion rather than the patient.

"Will you join me in prayer?" asked the Dean as he unfastened his cloak and draped it carefully over the back of the chair where the fire would keep it warm.

"Let us leave the Dean to minister to Sir Robert," said Lady Isabel with a hostile glance at the priest, "though I do not believe that extreme unction is needed just yet."

"As you wish," he replied and waited for them to leave before he opened the vial of oil to anoint Sir Robert.

Johanna was surprised that Lady Isabel was willing to leave her husband's side at all, but she followed her in silence up to her own chamber where Martha had lit the candles and added more logs to the fire. Lady Isabel poked the well packed embers into flames as if she wished she were poking at someone who had made her angry and

Johanna sat down and watched and waited until she was ready to speak.

"He has sent Geoffrey away," she said at last. Johanna stared at her, trying to make sense of the words.

"Away?" she asked. "Where to?"

"He has sent him to Rochdale, to take charge of the church of St Chad. He has also told him that he must marry Alys Nuttall or that he will disinherit him."

Johanna stared at Lady Isabel, unable to form a sensible thought with which to reply.

"Why?" was the best she could manage.

"What occurred between you and Geoffrey at Christmas?"

"He asked me to marry him and I agreed," confessed Johanna.

"You kept this from me and Sir Robert?" she asked in surprise.

"Yes. Richard knows. He told me it was not possible so I said nothing."

"Well, maybe Geoffrey spoke to his father..."

"No. The Dean saw us. He saw Geoffrey kiss my hand, and guessed, I think," said Johanna as the true gravity of the situation became clear to her. "I'm never going to see him again, am I?" she asked as she fought down the tears of anger, frustration and disappointment. The thought that she would never see his smile, or his dark eyes again; never touch his hands or feel his lips on hers or his arms around her as he held her tightly against him was more than she could bear. As she buried her face in her hands and tried to stifle her anguish she felt Lady Isabel gently stroke her hair and the comforted became the comforter once again.

"The physician!" said Lady Isabel some moments later and hurried out to greet him. Johanna sat a while longer before telling herself that there were more important things to attend to that evening than her separation from Geoffrey. At least Geoffrey was still alive and whilst they both lived there was hope that they could somehow be reunited. But Lady Isabel faced a more difficult separation as Sir Robert was surely destined to leave this earthly life ahead of her. So, wiping away her tears, she smoothed down her gown, pushed back her hair under a veil and with a deep breath went back to the bedchamber where Sir Robert lay so gravely ill.

The Dean glanced up at her as she came in, but she lifted her chin and tried not to catch his eye, wondering if it was simply because she was a FitzEustace that she found no favour with him. She knew that her brother Roger would dismiss Geoffrey de Wallei as being too low born to be considered as a husband for her and she wondered what the Dean had to gain by not allowing his son to take her as a wife. Perhaps he was afraid of being thought unworthy, or maybe it was just that he hated her for being a part of the family who he thought were intent on stealing his rightful inheritance. His piercing stare made her look back at him eventually and she met his eyes briefly as he studied her from where he stood in front of the fire. Uncharacteristically, he let his gaze drop first as he turned to watch the physician who was unpacking his bag onto the coffer at the foot of the bed, helped anxiously by Lady Isabel.

"The humours are in complete disarray," announced the physician after his examination. "The blood which Sir

Robert coughs up shows that he is sanguine and his hot, moist brow confirms this. His blood urgently needs to be let to set his body back in balance."

"I will leave this to the learned man," said the Dean although the description sounded a little sour as it left his tongue. "My knowledge lies in matters of the soul rather than the body."

"Then pray for this man," said the physician as he assembled his basin and his sharpened knives and leeches. "For he is in grave need of divine intervention."

The Dean swept up his cloak.

"I will accompany you," said Lady Isabel. "Please stay with Sir Robert," she asked Johanna. "I do not want him left alone but I have no stomach for this," she confided, her lips already bluish and trembling as she headed for the door.

Johanna watched in fascination as the physician rolled back the sleeve from Sir Robert's arm and picked the first of the small black leeches from the jar. He dropped it onto the thin white skin and within moments it began to curl and swell as it gorged on the sick man's blood. He gradually added another and then another until the whole of Sir Robert's forearm was covered in the slimy creatures in varying degrees of size. Johanna wanted to look away but the sight seemed to compel her to watch until she jumped back with a squeal as the first leech suddenly dropped off, satiated, and the physician frowned at her before picking it up between his forefinger and thumb and dropping it back into the jar. As the fattened leeches dropped one by one from his patient's arm, the physician collected them in silence and then wiped and bandaged the bleeding wounds. With his arm wrapped in the swathes of linen and his face even whiter, Sir Robert appeared to slip into a deeper sleep and the physician announced himself satisfied for the time being at least.

Bertram came in to tell him that a bed had been prepared for him and that his supper was ready.

"I am obliged," he said. "I will eat and then examine my patient again before I sleep, but I believe that he will rest well until morning now."

After they had gone Johanna sat down by the bed and gently wiped Sir Robert's face with a cloth. Although she was afraid that he would die that night it seemed that the physician knew his job. By morning he was breathing more easily and, as the sun rose late over the winter landscape, he roused and asked for a little soup to warm his bones. When she had helped him sip a little of it and had made him comfortable the old man drifted back into sleep. As she sat and watched over him, Johanna heard Richard come in quietly.

"I have prayed all night," he said.

"And it seems your prayers are answered. Sir Robert seems much improved."

"And you?" asked Richard.

"The Dean has sent Geoffrey away," she told him, and he gently caressed her shoulder in reply.

"I am sorry," he said. "I wish that I could have intervened in this for you."

"You cannot protect me forever," replied Johanna. "Perhaps it is time for me to accept that." She smiled up at the brother she loved so much. "Perhaps the stars do not hold that kind of happiness for you and me," she said.

As the weather improved Johanna took to riding Etoile down to the river again each morning. Every day as she slipped from the saddle and made her way to the river-bank she hoped that Geoffrey's stone would have been placed on the boulder to show that he had been. But every day it was her pink rock that sat there and his stone remained on the ground exactly where she had left it. At last, in a fit of temper, she snatched it up and flung it into the fast-flowing current with a curse on the Dean so loud that it startled Etoile and made her toss her head in distress.

"Sh... shhh," she soothed the mare and then began to cry because she suddenly felt that she had been unfaithful to Geoffrey and thrown away a part of him. Sadly, she left her own stone on the boulder as a sign of her stead-fastness but, knowing that to keep returning to the spot could do nothing to make her feel any better or improve her situation, she bade the place a farewell and mounted Etoile to return to Cliderhou to where the pollen from the spring grasses was once again preventing Sir Robert from catching his breath.

As the summer solstice came and went and the villagers held a celebration that was disapproved of by the Dean, Johanna was kept busy nursing Sir Robert. He was in need of almost constant attention and seemed to want her more than Lady Isabel, calling for her and asking for her even if she only went out for an hour to ride Etoile and feel the summer sun on her face after being enclosed within the gloomy castle walls. Sometimes he became confused and called her Isabel, mistaking her for the young girl who had been his bride.

Every time the Dean came to visit him she hoped that

Geoffrey had come too but, although the Dean occasionally mentioned that his son had come home to visit his mother, he kept him well away from Cliderhou and, to her dismay, Johanna began to find that when she closed her eyes as she lay in her bed at night it became harder and harder for her to see his face clearly. Yet he came to her in her dreams, as well defined and as loving as ever, until she came to believe that her dreams were her real life and her wakeful days only a purgatory that she must endure. Every morning she woke with a sense of disappointment that she must face another long and uncertain day until she could regain the peace of her bed and the arms of her lover.

Each morning she dressed with trepidation and tiptoed slowly to Sir Robert's chamber where Martha nursed him through the night, with instructions to wake her if he worsened. And every morning she was filled with the dread that she would find him no longer alive and Martha asleep at the foot of the bed.

As usual she paused and listened at the door. She could hear Martha moving about and Sir Robert's unsteady breathing. The stench of the sickroom grew worse each day despite the strewing of herbs and spices and Johanna longed to let in some fresh air, but the physician said that the air was bad for him and the window remained firmly shuttered.

"How is he?" she asked. Martha shook her head and Johanna caught the look of despair in her eyes.

"It will not be long now," she said. "Will you sit with him awhile?"

"Yes," said Johanna, gathering one frail hand into hers

and feeling a faint pressure in return as she gently rubbed some warmth into it.

How old he looked now, she thought as she stared at Sir Robert's gaunt face. How different he was even from the man she had first met only a year ago, and how much she had come to love him in that short time. It was as if he had replaced her father, or been the grandfather she had never known. Yet it seemed that it was her fate to lose those she loved the most and she wondered how much pain a person could take before it crushed them completely.

"Go and break your fast," said Lady Isabel when she came a little later. "Then ride Etoile and get some fresh air. The summer has almost passed you by, child, and your cheeks are pale as the newborn lambs."

"I'll eat," she said. "But I will sit with Sir Robert today. There will be other summers for me."

"But not for him," agreed Lady Isabel, gently stroking her husband's face.

She returned soon after and found Richard in prayer at Sir Robert's bedside.

"I have chosen not to send word to the Dean," said Lady Isabel.

Johanna raised Sir Robert's hand to her lips and softly kissed the gnarled knuckles, but now his hand was unresponsive. His eyes were half shut and half-open. He did not blink. The air began to rattle in his throat with every intake of breath, each one pausing longer than the last, and the gap between enticed her to count, as Richard had taught her when they were children, between the flash and the thunder of a storm to see how far away the moment was. Each new breath was a relief and a disappointment – a fending off of the inevitable, a prolonging of the awful.

His breath rattled again and they all waited, holding their own breath. Lady Isabel on the far side of the bed and Richard standing at its foot, his leper's cloak cast aside on the chair. The chamber remained silent. How much longer would it be, wondered Johanna. The gaps had been lengthening but this was the longest. It was too long. How much longer before it came again, the labouring gasp of that wasted body? How much longer? How much longer?

Her heart began to pound wildly and she tried to will him to breathe again, but then she realised that he was dead. She kissed his warm fingers one last time as Richard stepped forward and gently closed his eyes.

"It is over," he said as Lady Isabel began to sob. "His suffering is finished."

Chapter Fourteen

After Johanna had kissed Sir Robert's forehead in a last farewell, Richard gently took his sister's arm and led her out into the hall so that Lady Isabel could say goodbye to her husband in privacy before the body was prepared for burial.

He was a little surprised and concerned to see how distressed Johanna was as she sobbed inconsolably into the hands that covered her face, gulping and sniffing and unable to say a word to him. When she had been told that their father had died she had shed no tears, at least not in public, and had seemed to be the one in the family who was strong for their mother, who had wept uncontrollably when the news came and even more when he had left to replace his father in the Holy Land. He recalled again how his mother had thrown herself down in front of his horse in an attempt to dissuade him from completing his duty and he remembered how much it had hurt him at the time to leave her. It would have been much easier for him to leave for battle with the Infidel and to avenge his father's death had he gone with her blessing and support. Yet, he remembered that it was Johanna who pulled their mother to her feet as he rode away. He remembered that he had been proud of her self-control and maturity at such a young age. But now she cried like a child at the death of a man whom she had known for little more than a year.

He sat beside her and rubbed her back gently as her convulsive sobs began to subside. She wiped her face on one of the cloths from Sir Robert's bedchamber that she still clutched in her hand.

"Don't leave me, Richard. Never leave me," she said, reaching out to grasp his arm.

"I will always be here for you, Johanna," he promised. "For as long as I live. And after that I will watch over you from heaven to keep you safe." He took her hand in his and pressed it to his chest. "I promise," he said, catching and wiping away with his thumb a tear half way down her cheek. "Why are you so upset by this?" he asked. "I know that you had grown fond of Sir Robert, but these tears are so unlike you."

"I... I do not know," she struggled. "I have never seen anyone die before. It was so... so moving."

He nodded. "Perhaps I have become accustomed to death," he said sadly. "I have seen so much that it begins to lose its meaning. And you are so young. I sometimes forget how young."

"What will happen now?" she asked.

"The Dean will have to be told, of course. Though he will be angry not to have been summoned before Sir Robert died and I fear we will have excuses to make to him. Then, Sir Robert's body will be embalmed and wrapped and taken to Kirkstall Abbey to be buried alongside his father."

"It will be an arduous journey for Lady Isabel," said

Johanna, looking towards the chamber where the widow still sat beside the body of her husband.

"And once again you will be asked to be strong," said Richard, wondering how much resilience this slight young girl had. "My prayers will be with you."

"But you will come?"

"Everyone will go. But I must walk behind, at a distance, as the law dictates. Though my heart and soul will ride with you," he promised.

The sound of footsteps interrupted them and Bertram stood nearby with a pained and enquiring look on his usually cheerful face.

"Sir Robert is gone," Richard told him. "Be so good as to send a messenger for the Dean and then to begin to make the arrangements for our journey."

Bertram nodded, words seeming not possible for him at this moment that they had all dreaded and yet had known would come.

Richard turned back to Johanna and squeezed her arm. "Go to Lady Isabel now and give her what comfort you can. Help to wash the body and prepare it. I will go to my cell and pray for Sir Robert's soul. And if the Dean should ask why he was not sent for sooner, assure him that Sir Robert was alive when the message was sent and has only just passed on."

She nodded, calmer now, and returned to the bedside whilst he slipped like a shadow through the secret doorway to pray before his small altar that Sir Robert's soul would be spared purgatory and ascend straight to heaven.

Richard slept fitfully that night, dreaming that he was back in the Holy Land being attacked in his sleep by a faceless foe. When he woke on the hard cold floor of the cave and gathered his reasoned thoughts he had no doubt who that foe was. He supposed that the Dean would refrain from making any claim on the castle until they returned from the burial, but he knew that when they did he would make his move.

He stumbled across the cave and checked that his copy of the will was still safe where he had hidden it away. It was only this roll of parchment and the one held by his grandmother that could prevent the Dean laying claim to what rightfully belonged to the FitzEustace family. This was the task that both his grandmother and Sir Robert had given him to complete and he prayed to the Lord that he would be able to fulfil their wishes with success and without any bloodshed.

As light dawned, Richard washed and made his Matins prayers before gathering his few belongings, including the will which he had decided would now never leave his person until the inheritance was made legal. Taking his staff and his cup and clapper, he stooped out of the cave into the bright summer sun and walked down the path through the tangled grasses to the castle gate where the procession was forming.

At its head was the Dean of Wallei, dressed in black and bareheaded in respect to the deceased. He was struggling to keep his prancing stallion still as the body of Sir Robert, wrapped in waxed linen cloths, was carried out and placed on a litter slung between two horses. An aged Lady Isabel leant on Johanna for support in a scene that reminded him of the day he had left Halton Castle in his leper's cloak.

Bertram stood straight and still in front of the horses holding Sir Robert's sword upright before him and the other servants from the castle grouped behind Sir Robert's knights, softly singing psalms. A priest stepped forward holding a cross and censer and it took Richard a moment to recognise Geoffrey de Wallei. His eyes strayed back to where his sister was helping Lady Isabel into another litter that would take them over the Pennine Hills into Yorkshire. He saw from Johanna's steady gaze in the direction of the black-clad figure that she too had recognised him and he hoped that the presence of the man she loved would give her the strength she needed for the long journey ahead which would take several days, resting each night in a house of the de Lacy family along the way.

At last they moved off, the bright sun at odds with the mood of the day. It should have rained, thought Richard, as he watched the Dean's horse leap forward, frustrated at being reined in to keep its gait to a sombre pace. Bertram moved steadily off, his grim face concentrating on the bearing of the sword as he was followed by Sir Robert's body which swung gently between the horses' legs. The litter creaked forward with a jolt as the horses moved off and he saw Johanna reach out a hand to steady Lady Isabel. Neither cried. Their tired white faces looked simply blank and uncomprehending. The last of the knights scraped the castle gates closed behind them and Richard waited until they had passed before following behind. They turned slowly northwards to take the easier route around the hill towards Colne, where Sir Robert's grandfather had built the church of St Bartholomew. Richard glanced back at the almost deserted castle and to where the villagers stood sadly by to bid their own farewell and watch them go, and he wondered what would transpire on his return.

The journey was arduous and prolonged. Lady Isabel's frail health meant that each day could not be rushed; she needed frequent stops to rest and their progress was laboriously slow. It was four days before the imposing stone walls of Kirkstall Abbey came at last in sight.

Abbot Lambert and his monks came out from their cloisters to receive the body of Sir Robert. And by the time Richard reached the gates the shrouded corpse had been taken into the church where he could only imagine it laid out in front of the altar and surrounded by candles as the monks kept their vigil and offered up prayers for Sir Robert's soul.

He stood outside the church door and felt for a moment as if God had forsaken him, until he heard a movement behind him and a soft voice spoke.

"Hermit. Lady Isabel has asked me to make you welcome and show you our hospitality. Come. We have a small cell where provision is made for those with your affliction and you will be comfortable and cared for there. Come," he repeated as Richard continued to stare at the closed studded doors that shut him out from God's house.

The monk held out an arm but was careful not to touch him and, for a moment, Richard was tempted to wrench off his stinking garb and show him his face and shout that his skin was unblemished, that his affliction had been cured through the power of prayer, that he was clean and could be declared wholesome once more and allowed into the church to give thanks to God and to pray on holy ground for the salvation of his friend and relation. But

Sir Robert had left him with a more important task to see through and it was still too soon to show himself. Instead he gave a nod, pulled the hood around his face and tucked his hands into his sleeves as he followed the monk to the small leper house where he was given food and water and a pallet bed on which he gratefully lay, his aching feet and legs grown heavy and awkward, although sleep eluded him for some time as he watched the rising moon and listened to the tawny owls exchanging their cries in the trees nearby.

As the sun rose and he heard the ringing of the abbey bell, he got up and stretched his stiffened body before kneeling before the cross on the wall and joining in the morning prayers. The day ahead would be difficult for him, he knew. His exclusion from the burial was already stinging his own soul and he did not even dare to imagine how he would feel as he waited outside the church as the office took place. Forced to watch from a distance, as the mourners slowly followed the priests and the monks into the church where the Funeral Mass would be read and Sir Robert's body placed reverently in a stone coffin near that of his father, he could not hold back his own tears.

Afterwards they stayed one more night. Richard was dreading the long walk back to Cliderhou. He knew that the Dean had tried to persuade Lady Isabel to ride on to Pontefract Castle and take Johanna with her and that, according to his sister's words muttered in passing at various pauses in the journey, he was angry that she had not taken his advice. But the decision was one he had asked Lady Isabel to make: it meant that the Dean would have to temper the pace of his return to ride alongside her and therefore give him a chance of arriving back at Cliderhou not too far behind his enemy. To leave the castle empty would be an invitation for the Dean to take up residence immediately on his return, and that was something that Richard knew must be avoided; for once the Dean had physical possession of Cliderhou it would be difficult to remove him despite the written will. He also guessed that the Dean had a key to the strong-room and that he would take the opportunity to search for and destroy any documents of Sir Robert's that were not to his satisfaction.

As Cliderhou came into sight once more, Richard gave thanks that their long journey was over. He had walked behind the litter and the horses each day, despite Bertram's offer of Edric and the urgent exhortations of Johanna for him to accept the horse whenever she managed to catch a moment alone with him. He had refused, saying that it was not fitting for a leper to ride and he did not want to arouse any more of the Dean's suspicions, but now that the castle appeared in the distance as they rounded Penhull Hill at last, he allowed himself the luxury of admitting that he was indeed exhausted.

The horses seemed to increase in speed as their destination came into sight and Richard found himself lagging further and further behind as his weary body struggled to climb the last incline. His legs seemed weighed down and he leant heavily on his staff as he hobbled the last steps into Cliderhou.

Beyond them he could just see the Dean and his entourage as they made their way back to Wallei. Much earlier in the day the Dean had urged his party on so that the distance between him and Lady Isabel became greater. Richard knew that he had become increasingly angry and frustrated with the speed of their return and, according to Johanna, he suspected that the hermit had been instrumental in Lady Isabel's decision to return to Cliderhou.

Richard woke stiff and sore after his first night back in his cell. He had become unfit, he mused, as his legs ached on his walk down to the well to wash. As he returned up the hill, slipping on the wet grass, he heard the sound of horns and trumpets in the distance and, abandoning his bucket by the side of the steep path, he hurried up the slope to the castle walls from where he could see further down the valley.

A string of horsemen was approaching and Richard could make out the familiar red and gold colours on the banners that fluttered in the bright morning sun. At the head of the procession was an imposing figure on a huge grey destrier. He was wearing a gilded helm and, as he came closer, Richard saw that he wore the FitzEustace surcoat over his chainmail. Behind him his armour bearer carried his huge broadsword and he was followed by an escort of archers and crossbowmen. Behind them came horses laden with provisions, cooking utensils and even furniture. There was no one other than his brother Roger who would arrive in such an ostentatious fashion.

He watched as the villagers threw down their tools and came running up to the castle gates to view the spectacle, calling and talking loudly amongst themselves as they pointed anxiously towards the coming nobleman. The servants within the castle walls came down to the bailey to meet him too and, as the huge grey horse approached, the gates were heaved open without protest to allow him inside. Richard watched as Bertram came down the outer steps from the keep to see what was happening and could imagine his baffled and frightened face as Roger waved his hand and shouted words of instruction at him.

Of Lady Isabel and Johanna there was no sign, but Richard could picture them waiting inside, peeping out through the windows, unsure what to do with no one to advise or protect them. He turned from the compelling scene that was being played out before him. Leaving the bucket where it had fallen, he ran back to his cell and found the bag he had brought from Halton Castle.

Richard pulled off the leper's cloak and tunic and stepped into the fine linen underclothes, allowing himself a moment to enjoy the sensation of the soft cloth against his skin, before adding the padded gambeson, his chainmail shirt and his own FitzEustace surcoat. Then he covered himself completely with the leper's cloak and checked that his copy of the will was safely stowed in the pouch attached to his belt with the key to the door that led into the castle. He lit a candle from the embers of his small fire and pushed his way through the damp passage. He turned the key and slipped like a shadow onto the steps from where he could hear his brother entering the great hall as if it was already his own domain.

Richard waited behind the screen and watched as Roger lifted off his helm to reveal his thick brown hair, darkened and damp beneath his protective cap. He bore the beginnings of what promised to be a luxuriant growth of beard and his greedy eyes, which were a slightly darker shade of green than Johanna's, dulled slightly as he gazed around.

"It is much smaller than I imagined," he announced to anyone who was prepared to listen. And although Richard could not catch Bertram's words he saw that the man seemed to be apologising for the castle's shortcomings as if they were his own responsibility.

Richard crept nearer silently, pulling the dark cloak tightly around him, blinkered by the hood that concealed his face as he shadowed the contours of the stone walls. At the sound of light footsteps from above he paused and glanced to see Johanna, with a determined expression set on her anxious face, precede Lady Isabel down the stairs to greet the visitors.

Roger saw them too and Richard was close enough to see his expression turn to a mixture of amusement and malice as he recognised their sister.

"Well, well... at last the quarry is hunted to its lair," he smiled. "Good day, sister. I trust you are well? It is indeed a delight to find you after your various journeys around the houses and castles of Lancashire and Yorkshire in your quest to avoid me."

"And I see that reports of your demise by the sword of the Infidel are mistaken," she told him, with a slight and mocking curtsey.

"You are grown bold," he remarked, obviously surprised at her confidence. "And brother Richard is not even here to protect you. Just the widow," he said glancing dismissively at Lady Isabel, "and a household of elderly retainers and useless sentinels. Do your guards fling open the gates for any enemy who demands entry?"

"Enemy? How could I fail to recognise my own brother as he approached and give orders that he should be made welcome?" she retorted. Richard watched as she betrayed her fear by shifting restlessly from foot to foot under Roger's gaze.

"Then perhaps you could persuade your servants to find us food and wine, for the journey has been a long and tiresome one to this God-forsaken place and I am both hungry and thirsty."

"Of course," she said, with an obliging smile. "Bertram, will you attend to our visitors' needs? Though," she added to Roger, "if you had sent word ahead of your coming we would have been prepared for you."

"And have someone fill a tub with hot water so that I can bathe – in the best bedchamber," Roger told Bertram as he moved away towards where Richard was watching. "My men will bring in my bed," he said, indicating the large retinue of attendants who accompanied him, "for I do not want to catch a plague from the previous occupant. And my cook will prepare my personal food. And you, madam," he said as he turned back to his sister, "had best prepare your explanation of why you disobeyed me when I sent for you. I had a husband picked out for you. But he got tired of waiting. Which is a shame as he was of a good family that I would have liked allied to ours. But there are plenty more who seem willing to take you on and might enjoy the challenge..."

Richard watched as Johanna's eyes hardened and her fists clenched and, for a moment, he thought that she was about to spit in Roger's face as he closed in on her. But she straightened her back and lifted her chin to merely meet his eyes in wordless defiance before stepping aside to allow him to pass and sit before the fire in his own chair which had been carried in for him. Though barely had he seated himself and instructed his page to bring him some wine than the door appeared to fling itself back on its hinges and the Dean of Wallei strode into the hall.

Pushing the page to the floor, Roger leapt to his feet and turned to face the intruder whose expression was as dark as a summer thundercloud.

"Who are you?" he demanded as his hand rested on the hilt of his sword.

"Forgive me," said the Dean smoothly and made an exaggerated bow, completely at odds with his furious face. "I am Robert, Dean of Wallei. And you?" he asked.

"Your new master and lord of Cliderhou Castle and all the former de Lacy lands," he said, and as Richard watched, tight-lipped, he knew that Roger was expecting an apology and words of respect and obligation. But the Dean stood silent for just a moment longer than was polite before a slow smile of superiority spread across his face. He waved the feathered hat in Roger's direction in a gesture of contempt.

"I think not," he replied. "The last will of Sir Robert de Lacy leaves all his lands and possessions to me."

Chapter Fifteen

Johanna had been dreading the thought of the journey to Kirkstall Abbey until she caught sight of the priest who was to accompany them. Even dressed in black and with his back turned to her she recognised him immediately and felt a rush of excitement and desire. "Geoffrey," she breathed to herself, and his name was like a prayer on the soft morning wind; a prayer that had at last been answered.

Seeming to sense her eyes on him, he turned and they exchanged an inexpressive glance before he moved to his place in the procession with the cross and censer. Johanna helped Lady Isabel into the litter and then had to reach out to restrain her as the horses jerked them into motion, but all the while her eyes strayed again and again to Geoffrey.

He seemed to have grown and become a man during the months they had been apart and she studied every discernable muscle of his body as he moved forward slowly, swinging the censer which released the powerful aroma of incense all around them.

She began to ask Lady Isabel if she had seen who the priest was, but when Johanna saw that her face was still blank with the numbness of bereavement she realised that this was not the time to speak of her own feelings. Looking back at Geoffrey she felt a smile twitching at the corners of her mouth and, aware that the expression on her face must not look unfitting, she bowed her head as they moved off under the gaze of the villagers. She was bewildered by the ever changing emotions that circulated through her like the darkening of the night and the dawning of the day. As she watched Geoffrey walking ahead of them, she longed to leap down from the litter and run to him and feel his warm, strong arms grasp her and hold her close to him as if he would never let her go. But how could she allow herself even a moment of happiness when she felt so saddened by Sir Robert's death?

That evening they reached Colne as the sun began to redden in the west and Johanna gently woke the sleeping Lady Isabel. How anyone could sleep as the litter swung and jolted along the uneven road would have been a mystery to Johanna except that she knew Lady Isabel was so exhausted and distraught that she feared for her sanity.

As Johanna helped her out of the litter she became aware of someone at her side and knew that it was Geoffrey.

"How are you?" he whispered in passing.

"I am well... *now*," she replied without turning, and she felt the back of his hand brush against her own knuckles. His closeness made the fine hairs on the backs of her forearms prickle and despite the warmth of the evening she felt a shudder run through her before he moved away to escort the body to its overnight resting place in the church.

She glanced back as they were welcomed into the manor

house where a hot meal, a steady fire and soft beds awaited them. Richard, enveloped in his leper's robes, climbed slowly up the hill and followed the horses around to the stables where she hoped someone would find him food and a safe place to sleep. It would be a long walk for him and she worried that he was becoming weak from his constant fasting and penance.

Day after day the litter swayed and lurched along the rutted roads and Johanna watched in awe as the vast desolate moors opened up on either side of them as if they were travelling over the very top of the world. They seemed so high that Johanna felt that she would only have to reach up on tiptoe to touch the clear blue sky. She kept wanting to tell Lady Isabel how beautiful she thought it was in its bleakness, but Lady Isabel stared into the distance as if the only thing she could see was her own loneliness. She spoke rarely and often did not even seem to hear what was said to her. It was as if her grief cut her off from everything.

At last they came in sight of Kirkstall. It was very late and evening was already casting its long shadows across the fine stone church as Johanna watched the cloaked monks come out to receive Sir Robert's body. As she heard Lady Isabel's sudden sob at the sight of them she was starkly reminded of their purpose and she made a conscious effort to put aside her own feelings and concentrate on supporting Lady Isabel as they both grieved for the loss of Sir Robert.

It was full dark by the time they were shown to the simply furnished guest house just outside the Abbey. After Johanna had helped Lady Isabel to retire she went to her own cell. There was a simple bed and stool and a cross on the wall. A small candle was guttering on a plain wooden table which held a jug filled with scented water and a brass bowl in which to wash. Johanna pushed open the shutters on the small window and gazed out into the gloomy courtyard until her eyes adjusted enough for her to see the dark figure lurking there.

"Richard?" she whispered.

"No. It's me," said Geoffrey's voice and she quickly looked around to check that the door behind her was closed before she stretched out her hand and touched his fingertips with her own. "I cannot stay. My father has been watching me closely, but there is something that I must ask you."

"Ask me anything," she breathed.

"The promise you made to me at Christmas? Will you still keep it?"

"You know that I will. Ask me to climb from this window now and go away with you and I will come."

"You would leave everything? Even your fine clothes and your mare Etoile?" he asked in his familiar teasing way.

"Be assured that I would," she replied firmly.

"I will find a way that we can be together," he said after a pause. "Believe me, Johanna. I *will* marry you."

"And Alys?" she asked, hardly daring to form her rival's name upon her lips.

"A pretty girl," he replied, and Johanna could hear the smile in his voice, "but she is not you – and it is you that I love."

"I love you too," she said, searching the darkness for

a glimpse of his face. Yet the way his fingers found hers and caressed them as they both stretched into the night gave her all the reassurance she had longed for during the lost lonely months since he had been taken from her.

"I must go," he said as the abbey bell chimed Compline. "But never doubt that I will come for you at the first opportunity. Promise me that you will wait for me, Johanna."

"I promise," she vowed as his fingers slipped from hers and his shadowed figure appeared to float across the cloisters towards the stone church that was now illuminated in the glow of a rising moon.

She slept little that night, lying on the strange hard bed, knowing that he was so close and yet so untouchable. She was relieved when the sun rose and the bell began to ring for morning prayers. She threw back the thin cover, made a quick prayer of her own to thank God for bringing Geoffrey to her and, after splashing the cold water on her face and dressing in her dark gown, she went to see if Lady Isabel was awake.

She found her lying very still and staring wide-eyed at the bare ceiling.

"Lady Isabel," she whispered, reaching out to touch her hand, fearing in one wildly heart-racing moment that she too was dead. But her hand was warm and at the touch she turned to Johanna as a single tear rolled down her face.

"What am I without him?" she asked. "My life has lost its purpose. I wish that I were dead as well so that I could be laid beside him and my hurt would be healed."

"Hush," soothed Johanna, wiping away the tear. "Do

not say such things. Look how the day dawns and the warm sun rises; listen to the birds in the trees and the sheep calling to one another; life is good, do not dismiss it yet."

"Oh, but living is hard," she said. "It is easier to die. It is easier to be the one that dies than the one who is left alone."

"Hush," she pleaded. "Sir Robert would not have wanted you to speak like this."

"He was everything to me. I have loved him since I was a girl and I will love him in this life and the next. All there is for me now is to look forward to the day when we can be together again. Until then there is nothing for me but sorrow." She paused and reached out her fingers to touch Johanna's face. "Do not look so sad, child. I have had my love, and yours is yet to come." She smiled. "I have seen the priest," she said, "and I have seen the flush on your cheeks and the light in your eyes. I had that with Sir Robert. It is precious; never let it go, for being parted is unbearable. Be happy, Johanna, for as long as you can; for it is only the memories of my happiness that will sustain me through this day to come."

Johanna shivered in the church as the monks sang their prayers over Sir Robert's body and when the moment came to put him inside the stone coffin and lower the lid that would entomb him there she closed her eyes. She could not bear to look and think of him, with his sparkling brown eyes and bushy eyebrows, lying there in the cold and the dark as the flesh slowly rotted from his bones. Beside her Lady Isabel sobbed and as she patted her hand to comfort her Geoffrey looked at her across the church.

What Lady Isabel had said earlier was true. She resolved to find her happiness with him in this life, no matter what.

Back in her bed at Cliderhou Castle following their return, Johanna woke from a dream where she was lying in the sun by the river and Geoffrey was calling to her as he came nearer and nearer. For a moment she thought that it was real, but as the images faded she realised that it was voices and shouting from the courtyard below that had woken her and, after a momentary disappointment, she went to see what was happening.

Unable to see anything from her own chamber, she hurried barefoot to the small window at the top of the stairs. She was almost physically sick when she saw her brother Roger.

She ran back to the bedchamber and dressed quickly without washing and caught her hair up into a braid. Below she could already hear her brother complaining to Bertram. What should she do, she wondered, as she went down to the lower floor, unsure whether to awaken Lady Isabel. Should she go down to the great hall or should she find Richard? As she paused, undecided, Martha ran towards her.

"What am I to do?" asked Martha, wide eyed with fear.

"Waken Lady Isabel, gently. Do not alarm her," said Johanna.

"Who are they?" asked Martha.

"It is my brother Roger," she replied, frowning. "I think that he has come to claim the castle."

Behind her she heard a door open and Lady Isabel came

towards her, fear clearly visible across her pinched features and in her reddened eyes.

"Who are they?" she asked in a quivering voice.

"My brother, Roger FitzEustace," replied Johanna as the shouting of orders from below intensified.

"And this is the man who is to inherit my husband's lands?"

Johanna hesitated as Roger continued to issue instructions in the hall below, sending the servants scurrying to do his bidding. "I suppose we had best go down," she said at last, wishing that Richard was there to protect her and hoping that he was nearby.

As she went down the steps, she glimpsed a shadow from the corner of her eye and it gave her the courage to face her other brother.

Lady Isabel hung back and Johanna found herself standing alone when her brother's gaze alighted on her and his contemptuous words echoed around the stone hall. As their eyes met in combat she wished for a fine sharp sword in her hand, but had to make do with the involuntary clenching and unclenching of her fists as she restrained herself from flying at him in a fury and gouging out his impudent eyes.

Although conscious that she was trembling she managed to keep her voice steady as she answered him; the nearness of Richard gave her courage, especially when the talk turned to husbands. She wished and prayed in that moment that Geoffrey would come in through the outer door and publicly claim her as his own, though she recoiled as the door was suddenly kicked aside and a black clad figure burst in. She almost cried out, but her bitten fingers flew to her lips to silence them as everyone in the hall looked at the Dean of Wallei.

Roger, who had seated himself by the fire, jumped up and reached for his sword and, as the two men she hated most in the world faced one another in fury, she felt a sudden thrill of expectation that one might just kill the other and she was unsure which one she would have preferred dead.

The adversaries managed to keep at least a thinly veiled layer of civility as they introduced themselves, though Roger, having stated his claim to the castle, stared in incredulity as the Dean calmly explained that he was mistaken. Surely it was not true, she thought. She had no knowledge of such a will and she glanced towards Lady Isabel whose face betrayed that she wanted neither of these claimants to become her protector.

But as the two men stared at each other in a tense and expectant silence, Johanna saw a movement behind her and Richard walked forward into the hall.

"That Hermit," cried the Dean, as soon as he saw him, "is a trickster and a wizard. Sir Robert gave him his genuine will for safe-keeping because he believed he was a holy man. But he has already tried to trick me by producing a will that is a forgery. A false will of his own devising that leaves all Sir Robert's land and money to the church for the building of a huge abbey here at Cliderhou to rival Kirkstall. He believes that such an edifice will buy him forgiveness from God and cure the ravaged body that torments him for his many sins."

Roger turned to the figure of the leper with his sword extended.

" No!" the dean shouted, "he is possessed of magical powers and will reduce you to ashes should you touch him."

"Seize him!" shouted Roger to his men-at-arms, unwilling to risk his own life, "and hold him fast so that his magic will be bound as well."

Johanna watched as the men came hesitantly forward, terrified by the Dean's warning of a reduction to dust. As the first approached, Richard moved suddenly to grasp him by the arm and hurl him to the ground. The others jumped back in fear.

"Seize him, you clay-brained half-wits!" roared Roger. "Seize him before I have the lot of you hanged from the rafters here!"

More afraid of Roger than the devil himself, they moved forward as one and taking hold of Richard they succeeded in pinning his arms to his sides. To her horror Johanna watched the Dean stride forward and snatch a roll of parchment from a pouch beneath Richard's cloak. With sleight of hand he hid it beneath his own clothing and replaced it with one of his own.

"He has switched the parchments!" she objected stepping forward only to be pushed roughly aside by Roger.

"Get out of the way, girl! This is men's business, nothing to do with you. Get these women out of here!" he roared and Johanna watched helplessly as Martha and Lady Isabel shrank away from the dispute.

"Give that to me!" shouted Roger as he held out his hand for the parchment that the Dean held.

With a sly smile the Dean passed it over to Roger who opened and read it. A puzzled and unsettled expression gradually replaced his anger.

"This is the will that you have taken from the Hermit?" he asked, quietly now.

"This is Sir Robert's true will."

"But this says that the lands are left to Robert, Dean of Wallei and his heirs in perpetuity." Roger stared at the Dean in bewilderment. "But my grandmother, Albreda, has a signed will that leaves the lands to her."

The Dean gave a shrug and Johanna noticed a slight smile at the corners of his lips. "There was such a will," he admitted. "But Sir Robert called me to his deathbed and in recognition of my unfailing devotion to him, as well as my family connections, he made this new will in my favour. If you look closely at the date, my lord, you will see that it supersedes the parchment that your grandmother holds."

"Sir Robert made no such will!" cried out Johanna, slipping past the guard who reached out to restrain her. "He made no such will, did he Lady Isabel?" she asked and turned to see Sir Robert's widow sink slowly to the floor in her pain and anguish. "Look what you have done now! You lying, selfish men!" stormed Johanna glaring from Roger to the Dean and back again. "This will is false and you know it!" she accused the Dean, her anger giving her courage.

"My dearest, Johanna, do not distress yourself," replied the Dean, "for I would not wish you to fall into a faint as Lady Isabel has done. I am afraid that women are not capable of comprehending such matters," he said, turning to Roger. "They are far too excitable."

"Yes, be quiet, Johanna!" added Roger, turning harsh eyes to her. "You are not helping our cause by speaking of things of which you know nothing."

"I know that Sir Robert's genuine will leaves his lands to the FitzEustace family," she replied as calmly as she could, although she could feel her heart pounding in her chest and threatening to envelop her mind with the rising blackness that the Dean had predicted. "This one is a forgery," she added, breathlessly. "Sir Robert would never have left his lands to him!" She almost spat out the last word as she glared at the Dean who was standing watching her, arms folded, with a self-satisfied smile still lingering on his face.

"Enough!" said an authoritative voice from behind her. "I think that if you search the Dean you will find the genuine will that the ... villain... took from me a moment ago."

Roger strode forwards and catching the Dean unawares grasped him with one hand around his throat and backed him up against the hard stone wall whilst he tore open his expensive cloak with the other and produced the will that he had stolen. He pushed the Dean roughly aside so that he staggered and almost fell, grazing his temple as he struggled to regain both his balance and his dignity. Then Roger unrolled the parchment and read it quickly. His expression turned in an instant from pleasure and relief to thick anger as his gaze fell upon the Dean once again, and Johanna trembled as she watched his features harden into the expression that she feared the most. She shrank back as he bellowed at his guards to detain the Dean.

"You will hang! Here and now! Fetch a rope!"

Johanna watched in fascinated horror as a man was sent to the stables to find a rope. The Dean, white-faced, stared fixedly as his execution was arranged and Johanna felt sudden sorrow for him as he was grasped by the arms and pulled forward, a thin trickle of red blood running slowly down his cheek.

"No!" interrupted Richard, in a firm voice that caused everyone in the hall to pause and look at him. "I promised Sir Robert that I would protect the Dean. He will not be hanged by you, or anyone," he told Roger.

Johanna watched Roger's cheeks grow redder as if the anger at this unremitting contempt for his authority would physically burst from him at any moment.

"And who are you to tell me what I can and cannot do in my own castle, on my own land?" he asked, barely able to suppress his rage as he reached once more for his sword. Richard did not flinch, but spoke calmly.

"Although I am now an outcast, I too was once the heir to a vast heritage," he said. "But I vowed that if God would grant me forgiveness and cleanse me of my sins I would dedicate my life to Him. I was a leper, but God heard my prayers and I was healed. Since then I have lived in a hermitage below the castle, where I have fasted and prayed as well as becoming the friend and confessor of Sir Robert de Lacy." He paused and Johanna looked around the great hall to see that everyone's eyes were fixed on the robed figure. "It was at my desire that Sir Robert left his lands to the FitzEustace family," he went on, addressing his words directly to Roger. "But although you claim these lands for your family, you are not the eldest born son of your father."

Roger was speechless and the hall was silent, only a solitary rook could be heard calling from the trees outside.

"My elder brother is dead," he said after a moment.

"No," replied Richard as he pulled free from his distracted guards. He unfastened the leper's cloak and allowed it to fall to the ground at his feet, revealing the FitzEustace colours worn over his chainmail.

Johanna watched as Roger's face, reddened with anger just a moment before, grew suddenly pale as he stared at the only person in the world whom he feared.

"Yes," said Richard, "it *is* me. I am surprised that our grandmother did not make you party to our secret, or did you never stop shouting long enough for her to tell you?"

Petulantly, Roger flung his sword to the floor. "So now you declare yourself clean and snatch the inheritance from me, do you?" he asked. Johanna watched as Richard shook his head.

"No. I have dedicated my life to God," he explained again. "The money and the land is all yours, but," he said, as he turned to look at the Dean who still seemed unsure that his life was safe. "I have a stipulation."

"Which is?" asked Roger.

"The Dean."

"What of him?"

"Spare him," said Richard. "The man is not evil. He has a genuine claim to these lands, and until I arrived with my intercession from our grandmother he had been led to believe that he would inherit. Besides," he added, pausing to glance at the frightened figure, "he was compassionate to me when I first came here. He fed and sheltered me – and his son, Geoffrey, has shown me immeasurable kindness. The Dean is indeed kindred to the Lady Isabel and as such his blood is as noble as our own. He is no mere peasant to be hanged on a whim. Let him go," he ordered the guards that held the priest – and without waiting for Roger's acknowledgement they complied instantly.

Johanna watched as the Dean rubbed his sore arms where he had been held tightly. She had never seen him look so subdued and his reflective expression suddenly reminded her of Geoffrey in his more thoughtful moments. Where was Geoffrey in all this, she wondered. Had he been sent back to Rochdale on their return from Kirkstall Abbey, or was he at home with his mother, or waiting outside to discover the outcome of his father's claim on the lands that would, in turn, become his if the Dean were successful.

Feeling very alone as she stood and watched the drama unfolding before her, Johanna longed for Geoffrey's supportive arm around her and wondered what would happen to him now.

"The Dean will retain the lands at Wallei and you will respect him as your priest, despite this incident," Richard told his brother. "And in order that this rankling wound might be healed I suggest that a union is made between the two families."

Johanna held her breath at Richard's words and prayed that he was about to say what she hoped for. Hadn't he told her that he wished he could find a way to complete her happiness? He knew what it was she wished and prayed for more than anything in the world.

"The Dean's son is a fine young man who is also a priest, and I suggest that we join our sister Johanna in marriage with this boy and so unite the families and their lands."

"Yes," breathed Johanna as all three men turned to look at her. Then she ran to Richard and into his arms. "Thank you, thank you," she wept as he held her close to him and a babble of excited chatter broke out all around the great hall and Roger, never wanting to be out of control for long, called for scribes and witnesses to make written agreements, and for more wine and ale to be brought up from the buttery.

Johanna looked up into the smiling hazel eyes of her eldest brother and hugged him tight.

"I am in your debt, yet again," she said. "You have secured my future and made me the happiest sister on God's earth – or you would have if I could share this moment with Geoffrey!"

"So, I am no longer good enough," he laughed, holding her at arm's length.

"And you still so handsome," she told him as she stared up at him, restored to his old self in his chainmail shirt and the family colours. "Will you not have Father William declare you clean and claim Halton back for yourself?" she urged.

"No." He shook his head. "I am God's now, and my work is almost done. I will see you married and then I shall be content."

"So," said the familiar voice of the Dean from behind her, "you are to become my daughter?"

Johanna turned, still safe in the circle of her brother's arms, and met his recovered gaze.

"And where is my husband to be?" she asked.

"In Rochdale, about his duty."

"Then pray send a messenger with the good news," she said. "For I do not want to be parted from him a moment longer."

Chapter Sixteen

After the agreements had been signed and sealed, Richard told the Dean to go home and immediately summon Geoffrey back from Rochdale for his betrothal to Johanna. As he held his horse for him Richard was surprised by how much pleasure he felt to see the Dean so repentant and contrite. His usual arrogance was constrained and he mounted the stallion without meeting Richard's eye, waiting until he was settled in the saddle and able to look down on him before he spoke.

"I knew from the moment I saw you that you were no ordinary leper," he told him.

"I know that," said Richard, meeting his eyes steadily in an effort at reconciliation. "And there were many times when I believed that you knew exactly who I was."

"I suspected that someone might be sent from Halton to plead the case of the FitzEustace family, but I thought that person was Johanna. Young though she is, she has determination – and charm," he added as he gathered the horse's reins.

Richard was surprised at his words. Although he knew

that Geoffrey loved his sister passionately it had never occurred to him that the Dean himself might find her attractive as well.

"My sister has grown into an admirable woman whilst I have been away fighting in the Holy Land," he replied. "She grows more like my grandmother each day."

"And is that a good thing?" asked the Dean, recapturing a little of his former poise.

"Oh yes," said Richard. "My grandmother is a woman to be much admired. It is she who holds our family together."

"Then I look forward to meeting her," said the Dean as he turned his horse's head towards the Wallei road.

"It is a good compromise for you," said Richard. "And the two young people do love one another, and they are well matched. Good will come from this."

"Yes," said the Dean, circling his horse around. "But you must understand that Sir Robert always told me that the land would be mine. So you cannot blame me for feeling a little cheated by your intervention."

"I welcome your honesty," replied Richard, stroking the horse's soft muzzle as it pawed at the ground impatiently. "And I understand your disappointment. I too grew up expecting to be the heir of a great estate."

"But you are cured," said the Dean. "It only needs a priest to declare you to be clean. I would do it – and you could inherit."

"And my brother Roger?" asked Richard with a nod towards the castle keep.

"I have learnt today that he is a dangerous man to cross," smiled the Dean, ruefully.

"Indeed. Besides," said Richard, "I have made a pact with God and I will not see it broken."

"You are a good man," said the Dean, "despite your past sins. I will be pleased to see my son married to your sister."

"So it is a good compromise?" he persisted.

"Perhaps," agreed the Dean. "We shall see." And as he urged the impatient horse forward Richard watched him go and wondered if his first impression had been the right one after all. Perhaps the Dean was not such a bad man. He was keen to gain what he believed was rightfully his, and maybe willing to use a little cunning to get it, but not altogether bad and certainly not a candidate for a hanging.

Richard sighed and turned back to the keep. Inside lay the greater task of appeasing his brother. Roger was sitting by the hearth where several more logs had been added to create a huge blaze. His chair was pulled up close and his unbooted feet, stretched out towards the flames, were steaming slightly and adding an unsavoury aroma to the still air. He turned as Richard came back inside.

"Have you seen him off?" he demanded.

"The Dean has gone," said Richard.

"You ought to have let me hang the rodent. I didn't like the look of him from the moment he burst in uninvited," remarked Roger. "I think he must be the only person who has ever tried to cheat me and lived."

"Sometimes a degree of diplomacy and compromise is a better option," said Richard.

Roger snorted. "You always were too damned soft with these peasants and vassals."

"The Dean is not a peasant. His blood is as noble as our own."

"If you say so. Though I doubt it. His eyes are too small and his nose too large to be nobility," said Roger. "And you," he continued, fixing his brother with a stare. "Why was your part in this kept from me? When I rode to Halton and Grandmama showed me Sir Robert de Lacy's will she whispered that I would find someone here to help me, but I never thought it would be you. Our mother assured me that you were at the leper house at Spital Boughton and I always prided myself that I could tell whether she spoke the truth or not."

"Relax, you have not lost your touch," Richard told him. "Mother does believe that I am at the leper house."

"When I saw Johanna I thought she must be the envoy. It would have explained why, when I have been sending messengers to chase her all across the country, the wretches have all returned with myriad tales as to her whereabouts. Though," he added, "I thought it unlikely that she could have been the author of such devious plots."

"You always did misjudge her," said Richard. "She is cleverer than you imagine and more like you than you care to admit. Geoffrey de Wallei is a good match," he went on. "And I am sure you will be happy to settle at least a small portion of these vast estates you will inherit on them."

"I was hoping to find her a husband who would bring land into the family not take it out," he grumbled as he tormented the fire with a long stick. Richard smiled and resisted the urge to ruffle the hair of his little brother as he had seen his father do on the many occasions when he was a sulky infant.

Roger looked up and seemed hurt that his elder brother seemed to find his disappointment so amusing.

"I think it is better this way," said Richard. "And it is not as if it will leave you short of somewhere to live."

"And you?" asked Roger, suddenly." Everything that I will gain is your loss. How can you be so generous?"

"I have dedicated my life to God in return for His salvation and my redemption," said Richard.

"The leprosy? Was it a ploy?"

"No. I did indeed have leprosy."

"But not now?" said Roger, looking closely at Richard's face.

"No. By prayer and fasting and washing in the Holy Well here at Cliderhou the Lord has granted me a cure. But now I am His. I have dedicated my life to Him."

"You could be declared clean by a priest," said Roger.

"I will not claim your inheritance," said Richard, resting his unblemished hand on his brother's shoulder. For a moment Roger stared up at him and then a smile softened his quarrelsome features and Richard saw the boy he had once known.

"Thank you," he said and Richard knew that they had made peace.

He looked up as Johanna came down the stairs and across to the fire. There was an excitement in her step that he had not seen since before Geoffrey was sent away and she smiled widely at both of them although he saw that Roger only gave her his customary scowl in return.

"Thank you Richard," she said again coming straight

to him and once more plunging herself into his arms. "You are the best brother anyone could wish for."

"And I a poor second?" said Roger. "Though I am the one who is to provide for you and this Geoffrey, or are you content to live as a pauper, wife of a mere priest?"

"I would live in a hovel with him," she replied.

"It may come to that," he muttered and turned away from her as she pulled a face at his back.

"Come, let us discuss the wedding plans," said Richard. "What do you think, Johanna? Here or at Halton?"

"I don't mind as long as everyone can be together to celebrate, and be happy for us," she added with a glare in Roger's direction. "The Dean?" she asked.

"He is resigned. He knows that it is a good outcome."

"He knows he is lucky to have got away with his life," remarked Roger, throwing down the stick with which he had been stirring the fire. "But if you want all the family together then it will have to be Halton. Grandmama is frail," he said. "I doubt that she could make the journey to this... this place," he ended, indicating the castle walls with contempt.

"Then Halton it shall be," said Richard, suddenly filled with joy at the thought of going home once more. "Lady Isabel?" he asked, suddenly remembering her.

"She is asleep."

"Will she travel with us to Halton?"

"I hope so – and then I think she will return to Pontefract, for she says that there are too many ghosts to haunt her here and she would prefer to live with happy memories of Sir Robert."

"And as neither castle is hers she will go where I tell

her. Perhaps the nunnery?" suggested Roger, but as his eyes met Richard's and Richard frowned his displeasure he was pleased to see a moment of contrition. "She shall live at Pontefract until her death," he said. "It cannot be long coming."

"We shall make a benefactor of you yet," remarked Johanna, and Roger threw another log onto the fire with a snort as Richard watched his sister and brother, thinking how much he loved them both despite their shortcomings.

Johanna lay on her bed and could not stop smiling. Soon she would be on her way to Halton, to her wedding and Geoffrey would meet her there, at the church, with the blessing of both their families. It was an outcome she had prayed for endlessly but one which she had never dared to hope would come to pass.

Her baggage was packed and although Lady Isabel was to accompany them in a litter, she had insisted that she would ride home on Etoile beside her two brothers, Roger on his steely grey and Richard on Sir Robert's horse.

At last the sun rose and she slipped from her bed with anticipation and delight, anxious to be off. Martha, who was also coming to attend Lady Isabel, brought fresh water and Johanna washed and dressed in a gown that was the colour of the morning sky and ate bread and honey for her breakfast before going down to the kitchen to say goodbye to Wynn.

Everywhere was busy with preparations for the journey, though a portion of Roger's men were being left behind to guard the castle in their absence.

"I do not want some damnable Scots razing it to the ground as soon as it has been wrested from the treacherous hands of the Dean of Wallei," Roger had said as he had arranged to travel back to Halton with only part of his extensive retinue.

But at last they were ready and, with her cloak around her to fend off the early morning mist that was rolling down from Penhull Hill, Johanna settled herself onto Etoile and turned the horse's head towards Halton – and Geoffrey.

"Goodbye," she called to the spirits that dwelt on the hill and she kissed her fingers towards them as she rode south. "Do not fret. I will come back to you. For this land will be my home from now on."

Richard gladdened as Halton Castle came into view. His one-time inheritance never failed to lift his heart at every homecoming and the knowledge that it would never now be his could not mar his pleasure at the sight of it.

He urged the horse on at the gatehouse, eager to see his grandmother and especially his mother once more. Then he saw her, standing at the door of the keep, her hand shading her eyes against the lowering evening sun as she watched for them. He slid from the saddle as she hurried to him.

"Richard?" She hesitated for a moment then raised a hand to stroke his face as she gazed at him in incredulity. "You are cured?"

"I am clean," he said. "Come, let me hold you in my arms again, for this is the moment that I have prayed for." And she needed no more encouragement, but clasped him to her and reached up to stroke his hair as he held her close.

"My child; my son," she wept. "You have been restored to me."

Then as she allowed him to slip from her grasp he felt her stiffen with displeasure as she looked past him and he turned to see Johanna standing, waiting to greet her mother.

"Do not be reproachful," said Richard. "Make her welcome. She is your daughter and she has returned to be a bride."

His mother nodded and after Johanna had come forward to kneel before her she raised her up and briefly kissed her cheek.

"Where is Grandmama?" she asked, looking anxiously around and finding her missing.

"She is inside," said her mother. "We will go to her now, though she has grown frail with all this trouble," she added as if she thought the blame lay heavily on Johanna's shoulders.

Almost pushing her mother aside, Johanna ran up the steps and in through the familiar doorway. Throwing off her cloak as she passed through the great hall she ran up the stone steps to her grandmother's chamber. Breathless, she paused outside the door, hardly daring to picture the scene inside. But her grandmother was not propped up in bed as Sir Robert had been. Although she looked much older and smaller than when Johanna had last seen her she was dressed and sitting beside her fire, though whether she had made a special effort that day Johanna was not sure.

"Grandmama!" she said and ran to fall on her knees beside the chair and rest her head in her lap whilst Albreda stroked and kissed her.

"Oh, how I have missed your pretty face," she said, holding Johanna's head between her trembling hands and staring at her with eyes that looked blurred with a mixture of age and tears. "You look so well; so happy. You are in love," she concluded.

"Yes, Grandmama. I am in love," she confessed, stroking the hands that held her face.

"Then I am happy," she said. "For love is a magical and blessed thing to find in life. Who is this man? Not someone chosen by your brother Roger?"

"Indeed, no," laughed Johanna as she settled on a stool at her grandmother's feet to tell her about Geoffrey.

Richard had watched as Johanna barely greeted their mother before running inside. She always had been her grandmother's child, he reflected. Their mother had always found her incomprehensible. He turned and saw Lady Isabel and Martha coming forward hesitantly and realised that he had been remiss as he rushed to greet his mother. Lady Isabel looked tired and a little afraid and he offered her his arm as she came forward to be introduced.

"Come," he said as he felt a shiver run through her, despite the remaining warmth of the setting sun, "let us go inside."

Even though he too was anxious to see his grandmother he first made sure that the guests were comfortably accommodated and was then obliged to make a full explanation to his mother of what had happened at Cliderhou and how a marriage had been arranged between Geoffrey and Johanna.

"Well, I am pleased that someone has been found for her," she remarked, then suddenly got to her feet in alarm. "When will they arrive?" she asked anxiously. "We must make plans. There is much to do!"

"Hush, hush. Sit down," Richard soothed her. "There is no need to fret over this. We do not need a lavish affair. Father William will marry them at the chapel and a simple dinner to follow will suffice."

"When will they come?" she asked again remaining standing as if ready to run to the kitchen and begin the preparations that very night.

"In a day or two. The Dean and his wife were preparing to follow us in a couple of days and Geoffrey will ride from Rochdale to meet them here."

"We will need to air beds, find fresh linen, brew more ale and butcher more meat..."

"Do not fuss, mother," he said, catching her hand as she pointed in all directions. "It will all be done."

He looked round as he heard Johanna call his name.

"Grandmama wants you all to come to her chamber," she told them. "She says she has important business that cannot wait until morning."

Richard squeezed his mother's hand and nodded. "Come along," he said, "we will go up."

It was as if time had stood still at Halton as he followed his sister, brother and mother up the stairs. He recalled how they had run and played here as children, in the days when their father was still alive and he had believed that no harm could ever befall him. He smiled as he recalled how their grandmother would come out of her solar to reprimand them for their noise and end up joining in the game; then his father would tell her that she was as much a child as the children and she would laugh and tell him that he was too serious. There had been good times, he thought, despite the constant unease between Johanna and Roger and their mother's reluctance to form a bond with her daughter. He missed his father; he missed Sir Robert, and soon he feared that he would miss his grandmother too. But that was how life progressed; the cycle of birth and death never ceased. And though he knew that he would never again find the love that he had known with Leila, never father children to fill this castle with a new generation of laughter, he was looking forward to meeting Roger's young son John who was coming from Nottingham with Maud for the wedding, and if it was God's will Johanna and Geoffrey would provide him with a brood of other nephews and nieces.

He was shocked when he saw his grandmother. She seemed to have aged a decade since the night she had sent him north with Johanna. But despite her physical frailty her wits seemed as sharp as ever as she motioned them all to gather around a table where her clerk had laid out some written parchments.

"Richard," she began with a smile. "Thank you for what you have done; for taking my entreaty north and persuading my cousin Sir Robert to make his will in my favour. I am sorry that you are not to be my heir and in his letter Sir Robert said the same. He spoke warmly of you and told me that in his last days you were like a son to him, and that Johanna was like a daughter. Thanks to you the de Lacy inheritance is now mine to distribute as I choose and, as you already know, I have chosen to pass the vast estates of Lancashire and Yorkshire to Roger. However," she went on, "there are some conditions. First, Roger must give up his claim to the FitzEustace lands, so that on my death these may be divided amongst other members of the family. Secondly, Roger, I want you to take the name of de Lacy so that my family name will be preserved. And, thirdly, I want you to bequeath, on your death, a portion of the estates to Johanna and her husband." She paused and looked at them all in turn. "If you are all agreeable then the documents here are ready to be signed and witnessed."

Richard almost held his breath as he watched, in turn, Roger's impassive and Johanna's delighted faces. Then he let out a slight sigh of relief as Roger nodded and stepped towards the table and took up the quill to sign his name with a flourish.

"You shall have the villa of Tunlay," he told his sister, "and the manor of Coldcoats, with Snodworth."

"And I shall have a hawk," she told them, triumphantly. And Richard smiled at her shining eyes. Now his sister had all her wishes.

Johanna experienced a moment of terror when she opened her eyes and found herself back in the bedchamber at Halton. For a moment she thought that her escape had been a dream, and then she came gradually to her senses and remembered that it was all true.

As she lay in bed and stared at a spider mending its web in the corner she thought about the web that her grandmother had woven from her chamber here at Halton Castle that had brought Geoffrey de Wallei to her. She stretched out her arm across the empty space beside her and wondered what it would be like to wake next to him, his warm body against hers. She smiled as she hugged her arms across herself, imagining that it was him and a shudder of pleasure ran through her.

"I just hope he does not snore," she remarked to the spider.

A small army of women had been sewing and embroidering for days and the silk gown in sage green that Johanna had chosen to match her eyes was now ready. Today she would wear it; tomorrow she would wake with Geoffrey.

She heard footsteps and laughter outside the door and both Megan and Martha came in with knowing glances and jugs of hot water to prepare a scented bath for her, but Johanna was too absorbed in her own thoughts to appreciate their bawdy humour.

Already the aroma of the food being prepared for the wedding feast was drifting up from the kitchen and she imagined her mother, causing mayhem amongst the servants with her anxiety as she gave never-ending instructions about what needed to be done.

She allowed herself to be washed and dressed and when she was ready she walked down to the hall. Flowers had been brought in from the garden and the trestle tables, covered in crisp white linen cloths, were set with silver goblets and platters; the specially made loving cup from which she and Geoffrey would drink was waiting in the middle of the top table.

As she walked she could smell the aroma of the fresh herbs that had been crushed and scattered on the tables and across the new floor rushes. And by the door Richard was waiting, not in his leper's robes but in a fine tunic and hose of dark green. She paused and smiled as her eldest brother offered her his hand to take her to the chapel.

Early that morning Richard had abandoned the unaccustomed comfort of his childhood bed and, concealed only in his leper's cloak, had walked the short distance to the chapel to wait for Father William. As the sun rose the priest came from his cell to say Matins. He looked unsurprised when he saw Richard waiting for him outside the door.

"Good morning, my son," he greeted him. "What would you have me do?"

"You know what I want," said Richard. "I want you to declare me clean, so that I can enter the church and give thanks to God for His deliverance, and witness the blessing of my sister's marriage."

"Show yourself to me," he said and Richard allowed the cloak to fall to the ground around his feet before turning slowly in a circle.

"It is the miracle we have all prayed for," said Father William. "You are indeed clean. Come," he commanded, and as Richard approached him he took out a small vial of oil scented with hyssop that he had prepared in readiness. As Richard stood naked before him, the priest anointed the lobe of his right ear, his right thumb and the toe of his right foot. "Now kneel," he commanded, and as Richard knelt, the stony ground digging into his knees and shins, he felt the comforting hand of the priest on his head. "May the Lord bless you and keep you," he said. "Now go and dress yourself for the wedding."

"In a moment," said Richard as he looked longingly at the door of the chapel. "First let me join you inside for morning prayers."

He looked up and Father William smiled at him. "Come in," he said, turning to push open the heavy door. "Come inside." And gathering the cloak around him Richard stood and stepped over the threshold and under the archway into the cold interior that made him shiver as he dipped his fingers into the holy water. He touched the water to his forehead and felt a peace so strong that he would have been content to live the rest of his life within that moment of time.

"Father William?" he asked. "Is it possible for the soul of an Infidel to be accepted into heaven?"

"God will welcome all those who turn to Him," the priest replied.

Richard nodded and went to kneel at the altar. "Lord," he prayed aloud, "she is a good woman. Protect her; love her; give her Your blessing."

He opened his eyes to find Father William watching him intently.

"It is not your sister who is in need of such urgent prayer," he observed. "This woman you pray for? She is an Infidel?"

"She is the woman I loved; the woman I still love. I

once believed that God had punished me for it, but now he has cured me, although I have not stopped loving her. So is it wrong to kneel in His church, before His altar and pray for her?"

"No," said Father William. "Love bears all things, hopes all things, endures all things."

Dressed in her bridal gown and with a chaplet of fresh flowers crowning her loose hair, Johanna stepped out of Halton Castle and walked with Richard to the chapel. Geoffrey was waiting for her at the door. He was standing, tall and straight, his broad shoulders stretched under the dark ruby red of his tunic. Their eyes remained locked as she walked towards him and when she came within touching distance he held out a hand to her and she reached out to him and felt his fingers gently brush hers before they interlocked and his eyes ignited a smile that gradually spread to his lips and through both their bodies to her own face. There was no need for words to pass between them. She loved him and she knew that he loved her. With or without the priest's blessing, that was enough.

She paused to catch her breath and compose herself as their families and friends gathered around them. A silver penny was placed on a bible as a symbol of the dower that she would receive from her husband, and afterwards they exchanged their vows and Geoffrey slipped a simple ring onto her finger and kissed her on the cheek. Then they entered the chapel and she knelt beside her husband to receive the blessing of Father William and of God on their union. The Dean and her brother Richard held an altar cloth over them as the Latin words of the Nuptial Mass buzzed around her ears like mayflies. She looked up to watch Geoffrey's lips form his prayers and she waited, impatiently, for them to be pressed against hers.

Epilogue

After witnessing the wedding Richard waited at the back of the small chapel as the bride and her new husband were followed by both families back to the castle. There would be a huge feast with minstrels and music and dancing. Then Father William would bless the marriage bed and Johanna and Geoffrey would be undressed and put into it amidst much laughter and celebration.

He thought of Leila and hoped that they would find as much joy in one another as he had in that tent in a foreign land. He would not join the feast, but resolved to fast during his long walk back to his hermit's cell under the hill at Cliderhou.

When he reached the place where he had resolved to spend the rest of his life, he paused to take in the magnificent view from the top of the limestone knoll: the flat fertile plains of the Ribble Valley to one side and, to the other, the magnificent bulk of Penhull Hill crouched like an animal guarding its spirits.

Richard raised a hand and stretched his tired fingers upwards in a token of blessing. Beyond the hill lay the villa of Tunlay that would become the home of Geoffrey and Johanna de Wallei. He asked God's blessing on them both and, turning away from the scene, followed the path to his familiar cell.

He stooped unsteadily to his knees to make a final prayer:

"*Nunc dimittis servum tuum, Domine*," he prayed. "Lord, now lettest Thou Thy servant depart in peace according to Thy word. For mine eyes have seen Thy salvation..."

And having made his prayer he lay down on his hard rock bed and watched the crescent moon that hung above the hill as if it held all his troubles for him, and he closed his eyes and fell asleep.

Afterword

The story of the de Lacy inheritance is based on an old Lancashire legend that I came across when I was researching for my non-fiction book *Tales of Old Lancashire*, published by Countryside Books. Clitheroe Castle and the de Lacy family were already very familiar to me, but the story of the hermit who lived beneath the castle seemed less well known and when I realised that he was a real person and would have inherited a fortune except for his leprosy I wanted to know more.

When you go back a thousand years events are not always well recorded and that can be a good as well as a bad thing. Lack of finite detail gave me the opportunity to fictionalise what facts were available without being too restricted by them, although I did find that known facts had to be worked into the story. Suddenly discovering that Roger de Lacy had been the sheriff of the castles at Nottingham and Tickhill rather than being on crusade with King Richard I, as many sources claimed, proved a slight problem at one point, but in the end I think the threat of him sending for Johanna added extra tension to the story.

So where does the truth end and the fiction begin? That's

not as easy to answer as you might think. One thing you learn when you're researching for a historical novel is that there are many, many versions of the truth. Inaccuracies are often copied from source to source and sorting out the reliable from the unreliable is very difficult.

It is true that around 1193 the de Lacy estates passed from Robert de Lacy to his cousin Albreda de Lizours. Albreda was a member of the de Lacy family and, like her cousin, was a descendant of Ilbert de Lacy who was the first Lord of Pontefract Castle. Robert de Lacy and his wife Isabel were childless. Albreda was his nearest blood relative and after his death the ownership of all his lands across Yorkshire and Lancashire, including Pontefract Castle in Yorkshire and Clitheroe Castle in Lancashire, passed to her, and from her to her grandson Roger on condition that he change his name to de Lacy. Roger's life is well documented and you can read more about him on my website: www.elizabethashworth.com and at my blog: www.elizabethashworth.wordpress.com where you will also find a slideshow of some of the places associated with the novel.

The Dean of Whalley was a relation of Robert's wife Isabel and he had been appointed to the vacancy on the recommendation of the de Lacy family. At that time priests were styled as deans rather than vicars and their positions were hereditary so he probably did have hopes of claiming at least some of the de Lacy lands for himself to pass on to his son.

The lives of women and lepers are not as well documented as those of nobles. Although it is recorded that a daughter of Roger de Lacy married Geoffrey de Wallei and their descendants became the Towneleys of Burnley, I decided to make her his sister in my story as the timing and ages seemed more appropriate. There is no clear indication of her name and sometimes she is referred to as Maud or even confused with another family member, Helen de Lacy; so I took a leap of faith based on very flimsy evidence and named her with the feminine version of her father's name. A record of the Towneley ancestry was compiled by Christopher Towneley of Towneley Hall in Burnley in 1662 and in the Towneley Room at the hall there is a large chart displaying their family tree. Geoffrey and his wife had a son whom they named Richard and Richard became a common family name and includes Richard Towneley who was a scientist and conducted the Towneley Time Trials in 1675 when he plotted the course of the sun at noon each day in relation to a meridian line. You can read more about him in my book *Champion Lancastrians*, published by Sigma Press.

Records of Richard FitzEustace are even harder to find. He was a brother of Roger de Lacy and using the name Richard of Chester witnessed several documents signed by Roger. He is recorded in a chronicle of Norton Priory in Cheshire as a leper and he was buried there under the chapter house. I went to visit his grave and found that the ruins of the priory have been excavated and the remains of many of the burials removed from the site. There is one skeleton on display in the museum along with examples of bones which show signs of both leprosy and of Paget's disease (which was sometimes mistaken for leprosy). However only part of the chapter house has been excavated and personally I hope Richard's body remains where it was buried.